D0623324

THREE MINUTES ON LOVE

ROCCIE HILL

THE PERMANENT PRESS
Sag Harbor, NY 11963

For information, address:
    The Permanent Press
    4170 Noyac Road
    Sag Harbor, New York 11963
    www.thepermanentpress.com

Library of Congress Cataloging-in-Publication Data

    Hill, Roccie
        Three minutes on love / Roccie Hill.
            p. cm.
        ISBN-13: 978-1-57962-169-8 (hardcover : alk. paper)
            1. Women photographers—Fiction. 2. Rock musicians—Fiction.
        3. Music trade—Fiction. 4. California, Southern—Fiction. I. Title.

    PS3608.I43765T48 2008
    813'.6—dc22   2008004184

Printed in the United States of America.

Contents

PART ONE

ZACA CREEK

CHAPTER 1

We lived in the desert when I was a kid, in a climate without water where the plants looked like weapons and the sun-scarred colors of the soil and rocks were like none other on earth. Our neighborhoods had been drawn in graph-paper boxes across the parched Pinto Basin, with even, hot asphalt streets of air-conditioned stores and houses. Inside our town's shopping mall the developer had built a plaster waterfall and painted it turquoise, and all day long hundreds of gallons of water were pumped over it. This waterfall was where we went as children if we got lost; it was where we met our friends in high school. 'Meet you at the waterfall,' my mother would say to me, but it was not until I left the desert that I understood the irony. This was our community: fueled by someone else's water and someone else's electric power. Even then we were kids of excess, although we never knew it.

I grew up on a street of identical houses, and around ours my father had planted borders of bright pansies and geraniums, red and purple and pink. He set the automatic sprinklers to water three times a day to keep them alive, laboring over those frail flowers. Most families on our block had kidney-shaped swimming pools the dark turquoise color of sweet Hawaiian cocktails, and I remember that my father wanted a garden of ferns surrounding ours. Year after year he would plant new ones, drench them, and watch them die. Our town was a shield against the sun for spillover GI families from the California coast, with an air-conditioned house for each one, where only hot rocks and rattlers should have been.

Each year new people came, building new schools and cutting more lush green neighborhoods across the empty, dry horizon. People with real estate dreams dug huge trenches into hundreds of miles of land too dry to farm, and into these trenches they sank great pipes to bring the water from faraway snowy rivers to our homes. And this is how I grew up, playing in the heat among those stacks of enormous, sun-warmed concrete pipes that were waiting to be sunk into the cracked desert ground to bring more water to us.

I used to dance to radio songs across rows of them, holding a transistor to my ear in the heat and skipping across those huge concrete hulls to "Cinnamon Cinder," a song I always called "Cinnamon Sinner" and whose words I still have memorized. And I remember the first day the water came through those huge pipes. After years of planning and digging, early one fall morning as I sat in my seventh grade classroom, our teacher suddenly stopped talking. I could hear it, or feel it, not a sound but a heavy vibration in my inner ear as though the earth was about to crack open. The water gates lifted high and brought the Sierra-fed rivers into the pipes to our desert, to irrigate the future.

My dad was a teacher. He taught math to soldiers' kids out there in the heat where the Air Force kept its secrets. He hated that he wasn't part of it; he had never designed a plane or a landing strip or thought up a formula for a bomb, and although he never got invited to their parties or included in their theories, he stayed to teach their kids algebra. In the hot evenings after school he would sit by our swimming pool drinking whisky and telling me and my mother about the principles of logic and the politics of defense. Sometimes he would drink half the bottle on his own; other times he would leave it and walk along the sloped concrete edge of the pool, and his shadow would be bouncing like a marionette's across the blue glow of the water. Often, my mother put him to bed, and I could hear him moaning down the hall to their room about the importance of logic. He was the first man I knew who told me his job would save the world, and because he was my father, I loved him and believed him for many years.

I had no brothers or sisters, so my mother took me everywhere with her. We would go in the car to the movies or out for long drives in the heat, and she would talk about the neighborhoods, when they were built, what ghosts had come since, and what men had slept with others' wives. She knew everything. She was like a witch taken out of her own lands, and when she told me she could mind-read, I believed her, too.

She read constantly: novels by American expatriates, political books about workers' rights and the destruction of McCarthy, and obscure religious books about Rosicrucians or voodoo or the lost secrets of the Vatican. She was obsessed with moral harm and secret truths.

She had grown up in the Hollywood Hills before the roads were paved, and as she drove through the desert she would tell me her cluster of morality tales about the movie people during Prohibition and how the Hollywood she knew could protect you if you could stay away from alcohol, although in her beauty years she herself had preferred to drink. Her favorite tale was how she, the bootlegger's pretty daughter, had become a movie socialite while playing drunken chess with Harold Lloyd at his crazy parties. She told me that our job was to seek out our one, true soulmate, and once she confessed to me that my father was not her true love. Her soulmate, she said, had been a poet from Hollywood High, a boy who hitchhiked to Arizona, where he walked with a burro for several years until he disappeared forever down a canyon. This was so outlandish that even as a ten-year-old child I did not believe it, although I was eaten by guilt for being disloyal.

My mother had left the coast with my father because he promised a decent, sober life, and that is what she had for as long as I knew her.

She spent a lot of her time waiting in the heat and the bright light, watching the landscape for a movement that no one but she would see. She taught me to gamble while we picnicked on the dry and dormant ground, to play draw poker and blackjack, and when I got clever at those she taught me to play mumblety-peg. It was a game she had learned from clients of her boot-legger father on the beach at Zuma: a dangerous game with a knife that you played to test your skill and your courage. It was not a game for children, but she always expected more of me. The object of this game was to bounce the knife blade from your body to the ground, where your hand lay flat, fingers splayed. The space between your fingers was the target, and my mother used to say this was more a game of geometry than bravery. She had a special knife with a narrow, long blade which cut easily into the brittle desert, and she was good with knives and never once let me hurt myself. After mumblety-peg we moved on to games like bridge and chess, which she said also took more intelligence than guts.

Once she took me out on a drive, early in the morning when you could smell the heat coming hard across the valley. The sunlight turned the creosote branches dark in the early day and the white light behind cut crisp and simple black lines across the land.

My mother said, "Look at that. The first pen and ink drawing. Everything you see now will be less."

We parked by an old train track and waited and watched. She said, "The desert is never boring. It changes every day. I came here in 1948 with your father, and I would have died from boredom in a city by now. If you can't drink you can't live in the city."

We squatted by prickly bushes next to the rusty track, and she pointed out some wildflower growing in the hard, dry dirt.

She said, "Rosie, look at that. You'll never see a color so red. How do you get color like that out here? But a change in the weather can kill it. Anything can kill it." And she was right. Even the water we piped to our neighborhoods could kill it. Those desert flowers soon disappeared, replaced by the petunias and pansies. Without my mother I never would have seen the last of the real desert.

We sat on a plastic tarpaulin that we had found in our garage, now so hot that it burned the backs of our legs and my mother made us move to sit on the scorched desert floor, because she said the heat of the earth was good and the heat of plastic could make you sick. She pulled warm lettuce and cheese sandwiches from a paper bag, and we ate in the dirt, watching the far, flat horizon.

"Do you know," she said, "there are creatures sleeping under us? Tiny worms you can't see, and when the rains begin they come to life across this whole valley, thousands and thousands of them crawling for daylight." I put my hand on the hard, hot ground, not even afraid but hoping I would see one of them.

She watched me for a few moments and then touched my shoulder. "Rosie," she said, "I want to tell you something. Do you see my ears? Do you see I have no ear lobes? My ears are connected, just like yours." I was eight years old and could not yet distinguish between truth and entertainment. "Well," she said, "this is because we are descended from an ancient race of aliens who came to this planet thousands of years ago."

"How did they get here?" I asked.

"They came in spaceships that they buried in India. This is how you tell our people, by our ear lobes. Whenever you see someone whose ears are connected like ours, you will know they are one of us."

My father didn't understand her stories, and so he was never part of them. But there was still some picture in her mind of a family, and she was afraid of not being good at it. Years later on the way home from a Saturday car trip she said, "Please tell your father you had a good time with me today."

I would have anyway. The others were the enemy. Cecilia was my mother's name, a saint's name, the goddess of music. That was the first day I understood that she needed me, the first time I knew I would need to take care of her. I guess I was about eleven.

When I was fifteen my mother put the first anti-war poster in our front window. The poster said "Another Mother for Peace," and my father hated it.

"You'll have to take that down," he said. "I teach their kids. You can't think like that here. I'll get fired."

"I'm tired of eating my dinner while our boys get killed on television," she said.

Eventually, she took the poster down, but began secretly to organize meetings against the war in the Lutheran Church hall. People from up north would come to help her; young guys with lots of hair would drive in from San Francisco to speak to her groups. My mother, who by then was wearing bead necklaces and strange Egyptian symbols for earrings, would give them dinner and find them places to stay. Because we lived in an Air Force town, the important anti-war people from the cities kept an eye on her, and when they needed someone to feed deserters on their way to Canada, it was my mother they asked. She helped them secretly for years, giving the kids food and clean clothes, sometimes a few dollars, and they began calling her Saint Cecilia. As long as the Vietnam War was fought, she had that secret nickname.

The first boy I slept with was one my mother disdained. He was Thomas J. Thomas, the son of a colonel at the base. Tom Thomas had virtually no hair, was a member of the Junior ROTC, the Eagle Scouts, and the Varsity football team. He was a simple kid from a family with simple desires, and he could not conjugate a verb to save his life, something which my mother never let me forget. But he brought me freedom through raging hormones he could scarcely control during daylight hours, and I can remember so clearly lying with him on warm, clean rocks in the purple desert afternoons.

It ended in 1967. Tom Thomas and I were walking across a patch of lawn at our school, which was known as the "Senior Grass" and on which only kids of our year could sit. The humor of it had escaped me until that day, when we found a group of younger kids sitting in a circle and holding hands on our grass.

They might have been of a different time, clothed in leather fringe and scarves, with so much hair among them. They were kids I'd seen one by one in the school corridors, isolated and strange, and all of a sudden they were sitting together before us, holding hands and doing secret things I knew nothing about. Tom Thomas told me they were dangerous; my mother thought they were beautiful and exciting.

Tom dropped my hand and walked to the edge of their circle, standing squarely on the grass.

"You ain't all seniors now, are you?" he asked. He wore his football jacket and walked with the loping, swelled presence of a boy happily destined for shopping malls.

He should have commanded respect among them, but he didn't. One of the boys said, "No man, but we're making a movie about what it's like to be seniors." Indeed, another boy had a camera, and turned it on me and Tom.

"Come on, Rosie," the camera boy said, "smile for me, baby."

"I think that's enough," said Tom in a hollow voice that reminded me of his father.

"How do you know my name?" I asked.

"Hey, everybody knows your name—you're Saint Cecilia's daughter," he said.

Tom Thomas scowled and stepped forward toward the circle. "Go on now," he said to them, and reached for the camera boy's equipment, "or I'll have to get someone."

But they laughed and began to sing the Donovan song "Catch the Wind," that sweet ghost tune, in the warm red backglow of the late desert sky. One girl waved a smoky stalk of incense through the still air, and the smell of sandalwood rose around us. I whispered to her, "You really need to go now. Please go." But they just kept singing.

Tom moved forward and lifted one of the boys to his feet.

"That's enough," he said. He shoved him hard, away from the lawn onto the paved walkway. He grabbed them, one after another, shifting their bodies like sandbags from that important line on the grass, and their music fell to the empty air while they struggled against him. Tom was bigger and braver, and although he was alone, he had been trained to win. I edged back toward the clean, grey wall of the math building, suddenly unsure of which side I was on. It took Tom only a few minutes to shuffle them away, leaving the lawn empty in the quickly falling violet desert dusk. By the time he had finished his job, I understood that I needed to leave the Pinto Basin and the people who had begun as my family.

* * *

In the fall of 1968 I went to San Francisco to art school. I left the desert and the painted rocks and the heat, and went to the cool Bay to learn how to take photographs. This was a year after the summer of love, and by the time I arrived it had all changed. Venereal disease and heroin were the issues, and any promises of peace and a new society were just disintegrating. The streets in the Haight-Ashbury were filthy; half the shops were closed and used only for sleeping and dealing. My first pictures were shaky ones of street rags on Haight Street, taken on an old Olympus Trip my father had given me. All I knew how to do was point and shoot, but I loved it, and I always had the Trip with me. I'd take half a dozen rolls and only come up with one good shot, but I tried everything. At that age every single thing I saw could have been art, and figuring out what made the one perfect shot obsessed me. Those first months I would go down to the Haight at dawn on the weekends, before the morning sounds began, while the damp and mist clung to the crumbling Victorian neighborhood. The druggies would be asleep by five AM and I would have the quiet streets to myself, shooting roll after roll of a secret garden of garbage discarded from the wild night before.

Rather than take pictures of the children I saw crouching in doorways, the easy shots, I stood on the gutter corners where I found rags, old Indian cotton, discarded and damp and greased over by sewer sludge and cars passing by. Shooting people was the easy way to record those days; everyone was doing it, but I wanted to get a picture of the people from their rags in the street. I was only eighteen then, and I believed that the harder I made the job the truer the art would be. I shot thousands of pictures of the dirt of the Haight, my garbage garden, and hardly any pictures of human beings.

In Golden Gate Park I met people who would sit in circles pretending to be ancient Indians, except they would smoke dope and talk of Lenin and the CIA and the war. For hours we sat in the wide Sharon Meadow with music around us and the mist moving in from the cold bay at Ocean Beach. We talked of music as though we had invented it and all of us were certain we would one day be heroes of something. Sometimes a girl would do an odd floating dance around us; sometimes the Krishnas came chanting to us; always the smell of sandalwood clung to our clothes. When the days finished we called ourselves a family though we might never see one another again. Most of us had left our own families, but we kept seeing their ghosts in everyone we met.

One Saturday I sat next to a Hungarian refugee named Peter who was older than the rest, although his unabashed excitement at being in America made him seem like a teenager. He had short black hair that receded far off his broad forehead, and a prominent straight nose, sunburned from those early autumn days in the park. He told me he had just escaped from immigration jail in New York and was now the editor of a new music magazine called *The Bay Scene*.

"Because a scene is cool," he said in a heavy accent I could scarcely understand, "and Bay people are cool." He grinned broadly and talked about Trotsky and the agrarian revolution, and he said, "You know, Rose, I think it is easy to make money in this city. There is moral money and immoral money, but in general, being poor is no fun." He was the only person I knew then who cared about money, and because of this I thought he was unconventional and honest.

I told him I knew a boy at college who had gathered up all the mediocre assignments from the pottery workshops and sold them to Woolworth's. With that money he bought marijuana to sell, and with the money from that he had gone to live in Tahiti.

"There you are," he said, "the new capitalism." He leaned back on the grass, stretching his long legs out before him. I could see even then that he was extraordinarily tall, and not quite at ease because of it. He wore a very old navy sports jacket that was missing its buttons, and as he lay beside me, he grabbed nervously at the old button threads and then suddenly stopped himself doing it. He had round black eyes, always a little frightened and quite beautiful. "There are lives for us," he said, "if only we had the money. I am only in this for the money and the women." I laughed when he said that; he spoke too loudly and somehow the words came out as a fantasy, like a piece of America he was trying on. Everything about him was dark, his hair and eyes and obscure cynical economics, until he talked about America.

"Would you like to work for me?" he asked. "I need a photographer. I am useless at taking pictures."

"What would I have to do?" I had never been offered a real job before, although I had sat in the park for weeks pretending that I was a published photographer.

"Come with me to concerts and take pictures of the bands. So easy. And free concerts for you."

"Does it pay?" I asked, and he laughed out loud.

"Sweetie-pops! This is America. You must never do anything for free. I will pay you five bucks a picture printed."

"I'm at school most days," I said.

"My people only work at night. This is a night business."

"I suppose I could borrow a good camera from school."

"Look, do you want this job or not? I am trying to do you a favor. You need to be more aggressive. You will never be successful unless you are pushy."

The next time I met Peter, we had coffee at Tosca's in North Beach where we sat in a smoky room on an old, fraying couch and put our cups beside us on a low table. Part of the room was given over to a piano, and customers would now and then play tunes, mainly jazz music that belonged to the past. Each group of people seemed to know the others and guys moved from couch to couch, straddling the arms and smoking and talking. Peter nodded at most of them, and when we sat down he said, "These are the losers of the city."

"Why?" I asked.

"Poets. They don't do anything. Most of them might as well pay rent here. There's no money to be made in here. The revolution will come from those of us who control this capitalist economy, not from these loser poets," and he pronounced that word "poots." Across the room, a guy was sitting alone at a table in the corner. A chessboard was set up in front of him, all the pieces in starting position, and he sat waiting, watching it and the door, and straining his neck at the people coming in from the street.

"Look at that one," he said. "He plays chess in here every day. And when he's not playing chess he's waiting for chess. You know, some people are the get-aheads, and some people are the fodder. You can always tell right away. I don't know where that guy gets his money from. What about you?"

"I get my money from my father, but he says he's running out."

He smiled at me. "I didn't mean that. Are you a get-ahead?"

"Of course," I said, but I knew that wasn't true. All I ever wanted was to take good pictures and have a family, and I knew that a real get-ahead had to want more.

Peter sat next to me, with his arm across the back of the couch and his fingers on my shoulder.

He said, "The music business will save us." He wore a tweed jacket and a red silk scarf and threw his head back when he spoke. He drank his coffee all at once in a gulp like the French at a sidewalk café, and said, "We will make the art of the revolution through rock and roll." As he leaned back, I could smell Old Spice on his clothing.

"Before we start our discussion, I want to be clear about something," he said. He coughed nervously, and folded his hands in his lap across his thick waist. His nails were bitten beyond the quick, and he lifted his fist to his mouth suddenly.

"This is a business relationship, Rose. We can never have more than that, no matter how much we may be attracted to each other."

He was so timid, his eyes black and scared like a young boy trying hard to be an old-fashioned gentleman.

I smiled. "All right, I understand."

He stood up quickly. "I'll just go get us more coffee." When he returned his hands were shaking slightly. He was holding two tiny cups of expresso on saucers, and the delicate rhythm of his nerves caused the cups to shudder like wind chimes.

"Would you like me to take those?" I asked.

"Please don't be offended," he said, watching the cups and not me. "I don't really know many people here. Why do I alienate new friends so quickly?"

"Peter, please sit down. It's okay. I'm not offended."

He nodded and stepped forward, and he looked down at me, placing the cups on the tabletop. He smiled broadly and helplessly, and as he did the cups tumbled from their saucers, cracking across the table, the coffee splashing over me and the couch.

Conversations around the room stopped; a quick silence focused on Peter, who stood motionless, his face flushing and sweating in the smoky, hot room.

"Don't worry," I said, and took a napkin to clean it up. He didn't speak, but stood shaking before me like a Market Street crazy, the broad, helpless grin still quivering on his lips.

He watched me clean the table and pile the empty crockery at one end, and finally, he said, "I think we had better leave."

"Peter, nobody cares if you drop a few dishes. This is North Beach. The losers of the city, remember?"

"I guess I'm a loser, too."

"Sit with me." I reached for his hand. "Dropping cups doesn't make you a loser."

"In my family it does. In Budapest."

"Well this is North Beach. It doesn't matter here. Sit down and tell me about these pictures you want me to take."

He hired me for that first paying gig and, being honest, it is still the best picture I have ever taken. We went to a cheap neon bar in the Haight to cover Robert Clay, an old piano player who had come to the city with a new, young band. He was one of the real blues people, and he was in San Francisco to showcase his new band and to get a recording contract. He had been on the road for so long, smoking and drinking and shooting heroin, and trying to make some money for that gold limousine. I thought he was ancient, but I guess he was about fifty years old.

The bar was called the Skyway Lounge, and the words were painted in pink and black swirling lettering on the big plate glass window. Inside, the room smelled of spilled beer; the smoke was tobacco and pot mixed together. It was a small bar, not a music club, but a paying gig anyway, and I stood like a gawky kid beside the door, juggling my camera bag out of my way to grab my purse, until Peter pushed through and gave our names to the bouncer who checked his list and let us in immediately. For a kid from the desert, this was a ticket to ride; I had become a member of the holy music union.

They seated us at a table in the front and brought us a bottle of scotch. Peter believed in the new journalism so he didn't take notes—he said he experienced the story and re-created it afterwards. He sat at the little wobbly table and started drinking out of a thick, short glass that had been put in front of him; when someone brought him some pot, he started smoking as well. He looked around the room, bobbing his head to the jukebox music, smiling like a child and waiting for the show.

"I'm going to look for a spot to shoot from," I said.

He nodded at me and leaned over to speak into my ear. "Make sure you're in place. When Robert gets playing you will have to be ready. He is the best living blues piano player. Of course, most of the others are dead. Go on, go do your work."

The band was playing, so I went wandering the room for angles and dramatic shadows, but there wasn't enough light to take a picture. I didn't know that this would always be the case, that light was the secret to taking someone's picture and that light was a demon I would chase my whole life. I was trying so hard to be professional, but I hadn't brought the right film for concert photography, and had loaded my only camera with film that wouldn't soak what little light there was. In the end I sat defeated on the grimy floor in front of the stage and held my camera and listened to the set while photographers from better papers slid into place beside me and cracked their shutters.

Lots of people had come for this old guy; the news had spread across the city that a real musician was going to play our town. He played without jumping or kicking the piano stool back, without moving much at all. He scarcely opened his eyes and his tunes were easy and soft; those simple, deep under-notes that ground into the room, all over the room, those heavy, clear notes that hung there just so easy.

He wore a shiny suit like from another decade, an old one soiled from weeks on the road; a handkerchief soaked with sweat was stuffed in his pocket. Everything about him was out of fashion, but he and his band loved what they were doing, and our San Francisco style at once became irrelevant.

After, because he wanted a record contract and he knew the riff, he came to sit with Peter and me at our table in the front of the room where everyone could see he was being interviewed. He drank bourbon and smiled and his voice was so old you could hardly hear him through the smoke. He brought his guitar player with him, a young kid from Canada he had picked up in some bar in the East. The two of them laughed and smoked together and talked about women.

The old guy said, "Dave, you gotta admit, I gave you what I promised. You ever seen so many women just dying for you?"

The guitarist only said, "No, no man," and smiled.

"He's a pretty boy, ain't he?" Robert asked, looking at us. "They'll love his pretty picture on our jacket. I was a pretty boy once." He was looking straight at me, and his voice was heavy and drunk.

He put his arm across the table and grabbed my hand, taking my fingers from the glass I was holding.

"I could do you. Get in that box. Bring you up, baby," he said. "I could do any woman in this room." He coughed after he spoke, and couldn't stop and the sound of thick phlegm rose from his throat.

I was too frightened to speak. I was eighteen then, only a few months out of the desert, and I had never even been in a bar before. Now I was sitting with three drunken men I hardly knew, hoping that the old guy would let go of my hand without a struggle.

The guitarist looked over at me. I was clutching my camera with my other hand, my fingers trembling around the casing. He saw this, and in a moment of uncomplicated mercy, he put his hand on Robert's shoulder and said, "But not this one, Robert. She's got to take our picture and make us famous." Robert turned quickly and drunkenly to watch him, letting my hand go free. He wiped the sweat from his face with his fingers and pulled at his nose. He grinned quickly at the young man showing all of his teeth.

"Are you telling me this pussy is for you?"

And that's when I took the first picture I ever sold, of the two of them in that dying bar in the Haight, and I took it because I was afraid. David, with dark shaggy hair and big green eyes, high and sharp cheekbones, glanced across at this old piano player, looked sideways at him, with this strange, calm smile in the middle of that filthy place, a smile that could have been about God. Just then the old guy was looking at David like he hated him, sitting at that grubby little table staring at him with raw jealousy. I picked up my camera and hid my face behind the lens, holding it still for a moment while the light passed between them, and then I took a picture of those two, musicians who lived in buses and motels together but never once trusted each other.

Peter published it the next week in *The Bay Scene*. The band had left then for another date, but a few days after, old Robert hanged himself in the San Joaquin Valley, in a motel in Bakersfield. I had the last picture of him ever taken, and it caught all the nationals, television, and the trade magazines. That issue of *The Bay Scene* even sold out and became a collectors' issue. Soon after that, the photo editors at a couple of national magazines called and asked me to do some work, and I never went back to art school. That's how I started out, and that's how I met David. And I loved that picture, the first thing I was ever paid for, because it caught the hardest truth of that business before we realized it ourselves. I've taken tens of thousands of photographs over these decades, but I never took a better one than that. You might say I peaked young.

CHAPTER 2

The next time I saw David I was living in Los Angeles. It was about six months later, and I had moved there because I could live near the ocean, and Hollywood record companies were asking me to take pictures for them. Only a few women worked in the business then. When the photo editors made the assignment calls we were always the last on the list, and the job was one that the men had refused. But I kept calling them, kept taking pictures, kept walking onto rickety buses and planes to follow no-talent bands into the rough state fair circuit while the men got the private jet jobs to clean New York palaces. For years I worked only with the young musicians who wandered around those windowless backstage rooms, waiting for their slots, juiced and begging for any audience. I had to bring home enough cash to pay the rent, and all I knew was that somehow I needed to say yes every single time or the editors would stop asking.

At first I lived in a one-room apartment in a development built on top of the old MGM back-lot in Culver City, across from the cemetery and the rusted down oil wells. I drove an old Ford from the '50s, and when I got home in the dark morning hours from working some club, I would drive around and around the unlit blocks looking for a parking space, all the time watching over my shoulder. That end of town was the rough part, where the middle class kids from Westchester and Playa del Rey came to make their dope connections with the kids from East LA.

The building I lived in was old, from the '30s, and my room was so damp that the cockroaches lazed around the kitchen in broad daylight whether I was there or not. Nowadays people in LA talk about how great life was back in '69, but this is what I remember: the smog, the sour night smell of that graveyard soil, coming home scared at 2 AM and trying to look dangerous as I picked my way through the streets to my own door.

I hit the Coast magazine offices during the days, hammering on doors looking for enough jobs to pay my rent, and worked the nights in clubs and studios in West Hollywood, teaching myself how to take pictures in the dark. Every time I went out on a job I shot through rolls and rolls of film, hundreds of photographs. I had left school too early and I was always scared of what I didn't know, that I would kill the light or miss the natural frame. That was the way I learned, by drowning myself in my own mistakes, pushing through so much film that finally I would understand and my fingers would react to the rise of a breeze without hesitation.

In the summer a couple of record labels put me on jets to shoot their bands in little nowhere towns like Pueblo or Iowa City. By then I knew how to stand behind a row of empty vodka bottles in a dressing room and shoot straight into clouded mirrors and still get those unborn faces of the bands. Sometimes I would watch them on stage, exploding to an adolescent crowd that could not even find middle C on a piano, and the band would sing so sweetly, their voices bleeding through the cracked nights. When I finally began getting hired for those jobs, I was making decent money, and one weekend I went home and moved away from the Culver cemetery, found myself a place up in West Hollywood where the new music clubs were just opening up.

By then Peter had sold his magazine to a young San Francisco hippie called Matt Rappaport. He sold it for $4000, and Matt renamed it *New Rock City*, moved it to New York, and today it is worth a couple hundred million. Peter went to film school and David stopped playing the blues. When I met him again, he had that contract that Robert Clay had ached so long for, and the band was his, but they were playing rock and roll now in bigger, cleaner clubs. He called me one morning at my apartment, got my number from his own record company who had started to hire me.

"Is that Rosie Kettle? This is David Wilderspin. I met you in San Francisco a while back. You took a picture of me and Robert Clay."

Of course I remembered him, the face in the frame and that slow, calm voice. "Yeah, how are you?"

"I'm okay. Listen, I'm in LA for a couple of weeks, and I was wondering if I could have a copy of that picture. I'd kind of like to keep a good copy. You know, in a frame on my piano or something," he said and laughed. "How are you, anyway?"

"Fine. Working like crazy."

"Would you have time to do a print for me while I'm here? Or you could just send it to the label later on." He still had that flat Canadian accent then, and I could hear his voice skid from nerves. "I'll pay you, of course."

"I can print it today. I'm at the pier in Santa Monica doing a shoot tonight. You could meet me there."

"We can go get something to eat after, if you want." Years later David joked to reporters that music changed his life because every single girl became a possibility. But that was only the story he told; what I remember that day was his shyness and his cracking voice as he set us up to meet.

I spent the day at Publimode, a photo agency off Melrose that was a honey pot for all the photographers in the city. We kept our negatives there in safe vaults, and all of us would show up whenever we were in town, standing over light boxes, talking about the latest offensive in Vietnam or actress or concert we had shot. I was one of the inventors of the job, and our pictures fell into three categories: beads of sweat on naked chests, friendship between the boys, and dissolute backstage lifestyle. With those three we defined the music business to the kids who were buying records. Of course, we never got to sell pictures of the real business, the lawyers and the executives, the guys who made the real money, but no thirteen-year-old with a dollar to spend would ever have put her money down on a picture of two suits shooting up over a gold-faucet sink in the executive bathroom.

The guys from Saigon would come in off the military planes and hit Publimode to find out about songs and bands that were charting, to sit around and hear the gossip. That day while I was getting my negatives out of the vault, one of them sat in a big chair beside me and said, "You know, Rosie, I'd like to have your gig. Take some pictures of druggies on a beach somewhere." He smiled quickly and added, "Course, that's what I do now, but people are always trying to kill me while I'm shooting." He was drinking straight from the mouth of a vodka bottle, not even looking at me. He would be going back in a month, and had only come home to see his wife and new baby.

"I could never do what you do," I said softly, knowing that I would never have the courage it took to make pictures of hundreds of scars across some churning landscape. "If it weren't for guys like you, we would never know what was happening over there. You're doing real work."

He stood up to lean over the light box, looking at the old picture of Robert and David and a string of some others from an English band I had shot the month before while this guy was in a jungle in Asia. He picked up the magnifying lens and cracked it down on the glass, putting his eye over it and staring into the silver of one of my negatives. He stood up, still staring at the strip of light and plastic, and I could tell he was closing off hard on some picture in his head of pain, chasing it to quiet, but proud of it at the same time.

"We both take thousands of pictures," he said, "how do you know mine'll be around longer than yours?"

"You're the hero here." I put my hand on his shoulder. "I'm going to print this now. Want to come?" I asked, but he didn't answer me. I shimmied between him and the table, holding the negative of David in its frame, and he didn't even move as I jerked past. I took a lot of speed then and was always thinking too fast, moving too fast, for those guys in from the war who still knew how to relax. I locked myself in one of the private darkrooms, where the enlarger and chemistry vats lay waiting on opposite walls. I flicked the light off and put the double seals over the door. The bitter, thick smells of developer and fix solutions surrounded me, and for a few moments I could see only black until the darkened red glow of the safe light took over. I love that smell, those places; everything else is extinguished when I am in such a room. The mechanics of a battle was never what I wanted; I chased light my whole life, orphaned myself beside it. I pursued such a small thing, but that was it for me.

The band I was shooting that night had decided it would be a good idea to trip for the session, so they took some acid, and by the time I got to the pier they were huddling with their arms around each other by the night fishermen, pitying the fish. One of the band didn't show. He had eaten peyote and had gone up to Topanga Canyon in the hot, brush hills above the city, and was pretending to be an Indian. The record company rep told me to go ahead anyway and shoot, and in that way the drummer guy up the canyon was dropped from the band. He wasn't there for the picture so he blew his music career.

The pier then was a carny, shooting galleries and cotton candy stalls and coconut throw games. It always smelled of urine and popcorn and rotting fish, but people would come from all over the coastal towns to walk the honky tonk promenade in the warm summer nights, eat some clam chowder, and have their pictures taken kissing in the photo booth. It was a southern California tradition: even my mother had met her soulmate on this pier. Close to midnight, when the fair was packing up, we were ready to close the shoot.

The rep took the band off, and I sat on a concrete fishing bench putting my equipment in the case. I must have looked like a child out beyond my bedtime. I have always been so thin, and in those days I wore my hair straight and cropped short to my ears and dyed copper. That night I wore old jeans and a thin cotton shirt, plain working clothes. There never was any point in wearing anything else. I know I always looked like some scrawny girl too short and small for fashion.

When David came, he stood against the guardrail opposite, watching me. He had grown a beard, a dark, full one over the sharp line of his jaw. Finally, he said, "You have the longest neck."

"What?"

"I saw you then," and he smiled slightly but wickedly with those almond-shaped, deep green eyes. "I have a camera, Rosie. Just like you."

"What do you mean?" I asked, because he carried nothing with him.

"I mean I was watching you work." His voice was low and scratchy, wild a little as though his words kept a lid on his thoughts, did not release him but contained him. He wore a black hat pulled forward across his forehead, and his eyes looked huge underneath the brim. His mouth was wide, and he smiled again, not like a drugger and not quite like a crazy man. "You're a fast mover."

I grinned at him. "Yeah, well I swallow a lot of speed."

"Is that why you're so skinny?"

"Probably. I drive fast as well."

He laughed and sat on the concrete next to me, so close I could smell the tinge of soap on his skin. "Tell me something," he said, "how do these clowns get to make records? Can they actually play music?"

"Listen, my job is taking pictures. If some guy at the company decides he likes the way they look and wants to promote them, that's what I do. If they can't play, there will be somebody to teach them. Half the time it's the picture that's important, not the music. You know the story."

He shrugged, "Well, I'm in it for the music," and it felt good to believe him.

I closed my case and stood up. "Your picture is in my car." He nodded and lifted my equipment, carrying it for me. His skin was Canadian creamy white, no California bronze. He wore dark clothes: blue jeans and a loose, black shirt. He was slender and tall, and walked like every step was part of a plan, nothing like the sunburned, heavy beach shuffle that was the LA rhythm.

When I gave him the photograph he said, "How much do I owe you?"

"Nothing," I said. "It's a present. We had the same break. I've got one on my piano, too."

He smiled at me. "I bet you don't even have a piano."

"No," I smiled. "You're right. I don't have anything that makes music at my place except a stereo."

"I'm going down to Venice now. I heard about a jazz club there. Want to come?"

We left my car in the parking lot below the pier and drove in David's rented Corvette through the back streets to the beach and then through the old town ghetto, out onto the crumbling old promenade. When we got to Venice and Main, he couldn't find the club. David didn't know LA, and it was looking pretty grim down there, ghetto kids huddling along the arcade dealing. These kids were scoring in a safety zone, knowing that the cops did not hawk the arcade at night. Winos were everywhere, day or night, in Venice, curled up in doorways or looking furtively for a free conversation.

We stood against one of the huge pink pillars by the old town hall. The paint had been scraped off and lay in brittle cakes around our shoes. Young boys from down the block were staring at us, grinning and shaking their heads. I said, "Let's get out of here."

He lifted his hand to my cheek, touching my jaw as though his touch would make me safe.

"These guys will roll you before morning," I said.

He chuckled. "You don't know what it means to be rolled. This has got nothing on some of the dumps I've played in the South. This is resort suicide here."

He was a year or so out of the dive gigs, loving his rented Corvette and the hot beach towns. "Rich white music only ever gets you into rich white doors," I whispered. "Here, it's only a shroud." I was facing away from the guys on the street, but I could hear some people shuffling toward us and laughing.

One of them called out, "Got any blow?"

David looked at the guy and said, "No, man. Just looking for some music." The guy laughed and David laughed with him, sinking back on his heels and putting his hands in his pockets. His jacket looked like a piece of cloth draped personally by Armani, and as much as he believed himself still a part of the gigs in dying seafront bars in San Francisco or New Orleans, his record company had bought all that away.

One of the kids whistled a long, shrill noise, a sigh or a chant, and they moved closer to us, quickly.

"Great car, man," said the guy. "Nice pussy, great car. Sure you ain't got nothing? Goes with the car, don't it?"

"Not always," David said. Then he smiled calmly and moved back quickly.

"Get in the car, Rosie," he said. "Just looking for some music, man. That's all," and we moved slowly and evenly toward the Corvette.

We got in and drove off, and when we got a few blocks on he said, "I'm sorry I got you into that."

"We're safe," I said. "It's okay."

"It's not okay. I should have known better." He was driving fast, covering blocks damp from the night mist, up the wet boulevard back to the hot, safe city. "I been beat up too many times, by guys in the business and guys like those, not to be careful." He stopped the car. "Come on," he said quietly, "we'll go down to the canals. I have a friend staying down there."

Down at the canals most of the little, ornate bridges were boarded up then, broken and unsafe. At the beginning of the century someone had designed shady waterlands with gondolas for the rich, but in the late '60s no one could even remember why they called the place Venice. The canals were clogged with thick mud and algae and weeds. The tenants were gypsies in old broken houses with no windows, and once in a while a houseful of painters or poets set up shop. All you could smell was damp earth and cesspool seawater that had flowed in one night without the moon to pull it back out.

David parked his car at the end of Washington Street, and we headed for an old, pink cracker box house on the other side of the inlet. We could only reach it by a little shaky bridge closed off by huge cinder blocks and covered with a city Keep Out sign. He climbed over the top, out over the sludge-wrecked canal, and held his arms out to me.

"Come on," he said. "It's okay. I've done this before." He lifted me up and over the sign and the intricate, old iron railing, and I followed him across and to the back of the house. He knocked hard and called out, "Sonia!" and from the other side I heard the sound of soft footsteps moving quickly back and forth behind the door.

Finally, he reached out and shoved it open, and in the slip of light stood a tall thin woman with long, uncombed light brown hair. She was older, in her late thirties, and wore tight jeans and a huge overstretched brown wool sweater.

"Why didn't you answer the door?" he asked. "I told you I'd come by."

She was smoking, and surrounded by swirls of sweet-smelling, heavy European cigarette smoke. Her hands were so small and delicate they almost looked disfigured, and her skin was pale like faded paper.

"I never know who is coming here," she said, and her accent was Russian, but flecked with upper class English. Suddenly she smiled, reaching out to me. "Come in. You are welcome here of course."

She led us through a debris-ridden kitchen to the front room, and we sat on cushions leaning against the cold walls while she served us a French licorice drink that turned the color of milk when she poured water over it.

All the doors and windows were closed tight, and the inside of the house was swabbed with a dank, soiled smell behind the cigarette smoke. The hum of low voltage was buried in the room, and one wall had been scraped of wallpaper to reveal arcs of olive and gold paint beneath, like some child's rainbow.

She saw me staring at the dishevelled space, and said, "David did that." She smiled. "My parents bought this house for me last month, and it was so awful when we arrived that David said he would redecorate it. He was stripping the walls one day when I was out, and found that painting there. It's like a fresco. I think it's very old, don't you?"

"You know, the house itself is only thirty years old," David said laughing, "so this wall is not exactly gonna be prehistoric." He was sifting through the records that were stacked on the far side of the room. None of them were in their jackets or protective sleeves, and he knelt beside them, trying to match them back to their covers. She watched him for a few moments without speaking, and finally he said over his shoulder, "I can't believe you did this, Sonia. We brought these all the way from London and you don't take care of them. What was the point?"

"You look a little different," she said, ignoring him. His back was to us and he did not respond. "David, I have just smoked the last cigarette. What are we going to do?" She said this suddenly, almost pleading, and a little shoulder of color crept across her cheeks.

"I'll go," he said. "I'm hungry anyway. I'll get some food for us. Do you want to come, Rosie?"

"You can stay here with me, can't you, Rosie?" Sonia asked. "Stay and chat with me."

"Sure," I said. "I'll stay." As he left, she called out to him, "Don't forget the eggs!"

She came and sat next to me, and said, "I really hate being without cigarettes, and it's so hard to find good ones. I don't know where he goes to get the Gauloises, but they're the only ones smokable here." She poured more pastis for us and held the tall narrow glass between both of her disproportionately tiny hands. "So tell me your story, then. You are American? How long have you known David?"

As she moved, the smell of soiled bedclothes encircled her, as if she had long slept in the clothes she wore.

"I'm a photographer," I said. "David and I met a year or so ago. We don't really know each other at all."

She sipped from the glass several times quickly, and put her head back with her eyes closed. "David and I are not together," she said. "I know you are thinking that, but he is only taking care of me a little. We met in London last year." When she opened her eyes, tears slipped down her cheeks.

"I didn't know he did a European tour," I said, and I put my hand on her forearm.

"He didn't," she said. "His father lives there. After Robert Clay died he was very badly off. He went to England to stay with his father for a while." She continued to cry silently.

"Are you okay?" I asked.

"I'm never okay," she said laughing. "I am a calamity. Like typhus. Finally my parents got used to it. I just can't stop it, though. I don't have the confidence to sleep." She swept her long, thick hair back from her face in a greasy arc. "It got worse when I went to London. I was living with David's father, his real father. That was not very good. Now I don't trust the food, either. Baked potatoes, maybe. And hard-boiled eggs. You can usually be sure of those, that no one has tampered with them." Her cheeks were thick and puffy like baby's cheeks, but ruptured with veins. Between us, the air was medicated with the smell of anise, and she flicked her fingers on the glass. She must have been frightened for a long time, and was now crazy because of it, or was now frightened because she had been crazy since childhood. People like this did not survive in my suburban desert, because there they crushed people who were different. I had never known anyone who didn't wash or who was permanently debilitated by fright.

"Do you know David's story?" she asked, glowing with a smile that had caught the lamplight like a mask.

"Nope."

"You don't know about his father? Well, he has two fathers. The good one and the bad one. The normal one and the crazy one." She pulled her legs up close to her chest, and reached across the old carpet for one of several empty matchboxes that lay at our feet, flicking it open and closed again and again while she talked. "His stepfather is a psychoanalyst in Toronto, and his mother is a housewife who used to be a ballerina in England. That's where he spent the early part of his life. I do not know them. I only know the bad father. He is a choreographer, a famous man. His name is Nikolai Paletzine. Have you heard of him?"

"No," I said.

"Well, I suppose he has a rarified audience. Europeans know him, even working class know that name in my country. We are educated so differently, though. And people like my parents, well they worship him in art circles." She poured the last of the pastis into our glasses and added a small amount of water. "Now what will we drink?" she asked, exhaling bluntly. "David has four stepmothers in different parts of the world, a stepmother in every major capital in Europe, he always says. When I met him I had been living with Paletzine for a few months in Hampstead. David came to us after Robert Clay killed himself. He was looking for a room where he would be left alone. That's why he didn't go home to his mother and stepfather. He had started playing with heroin then, and Nikolai did not try to help him, but just ignored it." She wore a necklace made of pea-green glass beads, and she took this off and began rolling them through her skinny fingers, pressing them hard as though she were trying to shatter the glass.

David soon came with the cigarettes.

"Here, Sonia. I'm putting the eggs on to boil for you. These will get you through tomorrow."

"You're so good to me," she said to him as he walked through the slip of light into the room. "What will I do when you go out with your band again?" When he moved past me I felt a damp breeze against my neck. He had a gentle, oval face, and when he knelt beside her he smiled as though he forgave her. "One night," she said softly, "Nikolai took my luggage and all my clothes and put them on the sidewalk. Then he pushed me out the door. He said I was insane and dangerous. He said mad people are dangerous."

"He's a crazy little old man with a bad hip," David said, "an old dancer with arthritis and a temper."

"An unimaginable temper," she said, "Except he was right. People like me are dangerous. Anyway, David left with me. You know, I had no idea he was a musician. We stayed together for a month at my parents' flat and he never made any music. Nothing. He read all the time and listened to the radio and shopped for me. When I stopped eating, he came up with the idea of eggs. That they are the one safe food. I was so afraid and he was the one who figured out how I could eat. Some time during the eggs, he stopped using heroin. And on the plane here he finally told me about his music."

"Here," he said, and opened the cigarette pack for her. She took one of the thick, filterless cigarettes and he cupped his hands to light it. "You didn't leave me any secrets, did you?"

Sonia shrugged. "You know my head is pounding."

"You need to eat something. And it's late," he said, and kissed the top of her head.

She smiled slowly and said, "It's so late, it's early," and they both laughed at this sweet, private joke.

He drove me back to pick up my car in the parking lot beneath the pier in Santa Monica. We stood against the base of the cliffs with the new light coming behind us toward the dark ocean like a rising fire.

"Do you miss Robert Clay?" I asked.

"Not anymore," he said. When I asked him if he was happy with the band on his own he said, "No, not really," and laughed. "You worry too much about being happy. I just want to make music and get laid once in a while."

He said he listened to the radio when he was a kid in Toronto, and learned to play the guitar from it. He left home when he was sixteen and went south to the States.

"I refused to go home and my mother didn't speak to me for a year. She had it in her head that I would be a doctor, a shrink like my stepfather. Eventually she gave in to the music thing. I guess now she's just grateful I didn't want to be a dancer like her." Robert had picked him up in Buffalo, New York in a bar, and they played music together for five years across the Midwest and the deep South. "I played every broken-down bar you can name. And they kept getting worse and worse because of Robert. He loved what he did like a lunatic, but most of all he loved shit. No matter how good a musician he was, he loved junk more."

He talked about mathematical theories, which he said were his hobby, and when he touched me, he put his hands on my neck and kissed me. He stopped when we heard some shouting from one of the old houses across the parking lot.

David said, "I better get home. I'm driving to Santa Barbara tomorrow for a gig. It's getting near dawn now." He put his fingertips on my temples and smoothed my hair back. "Want to take a photograph of me, then?" he asked, his voice shaking just a bit as though he were asking me to a high school beer party.

The smell of the rising morning surf blew across the parking lot, cold and coating our faces with a mist so salty, it could eventually dry the youth from our skin. I had put my case in the trunk and was looking at him, not making a move, not wanting to leave.

"I'm kind of tired."

"That's okay. You'll get another chance." I didn't know whether he was talking about going out again or about becoming famous. In those days, everyone you met believed they'd get the gold limousine.

I pulled out my camera and said, "Maybe I better take this one." The sky was clear by then, a dim, blue-dawn sky. "Take your shirt off. I'll do a rock and roll photo for you."

"A Rosie Kettle special?" he asked.

He took the black shirt from his shoulders, and when he turned around to sit on the hood of the car I could see through my lens a dark, long scar down his arm, stretching nearly from the bend of his elbow to his wrist. I didn't frame it, and he pushed himself quickly back against the windscreen, showing the clean muscles of his arms and broad shoulders.

"You're kind of pale for an LA rocker," I said, but I took the picture in that dazed, morning light, a greedy picture of this guy with beautiful eyes and no shirt, and it wasn't a rock photo at all, but a personal one for me.

He slid to the edge of the car and nodded at me. "Come over here," he said. I stood between his legs, and he put his arm around me and began to touch my hair. He was so close, his lips were on my skin and his breath was warm against me.

"You're a rough guy," I said, "aren't you?" And he put his mouth across mine and groaned as his tongue slipped into me.

He held my shoulders and dragged his moist lips down my neck to the collar of my shirt, then stopped, waiting, and pulled back slightly to ask, "Is that what you want? Some punk?" He started kissing me again, pulling me close. He sank his tongue deep into my throat until we both began to groan again.

When he stopped he kept his face close to mine as though he were afraid to move. He smiled slowly, lifted his hand to my mouth, and gently wiped the saliva from my lips.

"We want the same thing, Rosie. You know that. Neither of us wants anything that's easy."

I lived and worked in southern California for another year before I saw him again. I used to read about him when he came into town, but we never ended up at the same parties. He began to chart with his records, and my pictures were published pretty often, and that was how we knew each other that year, through the glass of other people's stories, the LA way.

CHAPTER 3

In 1971 I was living in an old, pastel blue stucco building off
Melrose Avenue, with brown grass bordering the front walk
and two stubby, dried-out palms offering a fake tropical invitation. My apartment, and streets of places like it, had been built
in the late 1940s to house all the waitresses and bit part actors
and soldiers who came to California after the war to be famous.
This was before we realized that coconut palms and African
fire trees and GI dreams would have to be replaced each year.

The music people had money to burn in those days. Up on
Melrose and Sunset new recording studios were being opened
every couple of months, and the schedules were so busy that
backed-up musicians would hang on the hot street corners
smoking and waiting on their studio time. McCabe's was still a
tiny guitar shop where Clapton and Robertson would buy their
strings when they were in town, and where clusters of wan-
nabe guys would hang to rub shoulders with them. Clubs like
the Troubador headlined the hottest acts on a tiny, bare stage,
and the audience lined up at the original, uncomfortable plank
tables. You could finish the warm late nights up the avenue past
Fairfax at Cantor's, where two guys sat in a booth night after
night writing the classic rules for smoking weed that became a
best-selling book and their ticket to Bel Air.

West Hollywood was jumping then, but it never had anything pretty or gentle about it, no parks, and no view of the
sea. The hookers and the gangs moved in on that end of Hollywood, and the police finally closed the tropical Cranley Hotel
because some children were found one Easter Sunday with a
rock band doing drugs in one of the rooms.

People in LA craved the sea. Year after year people in the music business and the movie business moved farther west toward the ocean, leaving the detritus of their lives behind on the streets in Hollywood. People moved in on the ocean towns like Malibu and Santa Monica, Hermosa, the Palisades, any place up and down the squirm of the coast highway where the cool, salted breeze came across at dusk to clean away the heat and dirt of the city.

A few more of my pictures became memories of dead people, singers under thirty died from drugs and vomit and heart attacks, and every time I printed up, I wondered if the face in the photo was still a live person. It wasn't music that killed them. The ones who died had tags on their toes from the start; lonely kids or greedy kids, kids who were always going to lose control. I would get assigned to the big funerals and the memorials, and sometimes I was even sent to shoot the sad places where they died. Going off with cameras was my job, and those deaths gave me more work. I would stand outside taking pictures of wild-eyed rock royalty in black mourning, while decent, normal people spoke messages to all of us, trying to give us wisdom about dying young and how to avoid it.

Often when I was in town, I would go out to the desert. My mother had died that winter, and for many months my father was inconsolable. I'd drive him out into the high desert to watch the land. He had me take him to all the places my mother had taken me, and we sat on the clean crust of earth watching that landscape for the ghost of her. We could hear the aching pull of hydraulic brakes from the Mack trucks on the highway across the valley, but we seldom made our own conversation. I was too callow to understand his silent efforts to bring my mother back, and it frightened me to see my practical parent so suddenly bereft of logic.

One Sunday I drove out from Los Angeles Airport at dawn, just off a tour plane, hot and tired and grimy from the weeks of stale travel. When I got to the Pinto, my dad decided to make me lunch by the pool, to barbecue in the cool of his tropical garden. He had bought me a trampoline when I was a kid, and it was still in its place in the sun, the canvas faded and torn now, and not functional. I sat on the edge and watched him fling raw, limp steaks onto the coals, while the smell of fire and smoke lay about us. He wore an apron that he had bought himself years before and he gulped whisky out of a thick, golden glass he kept on a rickety TV table. When he filled it the third time, he glanced over at me self-consciously.

"I'm not an alcoholic, you know."

"I know, Dad," I said, although this was a lie: my father had always been an alcoholic.

"This is just very, very good scotch."

I nodded and smiled at him. I was drinking beer, ice-cool down my burning throat; my hands were shaking from the speed in my blood, and my skin grey from the late road nights. I knew that I did not any longer have the right to judge him for his alcohol.

I sat with him on aluminum chairs by the pool, the smell of chlorine and fire burning through the sweet desert air, and he was looking out over the water at the dull red and yellow plastic things he had bought, a ball and a raft and a ring, the things he had owned for years, the things that made his home.

"Your mother loved this swimming pool. It made her feel like she was back in Hollywood."

"She loved you a lot," I whispered. "She loved being with you, even out here." I put my hand on his shoulder, and was surprised at how scrawny and fragile his body felt now.

He shook his head. "No, the only reason she left LA with me was because she loved someone else who disappeared in the desert. A kid she went to high school with."

"Dad, that was just one of her stories. That wasn't true."

Now he stared straight at me and said matter-of-factly, "Yes, it was, Rosie. Jed was his name. They fell in love in high school. They went to college together for a while, and then he left to paint in the desert. He died there. Not in California, but in the Utah desert. They never found his body. You know your mother—she believed she would find him one day in the desert. It didn't matter to her which desert she was in."

It was an instant between us that lasted forever. I understood then that he knew her better than I ever would, and that her passing had destroyed him.

I tried to think of the words that would cross the geography between us, but nothing I could invent was good enough to heal him. Finally I put my arms around him and said, "Whatever happened when she was young, she stayed her life with you. She loved you, Dad."

He kissed the top of my head softly. "No, but it didn't matter. She was my one, great love. And you're the proof of that."

* * *

Before the summer came to LA that year I started to hang at the Marina next to Venice; back then it was just an experiment, so clean it looked like part of Disneyland. People in LA thought it would be cool to have a little harbor, and to live near sailing boats. Decades before, the city fathers traded a lot of money to build the real shipping port down south by San Pedro, ruining that part of the coast forever. Then in the '70s, the developers drained the eerie old swamp at Bologna Creek and let it fill again with seawater. They built hotels and shops and restaurants, all to look like a Californian's dream of Cape Cod. People were hopeful and talked about the great outdoor dream of southern California. The real outdoor dream had already been covered with concrete and oil slicks, but you could look out across the horizon from Marina del Rey at the little herd of sailing boats on the water, those clean offshores blowing, and it almost seemed as though we could start all over again.

I spent most Sundays down there. The boat people would have conversations about rigs and winds, real things, and however late I had worked the night before I would go down to the Marina, this clean, cool place, and talk to strangers about sailing canvas.

It was in the late summer of 1971 that I met Peter again, at the Marina one Sunday. He was scrubbing the deck of a little sailboat, leaning hard across the blue and white fiberglass seats, rubbing the salty dirt around and around in circles. He wore bright green shorts, and his slender legs and thick chest were bare to the bright coast light coming off the water. I watched him work for a while, and when he stood up he saw me.

"Going to take my picture?" he shouted, but I had no camera with me.

I said, "How can you remember me? That was so long ago." We were a couple years on from my start in San Francisco.

"It was your picture that paid for this," he said and swept his arm in a great arc across the bow of his boat. "I sold out to a fellow who wanted to own your reputation." He stood elegantly, a Hungarian aristocrat in a little boating Disneyland. "Would you like to join me? Come on board. I am about to have some wine and chizz," he said and chuckled.

We sat in the sun eating off the deck. He put two slabs of brightly-colored cheese on a small plate in front of me, hesitated a moment, and found a third one which he squeezed in between the others. "We will have a three chizz lunch," he grinned.

He tried to put me at ease by telling me about himself. He said he had finished his Ph.D. dissertation up north at Berkeley while he was editing *The Bay Scene* magazine. "I never received my degree, though, because I left my thesis in a taxi one night." Then he smiled and said, "No, maybe I threw it in the bay. Oh, I don't know."

He thought quickly and spoke slowly, and I had never been so frightened of not keeping up with someone else's thinking.

"Do you like this cheese?" he asked. "It is from the east mountains in France. From an area where the French conspired with the Nazis during the war. Have you seen 'The Sorrow and the Pity'? You really must see that film. I like the cheese, but the people are so dangerous."

Peter was much older than I, nearing forty years old, an adult by my terms. He had grown up an aristocrat in Budapest, and his accent was tinged with all the countries where he had scavenged during the war. His parents had sent him to England before they were taken to the camps. In England, his uncle put him on the street. "Because I broke his favorite cream pitcher." When Paris was freed he went there to find his mother. The American soldiers were asking for Jews to come forward to identify their relatives, but he never did.

"You see, my parents led me to believe that I was not a Jew, and I only ever half-believed the truth."

In Paris he worked for a ministry cataloguing the art that was left in the city. When he left for New York, for another uncle, he still had not found his mother. In America, he was sent to immigration jail because he had no passport, and when he was released he hid in the basement of a friend's house, where he played symphonies on an old record player he had repaired. The friend threw him out for the noise, and he escaped to San Francisco.

He had changed his name twice since he was fifteen, and eventually he found his mother and now lived with her in Santa Monica.

"A happy ending," he said. "Now I make documentary films. But one day I will disappear again. In America you can always erase your past."

He would spread his fingers across his face, look straight at me, and grin. "Thinking is unimportant. Music and pictures, these are important. Art. Philosophy is nothing without art. What do you think is the greatest art?"

"Staying alive," I said.

He laughed. "That is not an art. That is a con. Any Jew will tell you that. Rosie, you must never tell my mother any of my story. Not any. She still does not admit that we are Jews. This is her secret."

At three o'clock we were very drunk and he began to talk of women. He stood up and walked around the boat onto the bow and sat in the bright sun, grabbing his tanned knees close to his chest, and leaning back so far that I thought he might fall into the dark shallow water of the harbor. "Last week I made a decision. I am so lonely, and I do not know how to meet women here. A couple of months ago I was in love with a woman, and I bought a tandem bicycle because I was sure that she would love me and we would ride up and down the beach together. Now I have the bicycle in my garage. Rosie, there are so many beautiful women in Los Angeles. You know, my friend told me to advertise. So I wrote an ad and put it in the *Free Press*. What do you think? I have said that I need a woman who understands film and classical music. I am so hopeful. Why is a Jew so hopeful?"

"Peter, I don't think you'll find that kind of woman in LA."

He shrugged sadly. "I'm going shopping now. Do you want to come with me? I love shopping. Do you like to shop?"

He took me to Thriftimart in Santa Monica, a huge twenty-four-hour drugstore that sold makeup, candy, and canned food as well. "I love America. My dream is to get an American passport so when I shop I will not feel like a tourist. I never make a list, but I always have a route card." We sat in the car in the blazing heat while he planned how he would move up and down the aisles. He put his pen, his list, a calculator, and a pack full of charge cards in a little purse, which he slung over his shoulder. "Sometimes, I worry that I am too much like a Dostoevsky character. What do you think?"

He filled his cart with odd things, boxes of toothpaste and Tampax, perfume, trash bags, and twelve cans of tuna. Most of what he bought was on sale, although the bill was over a hundred dollars. He paid for it all with American Express, and whispered to me, "Really, I only needed the trash bags."

By then it was early evening and we went to his home, because he wanted me to meet his mother. They lived together in a wooden house in the poor end of Santa Monica, almost in the shadow of the old pier. It was a white clapboard house with two floors and a long balcony, one of the few wood-built houses left among rows of stucco-covered apartment buildings. They had a little garden at the front filled with flowers that his mother tended. He had furnished his home with clean, white modern furniture, and his mother covered the contemporary surfaces with little Catholic icons arranged on lace doilies.

She wore an elegant navy blue dress and dark blue pumps and pretended that an influential guest had come. She served us tea and sang a Hungarian rhyme for me.

Afterward, she whispered to him, "You know they were here again. Looking in the window."

He smiled at his mother. "No, no, don't worry."

Then she said to me, "You know, Rosie, there are people who are after my son. People who believe he is a Jew."

She was small and dark, and her face was covered with wrinkles, ancient tracks run wild.

"After him for what?"

"Well, they know who he is and they want to put him in prison. He was in prison once, you know. I was not there at that time, or I would never have let that happen."

Peter walked over to the window and opened it. He stood peering out with his hands folded behind his back and a softened smile on his face.

"They want him again," she said. "I tried to tell them. I left them a note today, but they don't take any notice."

"What do you mean, you left them a note?" he asked suddenly, turning to look at her.

"The ones who live across the street. I left a note on their car. I told them the FBI are watching them."

In a very loud voice he said, "Shall we have something to eat? I will cook dinner for us. Hunger madness is setting in."

"They will be afraid now to take you if they think the FBI are watching," said his mother.

"Will you help me cook, Rosie?" he asked again in that same loud voice.

We walked toward the kitchen and his mother said, "It will probably be better now." She continued speaking to the empty chairs opposite her as we left the room.

In the kitchen he poured cold white wine for us, and told me not to touch anything. He said, "My mother is delightful," but he frowned when he said it. "I must do something. Find her a place that will take care of her." He moved behind me and carefully put his hand on my shoulder. As he did, he walked into the chair next to me and stumbled, grimacing from the sharp pain.

"There are innocent people across the street who now think a crazy woman lives here. They are right, of course. Sometimes it is much worse than tonight. I have to go out looking for her. She is fine sometimes, she was fine with you, and then suddenly she changes."

"Loving her is the best thing you can do," I said. "And it looks like you do that pretty well."

He smiled again, so gently that it only came from the bright gleam in his black eyes.

"Americans are so naïve." He moved near me and touched my shoulder. "Are you hungry? I'm making something you have never had, something which was invented here, the only food that was ever invented in Los Angeles, and this one is due to the bootleggers, an historic food. Would you like to hear the story?"

I nodded and he said, "Just don't touch anything." He threw what now looked like vomit into a frying pan and said, "During prohibition the movie people would get their liquor shored up on the beach, dropped off by the bootleggers who would boat it in from Mexico. I was thinking about making a film of this story. Bootleggers in Los Angeles? You know I used to be a chef. For a short time in San Francisco, I cooked in a very expensive French restaurant. Only I broke an antique cream pitcher and they fired me."

He didn't remember that the story had come out before in a different context, but the facts were never essential to Peter.

The gesture, the meaning behind the facts was the thing, and only when he was angry or crazy did he use facts.

"At Trancas Beach," he said, "is where this food was invented. It was the same year that Thelma, that actress, was killed in Malibu. A houseful of movie people were too drunk to pay for their liquor, so the bootlegger mixed together everything in the cupboards for them, fried it in a pan and served it. To sober them up so he could get his money. Spinach, shredded wheat, eggs, cheese. It's called John's Rendezvous. It's America, it's the movies."

I laughed and said, "You know so many stories."

"My problem," he said, "is I cannot forget any of them."

Afterwards, Peter became my closest friend, really my only one, and though we never slept together, I learned how to live like an immigrant with him, searching out tiny, strange bars run by Russians and wearing shoes to the beach and drinking free glasses of ice water at restaurants as though this were a miracle.

We lost his mother a few times that summer. Once we found her in a hotel in Beverly Hills, once she had gone to his boat, but the worst time she was gone for two days, and we found her on a Friday afternoon at a hotdog stand in Hollywood. She was always dressed elegantly in dark colors with matching shoes and pocketbook. That time she stood in front of a huge pink plaster hotdog which formed the serving counter, cars racing past her on La Brea Avenue, eating a chilidog and chatting to an old man about the War. We took her home and Peter changed her clothes from the soiled dark suit to a soft, white cotton dress and slippers. Then he made her chamomile tea, and when I left they were sitting side by side, he was touching her hair, stroking it and whispering, "You are so beautiful," while she told him a story about the great Magyar hero.

Peter was determined to keep her out of police stations; he believed her madness would be noticed, recorded, and would keep him from becoming an American. He was never quite sure how America worked, but he decided at the beginning that he wanted to be part of it.

"There is a list on a people computer," he would say, "and I am on it. We are all on it. You and your speed drugs are on it. If they find me, I will be deported." When I asked him why, he said, "Because I might be illegal, I can't remember." He said, "I must do something. I am very, very frightened."

When he finished film school, educational people gave him money to make short films about science and great historic moments. Peter loved directing these, and would schedule location shootings of lichens in forests I had never heard of, or he would re-enact the Battle of the Californios at the top of the Grapevine Pass into LA. That summer he had been given money by an eccentric English writer to make a film about the Hindu movement in the state. He was researching it in Ojai, and would go off for days at a time to temples in peaceful places on the coast.

I was on the road almost non-stop in July and August, but whenever the planes touched down in LA, I headed for Peter and his mother and their old wooden house in Santa Monica, where I didn't need anything to protect me. For four weeks I had been flying with an English band, going to El Nowhere shows in hot, stormy summer places like Oklahoma and north Texas, stopping in little towns with big stadiums where thousands of kids would drive hundreds of miles on the wide highways that connected one desolate town to another, just to hear the music. The label had us fly up and down the Midwest on a crazy man's tour that went from Omaha to Kansas City to Wichita to Oklahoma City and Fort Worth, then back to Albuquerque and Denver.

I learned the road on my own, spending that time in the climates of airports and planes and hotels, watching my skin and hair dry out from air that no human was ever meant to breathe. For days I would smell infection under the blankets on the planes, while I listened to the band yabbering about the last set or the last woman or the next drink. Nobody talks philosophy up in those planes, and nobody ever stays clean.

The guys in the band were shooting heroin most of the tour, and drinking bottles of vodka to chase it down. Three times during that trip, some roadie took my cameras and smashed them against hotel walls or plane hulls. That last night we were coasting in from Yuma, Arizona, and I was scrambling around the plane trying to get the very last shots for a *New Rock City* story. We were still taking pictures mainly in black and white then, and the label was pushing these guys as malevolent, so the grainy, smoky airplane light was perfect. While our pilot attempted a few landings over the clear, mountain night, I scurried from the front of the plane to the back, following them with my lens and shutter. Again and again we tried to hit that runway in Orange County, coming close down the black tunnel of the coast in the clear, hot air. A storm over the ocean held us up, although the boys only laughed like lunatics when I lurched with fear at the movement of the plane. Eventually, they ended up asleep or paralytically drunk, and only I was left at the window praying over and over to myself in a quiet voice as we dipped and rose into the electricity.

I took my blue proof crayon out of my bag and began greasing the inner hull of the plane with swallows and flames, tethered to the runway by my frightened drawings. The English drummer awoke suddenly, startled by an arc of color through the window. His vision had long since been scarred by alcohol, but now he watched out the window, confident in the record company's ability to bring him down safely. We landed, falling hard through grinding thunder and not at all like a dove's flight over the darkened sea. When we clattered to safety on the tarmac of the runway, the band members opened their eyes and began throwing food at each other.

That night Peter met me at the airport and took me to dinner with his mother at a little Scottish restaurant in Westwood. We ate fresh salmon and buttery shortbread, and his mother told us a story about children in Hungary who were so brave during the war that they eventually escaped the Nazis by hiding in the woods outside of Budapest. Although I knew she was not sane, I loved to hear those stories, because I was starved for her decency and her simplicity in contrast to the people in the bands I knew.

I saw David again on Labor Day. He had been touring his group during a hard spring and summer trip which swung across the north and western states, playing in decent clubs in most of the secondary cities. He wasn't yet playing the stadiums and he didn't have his own jet like the bands I had been working that year, but he was getting good money and good reviews. LA was the first and last stop he and the band would play, and by then he had the power to request the Whisky on his last date. Rather than a bigger, money-making club, he insisted on spending at least one night making music down in Hollywood with his friends.

On any hot Sunset Strip night, the bands at the Whisky could be the best in the world or they could be new guys from the beach who sang off-key. The atmosphere was rough and tanked, and movie people and music people loved going because they felt it kept them on the edge. To get the crowd going, crazy women with huge breasts still danced in cages, and the strobes and the bass would pummel you into the floor before the liquor was even served.

The girls in the crowd were mostly from the local high schools, and they would come up the Strip from the beach, long clean hair blonde from the sun, wearing tight jeans and see-through shirts. In the summer the girls wore white like village virgins, and they would beg the bouncers to let them in. The guys in the bands and the rich guys in the audience went for those girls, and a lot of life-maneuvering decisions were played out in the hot Strip nights.

David had a new record out and his publicist was working overtime placing news about him in the music papers and the locals, even some in the nationals. It was the time in between for him, when his memory and knowledge of himself was different from the image his publicist and label were cooking up. David thought of himself as a guy from Toronto who loved writing music, a guy who played the guitar and hung on Yonge Street for a wild night or got beat up in Texas for being too wise-mouthed. He still wore cheap jeans and might eat lunch at Denny's, but making records for a living was beginning to pay off. As he traveled the country that summer, at every interview his publicist gave him a new sheet of information he had to memorize about himself: his disdain for fashion, that the rhythm of his speech was slow and thoughtful, his favorite food was smoked salmon and as a child he had eaten it with the lords at Westminster in London. These were things that might have been true, but were not, and in that business the possibility was the reality. By the time he pitched up in LA he had memorized this new self, and he had to split the story of his life, like through a prism, into what was real and what was told.

Every day I drove by a billboard on Wilshire Boulevard that had his picture, one I hadn't taken, hovering over the hot road, and when he and his people checked into his hotel, all the main radio stations covered the moment. Thousands of kids in LA, from the valley and the beach and the hot smoggy towns in the east, were waiting to scrounge tickets to his shows.

A glossy color magazine called *So-Cal* asked me to do a shoot of him while he was in town. This was an expensive magazine for rich, avant-garde housewives, and the angle was that David's father was here from Europe to revive one of his old ballets, and I was supposed to get some shots of David and his father together. These were big, coffee-table spreads, magazines that would keep for months in the houses of rich guys who might remember my name. The magazine paid expenses which would include fees for assistants and day rates I had only ever heard about from the guys who shot for *Vogue*. I had never met the folks at *So-Cal* and didn't know why they offered me that job, but I took it before they could change their minds. It was mainstream work, not national but nearly, and it had the taste of a ticket out of rock photography.

To shoot for those publications you had to come with an assistant. I didn't have one, so I asked Peter.

He said, "Will there be famous people there?" I told him we would start at David's hotel, and then move to the Whisky. When he heard who was playing, and who might be in the audience, he said, "These are not artists, Rosie. These are the same losers I left behind in San Francisco, only they are richer now."

"Well that's the best I can do."

In the end he came because I told him about David's father, that part of the spread was to be with him, and that Peter would be able to meet him. He said with reverence that Nikolai Paletzine was a genius, and I didn't understand why Peter believed people with talent were worth more than those without.

We were set to start at three o'clock, when David's management was sure the band would be awake. We would shoot a few with his father, comparing the two performers, then move to the Whisky where I would shoot the gig. The following morning I was scheduled to return, to a beach house this time, and do some outdoor work.

I showed up at the hotel desk with Peter and my aluminum equipment cases.

The sun was a white-hot LA sun that reflected off the concrete of the city. We walked around the tropical poolside path to the band's rooms and Peter said, "You know, Rosie, we ought to have a swimming pool. People who live in the sun need swimming pools." He was carrying my silver-colored cases, knocking them against his knees and the pool chairs as he walked.

"Peter, everyone but us has a swimming pool."

Inside, the hotel corridors were cold from invisible air-conditioning and we stood outside David's door in the chill and the sudden, dim light waiting for an answer. The publicist hadn't shown up and the arrangements I had been given had not materialized.

"What do we do now?" asked Peter.

"Go have a drink. Wait around. Something will happen eventually."

"How can you do business like that? It's completely disorganized."

"It's casual, that's all." I took a prescription bottle out of my purse and swallowed a pill.

"What is that?" he asked.

"Just something to keep me going. If they're not here now, it's going to be a very long night and I need to be crisp."

He put my cases down and asked, "Are you addicted to something?"

"Peter, this is just to make me stay awake. Nothing to worry about."

He leaned against the corridor wall. "Why is it so cold in here? They really are over-the-top with their air-conditioning." We waited for a few minutes, I knocked again, and then we went to the bar.

Peter said, "Famous people come here. I suppose you know that." It was decorated as a tropical place, pots of huge ferns and palms and South Sea wicker chairs and tables. Beautiful women wearing swimming clothes were the waitresses. He put my cases down and folded his fingers together. "It's too bad you don't have your cameras out."

The speed was wiping me; I was shaking and darting and going hot in the cold and cold in the heat. Though I never shot it into me with a needle, I swallowed enough during those years so that everything I did or thought came at a howling pace. I was drinking pretty fast that afternoon and after an hour I had swallowed half a bottle of vodka. By the time the publicist showed up and took us to see the band, I was just short of passing out.

She was a rep from the label, an older woman about forty, with curly champagne-colored hair and she wore a mini-skirt over stove-pipe shaped legs. She called me "honey" and "darling" in a high-pitched old lady's voice.

She said, "The boys aren't here. They went to Malibu last night to stay with a friend. We can drive out and do the session before they need to get back to the Whisky."

~ 53 ~

"That doesn't give us much time," I said. "It's an hour to Malibu at this time of day."

She put her arm around my shoulders, teetering on very high platform heels. "I'll drive, darling."

We took Sunset in her open-top, black Morgan, and she drove it fast, slamming into the gears without care.

"I got this from my ex in the divorce." We were stopped at a light near the university, and she reached over and patted my knee. "Fun, isn't it?" The road wound on for miles past the frog farm that had become a meditation center and on down to Malibu Beach. Peter was shouting at her from the back trundle seat about Hindu monks in Ojai. We were cramped together with the hot wind heaving around us and I couldn't get away from their voices. When we got to the house off the coast highway she opened the door and led us into a marble-floored hallway. I went straight to the bathroom, threw up, and when I came out she was gone.

Two of the band were sleeping by a swimming pool that overlooked the sea. Eucalyptus trees lined three sides of the yard, framing the pool to the open horizon, and the sweet smell of the sap and the leaves hung in the heat. Peter and I walked around to the silhouette side where the sun had fallen half through the sky, making us dark outlines against the cocktail-colored pool. Peter sat on a chaise longue, and took off his shoes and socks.

One of the musicians awoke. "Oh, you're here. David's in the bedroom." Both of them were thin and pale, wearing trunks that would have fit men twice their size. They both had beards and hair to their shoulders.

The other one woke and watched us, then said, "I'm going for some synthetic assistance. I'll be back in a minute." He spoke with a Southern accent, and hissed through his teeth. He stood up and held his arms out wide to us. "Anyone coming?" He disappeared into the house.

"Where is he going? We haven't got much time," said Peter to the other. "The arrangements were changed."

"Arrangements?" asked the musician, "What arrangements?"

"Nothing," I said. "Never mind. Let's get to work."

"But we're here to take your pictures," said Peter, agitated and louder than before. "And where is Mr. Paletzine?" He didn't understand the way the music industry worked then; arrangements were always changed. Chances were the band had not even heard about the arrangements.

"Who?"

"David's father," I said. "He was supposed to be part of the first session."

"Yeah?" The musician looked at me with a big, empty grin. "Beats me, baby. I never met him."

"Where's David?" I asked.

"He's coming, he's coming. He's just waking up."

I sat down by the pool while Peter walked nervously from one end of the terrace to the other, his hands folded behind his back. My head was aching. I wanted desperately to do the shoot and leave, but I knew nothing would happen until the band was ready. There was nobody to control them, no publicist or manager. I'd seen a hundred sessions like this; musicians were like children in cages and it was the game of people like me and the road people to trick them into keeping to some secret plan, to tell them only the bit they needed to know just before it was going to happen, so late they couldn't change things.

I waited in the open sun for a few moments longer, in the hard, sharp afternoon light, and I thought I would be sick again. "Let's do it in the house," I said suddenly. "The light's not right here. We can at least set up." Inside, I arranged my equipment in a dark, cool corner of the living room, and then sat on a huge pink silk couch and waited for David to appear.

When he came, the rest of the band were dressed and waiting with me. He walked in smiling, wearing jeans and an open white shirt. His hair was damp from a shower and he carried a small white towel in his hands. He had shaved his beard.

"I'm sorry. I took a little longer than I thought." He was looking straight at me, grinning, but I was afraid to speak. I was afraid my words would come dazed and drunk.

Peter said, "Come on, we're shooting over here."

David ignored him and came to sit by me. "It's good to see you again." He put his hand on my leg. I was wearing dark shorts and a thin, sleeveless t-shirt, and his hand was resting half on my shorts and half on my skin. I looked down and stared at it. His fingers were getting bigger and bigger and then smaller and smaller the longer I watched. "It's really good to see you. Are you okay?"

I said, "No," without looking at him. My shoulders and arms were shaking, I couldn't keep them still, and my head was pounding.

"You been drinking?" he whispered.

"Yes."

"And speeding?"

I didn't have to answer; he could see by the way I couldn't control my shakes.

"Come on," said Peter. "We haven't got much time before you have to get to your club."

"Lighten up a bit," said David. "We can be late for the Whisky."

"Come on. Peter's right." I stood up and tried to walk to my equipment, but sat down again halfway across the room.

David took me into his bedroom and I lay down on the covers which were thrown back and crumpled. I remember I could smell his sweat on the bed, and I remember he sat next to me and said, "I'll get a doctor." Then I don't remember anything until the next afternoon.

CHAPTER 4

When I woke I was alone in a room, not any room I knew, a different temperature, a different smell. I had no clothes on, so I got up quickly and went to look for them. I stopped by the window to look into the sun, and saw a flock of wild ducks on a hill in the distance rise into the sky and disappear. I watched the horizon and did not recognize it. The hills were dry, covered with warm brown meadow, curved and soft against a clear blue sky. The room had a polished wooden floor and a small carpet woven with images of native America. A dark wood rocking chair was set by the window; I could not find my clothes so I sat in the chair and swung it gently, creaking against the wood.

My equipment and my clothes were not in the room. Nothing was with me. The sun shone in the window and cast a haze of dust across the floor. I could smell the years of must in the room, and I thought about opening the window but decided it wasn't worth the effort. I continued to rock in the sunlight, and realized that the terrible shaking from before my sleep had stopped.

I could not hear anything, and so began to speak myself. I said, Hello, and, How warm it is, to hear a familiar noise. And when I began to speak I heard another voice from another room, then laughter, and then the floor began to vibrate, because someone was coming to me.

The door opened and it was David. He asked, "How are you?" but I didn't answer. He was smiling, looking at my body and at me, gentle curiosity as he looked at my naked legs and breasts and shoulders. "You look pretty good for someone who nearly died." I smiled back at him. "I heard you talking in here. I brought you tea and grapes." He put the tray he carried on a small table near the bed. "The doctor will be back later to see if we've done our jobs."

I walked to the bed and lay down.

"Were you talking to somebody? I heard talking," I said.

He sat next to me. "To Peter. He's in the kitchen. We brought you here last night when the doc gave you the okay."

He wore bright red swimming trunks, and no shirt, and his body was strong and tanned. I could smell soap in the room now, a clean safe smell.

"Where is here?" I asked.

"My place. My ranch, I mean. I bought it a few months ago. Gave up on the snow. Did you know that?"

"But where is it?"

He laughed, took some grapes in his hand, and began eating. "Santa Barbara. Don't worry. This is my home. You're safe."

"Well, it's just surprising to wake up like this."

"The doctor told us not to leave you alone. He wanted us to make sure you kept breathing."

"What about the Whisky?"

"I cancelled that. Punked out at the last minute like you do when you're an egotistical rocker." He grinned.

"I'm sorry." He shrugged. "Is your father here?" I asked, remembering that I still needed to get those pictures.

"No. He came last night for a while. You know, it seemed like a good idea. He's my father, after all, but I just couldn't stand it."

"What happened?"

"Nothing," he said, and hesitated. "You remember Sonia? Well, she went back to him a few months ago. When he arrived last night he mentioned that she's been in a hospital for weeks now. Her parents finally committed her." He didn't speak again, only continued eating grapes and looking at me. "Somewhere in France. The kind of place that is the end of the line."

"I'm so sorry."

"I tried calling a couple times last night and this morning. Her parents said she's not allowed phone calls and they won't even tell me where she is." The shape of his mouth was distorted from anger that he was trying to contain. I put my hand on his warm, bare shoulder, vainly believing that I, a drug-riddled overdose, could bring calm to him. "This is the kind of thing that happened to my mother, only my stepfather came along and got her out." The sunlight had moved across the room, bringing shadow across the golden wooden floorboards and the bed.

"I am so sorry," I said again.

Suddenly he looked up. "It would have been a terrible picture. No love between me and old Nikolai."

"Maybe I should put some clothes on."

"They're in the closet." I turned to where he pointed and saw a door I hadn't noticed before. "And your equipment."

I walked to it and reached inside for my clothes. He didn't move to leave the room. When I was dressed I sat beside him on the bed and took the warm cup of tea in my hands. The smell of mint awakened me.

"Did I do any of the shoot?" I asked.

"No. You passed out. They thought they were going to have to pump you, but they didn't. Lucky kid. You ever been pumped before?"

"No."

"They shot you full of something and then you vomited all night."

I drank my tea and didn't speak, and for a few moments neither did he. Eventually he walked to the window and opened it, standing in the heat and the sunlight and the fresh air, with his back to me. He put his hands on the rough, unpainted window frame and watched the landscape.

"What's out there?" I asked.

"A couple of horses. I thought I'd learn how to ride so I bought them." When he came back to the bed, he came as a black silhouette against the light, sharpening to color as he got closer. "A lot of people are going to tell you what a fuck-up you were last night. But the magazine will listen to me, and I understand what happened. I saw Robert do it enough times to get the idea."

"It was an accident. It happens to people in this business. It was stupid, but it was an accident. You know, I wasn't counting what I had taken. Normally, I am what they call a light drug user." I laughed nervously.

"Accident or not, you nearly killed yourself. I don't call that light. You know, the guys who make the decisions in this business think you're a liability. There aren't any accidents to these guys. You have a reputation. Why do you think they send you to Texas and give other guys the glossies and billboards?"

"How do you know where I work?"

"Oh, I been keeping tabs, Rosie. It's a pretty small business after all. I asked for you. I wanted to see you, so I told them you were the only one who could get in my door."

I stretched my legs out across the bed and lay back where the sunlight cut across. He was sitting so close, his legs touching mine, and he traced the line of my leg with his hand from my ankle to my thigh.

"Your legs are so smooth. That day in the parking lot, I really wanted to stay with you." His hand felt like soft silk draping across me. "I didn't mean to wait this long. I don't know why it happened like this." He put his lips to my cheek and then my ear. Then he lay beside me, quietly, and for those moments we breathed evenly.

After a while, he took my hand and kissed it. "We should go let Peter know that you're okay."

I nodded. "I'm worried about this job, David. I have to file today. I have to give them something."

"You know, everyone's gone. My old man and even the band. They went off this morning."

"What time is it then?"

"About four."

"God, I blew that, didn't I? Where did they go?"

"Home. Back East. Relax, Rosie. You could sit in the sun for a while. We could go for a swim at the beach."

"I need a picture of you for this assignment."

He gave a long sigh. "So come and take your picture now. Let's get this over with."

"Without the band?"

"Why not?" He went to the closet and pulled my cases out. "Come on."

I followed him to the kitchen where Peter was sitting at the long butcher's table. The room was cool and dark, the walls covered with dark wood. The smell of mint was everywhere, and the counters were covered with bunches of fresh, damp leaves, crushed and filling the room with thick fragrance.

Peter looked up when I crossed the doorway. He smiled but barely moved, his hands folded on the piles of mint in front of him.

"Ah," said Peter, "Rosie, how are you feeling? You are walking, anyway. That in itself is better than last night."

"I'm okay."

David put his arm across my shoulders. "You're cold, you know. I'll go get you a sweater. The doctor said you shouldn't get cold."

David put my cases down on the red tiled floor, and went to the next room.

"I had a fascinating conversation with Mr. Paletzine last night," Peter said. He let his eyelids close at the memory. "He is a genius."

"Did you ask him if you could make a documentary about him?"

"It wasn't appropriate to ask him that. You can't just blurt these things out." He paused suddenly. "I am a very rude man. Sit down, Rosie. How are you feeling? You were a stupid girl, and if I thought about it I could be very angry with you."

David came back in the room and lay a soft blue cotton sweater around my shoulders.

"Maybe we oughta get away from these overdose conversations," he said. "Maybe Rosie's had her fill of all that. Anyway, she wants to get her photo of me. Where do you want to do it? Inside or outside?"

Peter said, "This is a fantastic place. Meadows and the sea and this old house. You could shoot your pictures anywhere; everywhere is a frame. What do you think? Fantastic, fantastic."

"I guess we could look for a good shot with a sun glow. It's a beautiful day," I said.

Outside, we followed a cobbled path bordered by high bushes of marguerites. Down toward the sea, the path opened to a dry grass paddock enclosed by a fresh-painted white fence. Within it two horses, a roan and a black mare, were standing alongside each other. They did not look up when we came.

"When did you do this?" Peter asked. "I thought you were touring these last months."

"There's a guy who takes care of stuff for me. Or the record company will."

"Do you mean you have servants? I could make an interesting film about that, couldn't I? Fellows who take care of your life when you're not in it. Like a mirror version, only empty."

David was smiling, and he had climbed to sit on the fence. "I'm planning to build a recording studio here. There's an old stone barn up the hill. Look," he pointed, "that's an Indian burial ground where that pile of stones is. Nobody's ever dug it, but the guys at UCSB want to come have a look before Christmas. Behind it is this barn, and down the other side in the hill is a cave with some Indian rock art. So after they've had a look, I'll put my studio together. This is the first time I've stayed here since I bought it."

I leaned across the fence next to him, and he glanced down and put his hand on my shoulder.

His eyes had turned light green and were set wide apart, so wide they appeared to hide nothing. His skin was brown from the sun of the summer tour, and the scar on his arm had gone light grey against that deep color. He seemed older than I remembered, but at least he had no tracks on his arms.

He grabbed my hand. "So where do you want me?"

I took my equipment out, and set the tripod by the fence. Peter said, "It's so boring when Rosie takes pictures. She never lets me talk." He walked off through the tall grass toward the hill.

"Stand wherever you want, but don't pose. I don't know how to take pictures of people who pose."

He laughed at me. "I thought that's all you did, Rosie. You been taking pictures of guys so long you forgot they're posing for you? That's half the point of doing a concert, Rosie Kettle gets you on film."

"I thought you said I was the drag-end these days."

"I said people think you're unreliable. No one thinks you're a lousy photographer. There's a difference." His voice was confident, but he was standing like a kid with his arms hanging limp at his sides, like I could have whatever I wanted from him.

"You know, I'm not sure I can do this," I said. I put my arm over my eyes.

"What's the matter?" he asked. He put his hand out to touch me. "Hey, baby," he whispered, "come over here a minute and rest."

For all the years I had worked in LA I had never been the center of anyone's attention. Shooting rockers was a job for people who could keep their problems and their hangovers to themselves. Now suddenly I stood in this hot, dry field, exhausted and sick from so many kinds of my own abuse, and David was pulling me close to him for safekeeping.

"I'm kind of groggy. It's hard to focus."

"It's way too hot out here for you," he said. "Let's go inside and get you some water." He took my hand. "I think you're burning out, Rosie. You were pretty close last night. You have no idea how scared we were."

"What do you want me to say? I really am sorry."

"I want you to say you'll be more careful with yourself. Because I'd like to know you a little better."

He stood by the fence, leaning on the hot wood. His hair clung damp with sweat to his face.

I nodded.

"Would you do something for me? Would you let me look at your arm?"

"Why?"

"I want to know what that mark is."

"It was a long time ago. It got smaller as I got older."

"Did it happen on the road?" I asked.

He looked at me suddenly, like I had said a few words of incredible stupidity.

"It was before I left home, before I left school." He pushed his sweat-damp hair straight back off his forehead. "Look, my father was always pretty crazy, and my mother got that way before she finally left him. He made her crazy. Completely. That's how she met my stepfather. You don't know any stories like those, do you? You come from some clean place out of the movies, people with easy lives who went to church and built airplanes. I got these marks from a knife, Rosie, and now it's over. Leave it alone."

We took my cameras up the hill to where Peter sat on the pile of stones. When we got near him he held up his arm for us to stop.

"Are you finished?" he whispered.

"Nope." It was silent on that hill, no wind, not even the sound from the sea, a needle of silence and heat on the dried-out landscape.

He sat very still, staring at us. Hidden in the spaces between the stones were four or five wild kittens looking out at us with sick eyes crusted with pus.

"I guess you found the secret of my ranch," said David, and when he spoke the cats leapt from the hot stones in different directions and disappeared into the grass. "The realtor told me there was a colony of wild cats I'd have to get rid of. There's a guy coming next week to do it."

I knelt in the brittle, stinging grass, holding a small camera. I pulled my arms tight to my sides to make myself rigid like a tripod. David squatted by the stones. He licked his finger and put it in the soft powder dirt surrounding the mound, and brought the soil to his mouth.

He said to Peter, "They say you can tell where the water is by doing this."

"But the sea is just down the hill," said Peter, and David began to laugh, he lifted his head back and laughed out loud against the warm red afternoon light, with crusts of soil clinging to his lips.

David drove us home that night and did not stay with me. The following afternoon Peter called me to tell me he had been at the police station. They called him in because his mother was dead, killed by a car on a street in front of Safeway in Santa Monica. When I got to his house I found him perched on a high stool in the kitchen. He had drunk a lot, and his face was flushed.

He said, "It was a way for me to kill her myself, not to find people to take care of her."

I lifted one of his hands from around a huge, brittle-thin brandy glass and held it.

"But you did take care of her."

"No, I only wanted the other mother. I only knew the one who took care of me. I was stubborn about her getting old and frail. I pretended she wasn't as bad as she was." He smiled slowly and put his hand across his face. "You know, Rosie, I was right about something else, too."

"What's that?"

"They do have a people computer. They have caught me on it, and I will never be an American now. I think I need a lawyer," he said.

* * *

~ 65 ~

For the next few weeks I watched over Peter, wandering the funky beach towns like Hermosa and Redondo with him. We scuttled over sandy blacktop streets down by the beach walls and the stucco taco huts, and he would recite for me the opening sequences of his dream documentary, a film he wanted to make about Paletzine and Stravinsky and Bakst in pre-World War II Europe. He was talking this out as a memory of his mother, because he believed that had been her life, although in truth he had not the slightest idea of what her life really was.

Down at Hermosa we sat on an empty beach in the warm September breezes, eating takeout pizza from the huge, flat greasy box on the sand. Peter would wave his arms in the air, mapping a scene, then finish a piece of pizza dripping with cheese while I gave my opinion. The only people left on the beach now that schools and colleges had started back were the out-of-work surfers who would lope by us on their way to the waves, carrying the big old heavy boards they still used in those days.

Peter was nothing like any of them. He still pretended to be a European, wearing heavy brown leather shoes without socks, carrying his purse, and sometimes arriving at the boardwalk in a taxi. He wanted so to be an American, and was obsessed about the people computer whose existence he had proven, but he would never allow himself just to fit in. He spoke of his film as though it were real life, describing it with wild sweeps of his hands and in a loud voice that made the surfer-boys jump.

"Paletzine is a genius. That was the best night of my life, Rosie. He was brilliant. That and saving you, of course."

"You said he barely spoke."

"Yes, but what he said was perfect."

"That's not what David said."

"Ah, well that is something entirely different. The father and son don't trust each other." He smiled. "A well-known literary theme."

"To hear David's story he's a pretty evil guy."

"That doesn't mean he is not a genius. We make allowances for people with artistic genius." He stuffed more pizza into his mouth. "When will you see your man again?" He looked at me and smiled then, his cheeks bulging with pizza crust and sauce and anchovies, chomping away at it all with a big grin.

* * *

This is what my mother used to say to me: Keep away from what you want. When your hand is nearly touching something, grabbing it, keep back from it for a moment. Think about why you want it, what part of you needs it. That's the way to learn about what you desire, by not having it. Having something makes you stop seeing it. This was how she stopped drinking, she said.

I had forgotten she said that.

I went back to Santa Barbara one night when the black country sky was mashed with grey clouds, glowing through by a moon backlight. Take it, have it: I went as a kid, showing up at his door. David had finished moving into the house, and his people were around, a gardener and a builder; even a gate-keeper who stopped me when I drove up, coming out of his smoky, tiny cottage at the bottom of the long drive to open the gates for me.

I hit the lock and sat in the dark for a minute. I was afraid of this young punk, but to be honest I was more afraid of David, of whether he would be alone and whether what I remembered of him was real or just my own loneliness. Suddenly, I realized that my surprise visit was likely just a grab at humiliation.

The gatekeeper knocked on my car window. "What are you doing here? This is private property."

"I'm here to see David Wilderspin."

"He's not expecting anyone."

"It's a surprise."

"Maybe he doesn't want your surprise." He was dazed by pot but young and cocky anyway. "Get out of the car. Come on, I'm cold out here."

I walked around to where he stood, near his open door. Music was loud inside and I could feel the warmth from his home spread toward me across the crisp night.

"Lean against the car so I can frisk you," he said.

I turned and rested my body across the cold curve of metal and his hands moved down my legs and up between them. I wore black sandals and a very short black knit dress. He put his hands on my waist, under my black leather jacket.

"Are you a friend or what?"

"A friend." I was aching in the cold against the car.

"Never seen you before. What's your name?"

"Rosie. Are you finished?" I asked. He stepped back.

"I gotta call up to the house. Wait here."

He went inside his cottage. I looked up the hill, but all I could see were rows of tall eucalyptus trees lining the drive, and their sharp, bitter smell filled the air.

When he returned he swung the huge gates open. I drove up to the front of the old house and stopped before a wide wooden porch that framed it. David stood in the open doorway, smiling. He wore wheat-colored jeans and a plaid shirt and he bent his head forward to see me in the dark.

I said, "Long way to drive on spec. Is this okay?"

He held out his hands to me. "Of course. It's good you came. Come in. You want something to drink?"

"Sure." I followed him into the kitchen and sat at the long table. The room was warm and I could smell the trace of fresh soap that followed him always. He stood behind me, taking two glasses and filling them, and the sound of his body moving, the soft vibration of his step and his shirt-sleeves sweeping against the counter, were like thunder in the silent night. I turned and put my hand on his sleeve and he stopped. He put the glasses down. I could never have stepped back then. Whatever

I wanted from him, I wanted so badly I was shaking just sitting near him.

"Were you in the middle of something? Am I disturbing you?"

He pushed the hair back from my forehead. "No. I was working on some songs, that's all. You know how that goes. One muse leaves and another arrives." He grinned. "How's Peter?"

"Worried. He thinks they'll deport him, but he hasn't got another country to go to. He needs a lawyer, but he's too lazy to go out and look for one."

"He's not lazy, Rosie. You ever been scared before?"

"I'm scared now."

I had not moved my hand from his shirt.

"I'll call my lawyer tomorrow," he said.

"He can't afford your lawyer, David. He hasn't got any money at all. He lives hand to mouth, like the rest of us."

"I'll pay for it."

"Why would you do that? You don't even know him."

"There are at least a dozen people I hardly know who are on my payroll. I hardly know everybody." He handed me the glass and stood behind me. "Would you let me kiss you?"

"I don't know," I whispered, "but I'm clean now, you know."

I put my hand on his face, and he moved closer and put his tongue across my lips, wetting them. I opened my mouth, but he leaned back and looked at me.

"I've been waiting a lot for you," he said and levered himself up to sit on the counter opposite me.

"Why didn't you call me if you've been waiting?"

"You know I don't call people, even my friends. I don't call anybody."

"Why not?"

"I just don't." He sighed softly. "I work a lot and sometimes knowing people takes a lot of time."

"There's a rumor in town that you have plenty of time for women."

"Yeah? Rumors are easy to start and easy to believe. I don't pay much attention to mine. You and I are too close for that."

"You think so?"

"We were close that night in Venice. Even that photo you took way back. We were always close."

"We hardly know each other."

"You slept here once and I watched you."

"What do you mean by that?"

"I've been thinking about it, about you. You looked so beautiful sleeping that night in my bed. I watched you a lot." He stopped then, and I could hardly breathe in the silence. "You're more frightened now than ever, aren't you?"

"Yes."

"I'm sorry. I haven't seen you in a long time. I've been thinking of all the things I could do to you, all the ways. I could come in here," he ran his hand down between my legs, "or here," and put his other hand across my butt. He sat on the table and faced me, putting his fingers between my lips. "Or I could just come into you here. What about that, then? Shall I start here?" He slipped his damp fingers from my mouth.

"What about me?" I asked.

"You tell me what you want."

He began to unbutton his shirt, and he slipped his arms from it. Then he sat on the chair and unzipped his pants. He spread his legs apart and put his fingers over his penis. "Look at this. Touch me." He took my hands and put them over him. "Touch me then. Put your mouth on it, Rosie, and suck me."

"I'm so thirsty."

He pushed his hands under my dress and moved them up to my breasts, holding them and squeezing my nipples. "What do you want, then?" I stood up and his hands slid to my waist. "You want me to do all the work?" he asked, looking up at me. "Okay, if that's what you want. Let's go somewhere soft."

I followed him to his living room, and sat on the couch, but he pulled me back up. He began to stroke my neck, then my legs, touching my thighs, and pushed my dress up to my waist. He pulled my underpants down and put his fingers into my hair. Then he knelt on the floor and put his mouth over me, and his tongue in me. He pressed his hands against my hips, warm, and reached high inside of me with his tongue. He was sucking, then pressing onto me with his tongue, he was pressing on my bone and my blood was moving in a rush. All the feeling in my body was rushing like a river to that point and his tongue, slipping around and again, not letting go. I tried to move away; my arms and legs were slicked with sweat and I needed to stand up for a breath, but he held tight, and all the time working his tongue inside my cunt, his breath getting hotter and hotter on the skin between my legs. I hated him more and more for not bringing me off, and I still couldn't move away and then he did it, and I let go of him, the muscles in my arms and legs slacked and caved, and I became him, became the power of what I desired.

CHAPTER 5

David's lawyer had a huge office in a new black-glass Beverly Hills building with floor-to-ceiling windows looking out on the yellow-brown smog horizon of the city. The law firm was filled with good-looking guys who were dying to be the celebrities, but who early on realized they had no talent and so worked the labels for clients instead. In a few years they did become celebrities, and the record company executives did as well, but at that time no one cared about the names of the lawyers or the businessmen.

We took Peter up to the twenty-sixth floor in a glass elevator. We could see the hot street sinking below us, and Peter said, "What if there's an earthquake? The one last year was terrible. You just can't get away from an earthquake."

"Don't worry, Peter," said David. "These big buildings are built on rollers now to move with the ground."

"Rollers? That doesn't really make me feel much better. Why do we live in places like this?"

"You don't," I said. "You live in Santa Monica in an old wooden house that's been there over a hundred years."

The lawyer's name was James Gallas and his private office was a corner one, spread wide across an area that was bigger than that of any record executive. The walls were made of glass and faced west, so that the afternoon sun blazed at the air-conditioned room. It was furnished in dark red leather couches and chairs, and the floor was covered in thick, white carpet. Mayan icons stood on a table and on his desk. The room smelled like laundry dried fresh in the sun.

"Sit down, sit down," he said. David and I took places on one of the couches, but Peter walked to the window. "Would you like a drink? Anything you want." He walked to a tall oak cupboard and opened it. He was slender and wore a suit which was cut to drape across his shoulders and hips, to drape even as he moved, like a statue. His hair was very blond, bleached from the sun and long as well, but precision cut with a razor. He had blue eyes and beautiful hands, and he spoke softly and precisely.

"What about some of that Sangria, like you had at your party the other night? I liked that," said David.

Part of the oak cupboard was a refrigerator, and James pulled a pitcher from it. "That was a good party, I guess. I'm glad we got the go-karts running in time. Everybody seemed to enjoy them."

"Don't know," said David. "I didn't get around to trying them."

"You should have. They were terrific. Terrific. Why don't you come out to the house this weekend, come and try them then."

"We'll see," he said.

"What would you like to drink?" James said, turning to me.

"The same. That'll be fine."

"And you?" he asked Peter.

"Me?" Peter was still looking out of the window, and was obviously surprised that he had been included. "Oh, nothing. Thank you though."

"Sure?"

"Yes, thank you. This is a fantastic view. It must be a fantastic feeling to float from here to the ground."

James watched him for a moment, and then walked to us with our drinks. "But you'd die," he said.

"Yes, of course," said Peter. He looked at me and raised his eyebrows. "I forgot about that."

"So," said James, "you've been having some problems with the immigration people. Why don't you tell me about it?" Peter began the story, starting with his birth in Budapest, and by the time he had finished the lawyer said, "That's pretty scary."

Peter looked at David and then at me. "Yes, I imagine it is. Scary, yes."

James said, "Well, the bad news is that the immigration principles in this country are very serious, but the good news is that the immigration people are not. Not for people like you. If you were Mexican we might have a problem." He had been taking notes on a yellow pad while Peter was telling his story, and now he began flipping the pages back and reading what he had written. "I can see a few points here. Things we can work on. But I'm not an immigration lawyer. There's a great guy two floors up who helped me with an English band a couple of years ago. I'll talk to him. Don't worry about it."

"Don't worry about it? I can't think of anything else."

"Don't worry about it," James said again. "Just be around to sign some papers. Leave your phone and address with my secretary and I'll get in touch in a couple of days. Don't stew about it. We'll fix it."

"Is that it?" asked Peter. James was standing up and moving toward the door.

"Well, yeah. If you could just sign a Power of Attorney, we'll get moving on it. And I need to have any paperwork you have on this, letters or orders, anything."

"But what if the immigration police come and get me."

James walked to Peter and put his arm across his shoulders. "They won't. Don't worry. Oh, and David, give me a call when you have some time. It's about time we started work on a new contract for you."

"I've got another record left on the deal, James."

"Yeah, I know. Just a little constructive hassle. Now or never, while things are going so great. Good to see you all. Give me a call, David. Don't forget."

"Sure."

James went into his secretary's office for a moment, and came back with some papers for Peter to sign and a small box. He handed the box to me.

"A little personal present." As I opened it he said, "It's fourteen carat. Corporate identity." He shrugged his shoulders. Inside the box was a necklace, a small gold triangle pendant with the initial "G" etched onto it.

"James is running for City Council," said David.

"Thank you." I put the box in my pocket. "Thank you very much."

"Have you been validated?" he asked, and Peter looked bewildered. "Your parking sticker, I mean."

James walked us to the elevator, hands on his hips and leaning forward as though he were ready to lurch off somewhere. He smiled a huge, sweet smile as we got in the elevator, and lifted his hand in a kid's wave.

The car was in the subterranean parking lot under the building, cool like the office but dark. Peter collapsed onto the back seat, spread-eagled across the leather.

"That was good," he said. "That was very encouraging. Wasn't it? Don't you think it went well?"

"It always goes well with the guys who work for you. That's their job."

"You mean he was lying? You think I should worry?"

"I think he'll keep you out of jail. I don't know about the rest. Although my father's an American. If they let him be American, you oughta qualify."

"Your father is a genius. That's why he got his papers."

"Anybody can be a genius, Peter. You just need a good publicist. Isn't that right, Rosie?" He started the car and pulled out slowly up the darkened ramp. "Don't worry, Peter. James'll take care of you. Now, if only I can keep him off my back for a couple months."

"Why?" Peter swung his legs onto the back seat, leaning against the side window with his shoes resting on the cream-colored leather.

"We'll be rehearsing and recording in a few months and I've got some songs I want to work on now. This is my vacation time. You gotta understand, I have a dozen people who pull paychecks from the band and all of a sudden they got nothing to do. The lawyer, the manager, the PR guy, the roadies. The roadies are the only ones who leave you alone. The rest of them are on my back trying to prove they're worth a paycheck for nothing. They'll be calling me with ideas or parties and I'll be wanting to work the new songs. James will be sitting at the top of this building thinking of billable Wilderspin hours."

"He seemed good to me," I said. "What about the business about your contract? That was pretty smart."

David shook his head. "No, that was just stupid. Rosie, there's a whole other side to this business from the photos and the stage. You've never been part of that. James can't renegotiate my contract now, not before the next album is out. I'm making some money, but I still don't get the best venues and I don't have control of the production. I need to find a way to the next level. And, for God's sake, he knows I don't want to leave my company. I got one of the best deals around when I went with the label. Sure, they still calculate the points on me like everyone else, but at least I know they're willing to put enough of a budget behind the marketing if I can keep delivering." We left the cool cavern of the garage and David stopped the car at the top of the ramp. "This isn't about the music anymore," he said.

"Most of the bands I know don't try to out-think their lawyers," I said.

"Most of the bands you know are gonna end up dead or broke."

* * *

By the end of that year, David and I had carved out a kind of silent understanding, and it was easy to trust him, easy to imagine him as my family. One afternoon in early December I went to a studio to watch him work, to a private place out by Zuma Beach that belonged to another band. David had borrowed one of the small rehearsal rooms that week to get some songs set for his own band.

Watching musicians work was part of my job, hovering against the wall of some studio, waiting for days through all the false starts and off-sync hash and pound of the instruments. A band might nurse the same bar hour after hour, and I would have to wait in that veil of painful noise until the moment when the gears of the music finally fell into place and I could get some good shots. The look of those studios was charmless, places filled with bright electric light where a shadow in a picture would mark a singer for death or a scowl might print up as madness. These rooms resembled warehouses, unadorned walls and floors covered with great knots of cords connecting the equipment and machines to each other and to the band, cords that could strangle you or trip you or fry you. Sometimes they would hole up for days and a technician or one of the women with the band would bring a bottle of vodka and takeout in paper bags; when the bands started turning real money from their audiences, the companies brought in single malt scotch and champagne, and later personal chefs catered huge tables of salmon and melon that would keep the boys healthy until the late, lost nights when they would decide to put guns into their mouths.

That week in December, a red tide had hit the coast. The water for miles had turned red overnight and it lasted for days, and fish by the thousands shored up dead on the beach, piles of fish stinking and rotting on the sand from this slapping, warm red water. This happened a couple of times a year, and the lifeguards told people to stay out of the sea, but this was a private beach, and a few guys from the studio who knew nothing about the ocean were out on boards trying to surf between the floating fish bodies.

The building was an old, converted beach house, and to get in I had to pass through an alley of white-washed walls covered with magenta bougainvillea, into a tropical garden lifted from the sea. The sandy path was tufted with rubbery ice plant, the roots precariously lodged in the dry salt-covered soil. A glaze of salt formed over everything on the coast, ate away at surfaces, whether skin or stucco. The back of the house was wood, with a wide plate of a window, and the paint on the wood had been scaled and crumpled by the salt spray. Out across the water, the surfers were floating on their boards in the calm, oily sea. Even in the winter, without the heat, the smell rose up from the beach and covered everything with a layer of red tide rot. In a few days the tide would disappear and the beach-cleaning trucks would come and scrape the fish from the hard, packed water's-edge sand.

One of the surfers began paddling in through the dull mist, and I stood by the door waiting for him to hack his board upright into the sand. The sun was crashing quick across the horizon and as he came to me I realized that I knew him, an engineer I had worked with a couple of times in West Holly-wood. He wasn't wearing a wet suit and he stood by me drip-ping and shivering.

"Hi, Carl," I said. "Good waves?" His face was bright red from running up the beach, and he was grinning, sparkling with the water and the exercise.

"I guess," he said. "You here to see David? Dumb question. You're not exactly here to shoot, are you? He's inside. Come on, I'll show you. Been here before?"

"No, never. I've never worked with the band that owns it."

"Ah, Rosie, you missed a good time, then. This place used to be a whorehouse, you know." He cackled as he led me through the corridors, beyond a room that opened wide with new couches and chairs, into a long hall with a chain of doors on either side. "Some of these are studios and the others are just places to sleep. This is where the naval officers used to come to get laid during the war." He stopped outside one of the rooms. "He's in here."

"Where are you working?" I asked. "Who else is recording today?"

"No one. I'm working with David. We're trying to get some songs down so he can play around with them back at his place. Look, I'll change my clothes and be back in a sec." He pushed the door open, and called in, "I'm back. See you in a minute."

When I walked in the room David asked me what time it was. The windows had been blocked and sealed professionally and the room padded in order to contain the sound.

"About four o'clock. Even the surfers are packing up."

He unplugged himself, put his guitar down, and took his headphones off. "Wait till I get my own studio built. We'll have some fun there." Whenever he talked about his plans for Zaca Creek, he was always light-hearted, like a kid with a great idea. "Want a drink?" He came close and put his arms around me.

"No thanks. What are you working on?"

"Songs for the new album. We'll be rehearsing in a couple months and I'm getting the material together." He sat down and said, "I'm tired, you know. I guess I'm about finished. Want to hear something?"

"Sure." I was expecting music, but he pulled out an old review that had appeared in the LA papers, a write-up of his second album. "It is hard to overestimate the importance of this work," it began. He read it to me and said with frustration, "What does that mean?"

"It means they liked it."

"I know that. But what does it mean? It's embarrassing. It actually makes my music sound stupid because it's so stupid. A song isn't a work. They make it sound like I discovered DNA."

Several canvas director chairs were arranged in a semi-circle around the old stool he sat on, all of them empty and facing him. The floor was covered with a scrawling mass of thick cords. I sat in one of the chairs, and said, "They liked it."

"Three minutes on love, that's all I do." After the sound of his voice fell, the room was immaculately silent. "Listen to this." He walked to the playback to run it. "I love this one." He waited a moment, and then flicked his switches. His voice and his guitar came hard through the room, cramming in at every wall, the back rhythm shaking and humping around me and his voice grinding with it. I watched him move calmly above the boards. His skin was tanned, but that dead light made it look the color of granite. The walls of the room were painted grey, the equipment was black and chrome, and the light gave a streaky harsh haze over this. He moved slowly, and I was thinking of the pictures I could take that would make his tiredness disappear. Suddenly, that hard beat subsided, and his deep, soft voice came off the tape, singing on its own almost a capella about a mad Frenchwoman. I could hear every breath, so close his voice seemed to press around us with mourning, because this was a song for Sonia. When the tape stopped, he lifted his head to look at me.

"What do you think?"

"It's beautiful," I said. "You really are better than the others in this business."

"Let me try something here." He sat down with his guitar to pick out a new top line against the old rhythm. He did that again and again for an hour, dissatisfied, and each time destroying the lines he had just created. I sat in a darkened crack of the room, and he didn't speak to me. He just kept furiously slicing pieces of his own voice into the silence, and then beginning again.

When he stopped, he did so suddenly, letting the tape stutter through the reels. "It's fucking hard to do this without an engineer. Where the hell is Carl?"

"I'll help. What can I do?"

He smiled, "Working the boards is more than pressing buttons, baby." He walked to me and put his hand on my face. "Is it foggy out there?"

"Not when I came in."

"Want to go for a walk?"

His clothes were wrinkled, and the great empty room around him smelled like his sweat and his cigarettes and the faint, bitter odor of his coffee.

"I brought you some vitamins," I said. "You don't look well, you know."

"I'm shattered. I've been here for days now. Do you think the vitamins will help?"

"I don't know. I think the sun would help."

"We don't get to see each other much, do we? When the band comes and we start rehearsing it will only get worse."

"It's okay. I'm not complaining."

"You know if we lived together you wouldn't see me much more. I travel a lot."

"I travel a lot, too."

"Yeah," he said. "But when you're home you're bound to be lonely. Do you think we ought to live together?"

"Where would we live?"

"I was thinking in Santa Barbara. I guess I should ask you, though."

I laughed. "So you want to know if I'll move in with you?"

"Yeah. That's what I'm asking. I guess it's time for me to settle down now. All those years driving around the South with Robert Clay, you know, I just kept thinking one day it would get easier. I watched him on the road with these hookers who would fuck him silly for five bucks. Every night he'd be drinking himself paralytic. He kept promising me that he would get us a contract, but he was way past it. Just one more bluesman nobody took care of; nobody on his side. And he had no idea when to stop. Look, what's important to me is music and you. Maybe the whole thing, maybe a family. Did you ever want that?"

The tape had run out and the room was quiet and cool. I said, "Yes."

"So what do you think?"

"I think it sounds good."

"You can do whatever you want to the house, redecorate or whatever. But I would expect you only to be with me. Nobody else, Rosie. For good."

I walked to where he stood over the control boards, and put my arms around his waist.

"Then it's settled," I said. "We belong to each other." My voice did not echo in the room because the walls were padded.

David grinned. "I had another idea. Do you think Peter would move in with us? It would be good to have him around."

"Why would you want to do that?"

"We don't have to if you don't like the idea. It's just, there's no rule that the only people who get to live together have to be related."

I put my hand on his shoulder. "Peter's my best friend. I love the idea. Ask him. He'll be back at Christmas."

"Baby, let's get out of here. I'll go tell Carl we're finished."

The engineer was in a living room that looked out onto the sea, and when we found him we thought he was sleeping. He sat on the couch with his head dropped forward against his chest. His mouth was open and his arms were crumpled in his lap. He had been drooling, although the drool came in spots of froth and lay at the corners of his mouth and around his nose. He was still wearing the trunks he had worn in the surf, and his arms and legs were red and covered with goose bumps. David spoke to him and then tried to shake him awake.

"Ah fuck," he said, and knelt quickly before the couch. He put his hands on the sides of Carl's neck, then on his wrist. "I can't get a pulse. Shit. There's nothing."

"He's taken something."

He turned sharply to me. "Of course he's taken something," and he put his thumbs on the thin skin of Carl's eyelids and lifted them quickly, one at a time. "There's a phone in the room next door. Call an ambulance," and he began slapping Carl's cheeks hard.

When I returned he was running his hands up and down Carl's arms, looking for newly-pierced holes in his skin.

"Is he dead?" I asked.

"I don't know. I can't get a pulse. I think I can feel his breath. I don't know. I don't even know what he was taking."

"Has he got any needle marks?"

"Everyone has needle marks, Rosie."

David stood up slowly from the spot before the couch where he had been kneeling. "We better go wait on the highway. The driver won't find the entrance otherwise."

"We can't leave him."

"What can we do? I can't wake him. I think he must be dead. We don't know how long he's been like this."

"What if he wakes?"

"Rosie, he's not gonna wake up."

"I'll stay here. You go. They'll be here any minute."

So I waited with Carl, a guy I'd shot accidentally a few times, whose arm or scalp or grin figured in the background of some of my prints, the old ones, the black and white ones. I sat on the couch beside him, and put his head back against the wall thinking he would wake more quickly if he were sitting upright. I held his hand and stroked it, because I believed his soul was waiting to be awakened. I could smell the fishy sea still on his skin, and as I warmed his hand, I felt his arm move, pull quickly against my grip. I put his palm close to my face and blew on it, warm breath again and again, believing that some life could pass between us, a connection without any visible thread.

Of course he was dead all along, and when the medics came they told us this. David brought them in the room, two men in crisp white clothes, and they moved me aside and began to touch Carl's body.

One of them asked, "What's his name?"

"Carl," said David.

The medic shouted, "Can you hear me, Carl?" in his ear, but at that point the name of the engineer was irrelevant. He no longer had a name, or a wife or a house.

"He's gone," said one of them. "I'll call the police. We can't take him in."

"What do you mean?" asked David.

The man began to smile nervously. "This is not an emergency now. It's stupid, isn't it? We go through this a lot. Being dead is not an emergency. A different team deals with this. You'll have to pay for it, though. They charge you for anything that isn't an emergency. It's about fifty bucks to call them out. Anyway," he said stepping back, away from David, "it looks like a massive pulmonary edema. You know, mega heart attack from mixing drugs. I've seen a few. We'll have to get the police."

David showed him the phone and went immediately to the studio room to make his own phone calls. He talked to the guys who owned the place, to his manager, to his record company, and to James. By the time the cops arrived, James was with us as well as a publicist from the company. A police doctor arrived and began looking at the body, and while he did James went to work on the police. They stood together in the living room around an empty body bag which was waiting for Carl, and James was talking fast. From the distance I couldn't hear his words, but I saw the worried look, the innocent smile, the expressions he designed for the police. By then the light had fallen in the room to a dim, dusk blue and we waited in the soft shadows with the noise of his high-strung voice shooting across us.

James had come straight from his office and wore a light grey linen suit that brought out his deep tan and made him look healthy and respectable. He looked like one of them, and when he smiled it came as an honest smile, a big gleaming innocent grin.

When the police left the room James walked to us bent slightly forward, and a shock of glossy, blond surfers' hair fell across his face. Behind us a large Confederate flag covered the whole wall, and David stood quietly staring at it, as though he didn't quite understand. He didn't move and didn't speak, but leaned against a chair and stared at that flag.

"You know the problem," James said to David. "If the doc says it's a drug-related death they'll search the place. They know your face and they know about this place. Are they going to find anything?"

"How the hell do I know?" said David. "This place is used by loads of people."

"Well if they find anything, you're the one they'll go for."

"I know that. What do we do?"

"You should get rid of Rosie for a start. You never should have let her stay. Now she's on their records."

"I've been on their records before," I said.

"This isn't a joke, Rosie. If they find any drugs in this place they'll try to carve both of you up. Rosie shouldn't be here at all."

David looked at him quietly, but didn't move.

"I'm explaining the situation to you, David. You are now in the middle of a complex police situation."

"Well, we're out of here as soon as they say," said David.

"You know, they might take you in. If they don't, you'll even have to ask permission to go home. You live in a different county."

The publicist said, "We'll get our own stories running right away. The cops are going to love getting in here. Everybody's going to love this story. We'll have to move pretty quick to counter it all."

One of the policemen came in and sat down beside us. "Mr. Wilderspin, have you been at this location long?"

"He arrived early this morning," said James quickly. "About eight, wasn't it, David?"

"Where did you travel from?"

"He lives in Santa Barbara," said James.

"And when did Carl Shapely arrive?"

"David?" said James.

"About the same time. We were doing some . . ."

"David was rehearsing."

"Right," said the policeman. "Can I see you outside, Mr. Gallas?"

"Yes, of course."

They were gone for several moments. The publicist picked up the phone and called the company.

David said to me, "Don't panic, Rosie. We'll be okay, you know. I've been in tighter situations than this. Now I've got James, and I pay him to make sure things are smooth. I pay him a lot of money to do it. The more you pay, the better you get."

"We're in trouble here, David."

"No, not really. The C-harp was trouble." He hardly moved his lips as he spoke. "When I was a kid and Robert Clay and I were on the road, once we got stopped by the police in Texas. You know, young white guy, old black guy; unnatural situation in Texas. We were holding then, Robert always was. He kept his works in a little box under the seat of the car. Well, the police decided to search us, and they tore everything apart looking for something they could bust us on. They came to the box, and man, Robert was shaking and pissing himself. One cop said, What's in this? and I don't know where it came from but I said, That's my C-harp. They handed the box back without opening it, finished looking at the rest of the car, and off they went. That's when I knew I was going to have to take care of Robert. He was past it then, not the music, but life I mean. So we've got James now, and he's the best available."

Eventually, James came back into the room. "That's it then. They're going. The doctor is finished."

David asked, "Are we clear?"

"Doctor says it was a heart attack. Thought it was heroin, but it wasn't. Just a heart attack. Young, wasn't he?"

When they had taken the body away in its bag, and cleared out, when the publicist had gone, and David, James, and I sat alone with our coffee on the couch in the living room, David said, "Man, that was a piece of luck."

"There's no such thing as luck," said James.

"Well, we're out of here," David said. "I'll go pack up."

When David had left the room, James said, "You know, Rosie, guys like him can't get away from it. You go with him, you'll be the same."

"David's not a drugger."

"I'm not talking about that. There's worse things than drugs. They're all psychotic in one way or another. Do you really want to be part of that life?"

"I already am. Before I met him."

"You're not listening, are you? Think about it; give me a call if you want to talk." He touched my hand and smiled. "Anyway, I'm going back to the office. Interesting evening." He smiled and walked to the door. "Listen, I'm having a New Year's party. Be great if you two could make it. Go-karts and all, you know. What do you think?"

CHAPTER 6

It rained continuously after I moved to Santa Barbara. Eventually the sky drained of any autumn color and stayed washed in barren grey through to Christmas. Even that paltry daylight dimmed early, giving over to evenings filled with unnatural frost, brittle against the hills. On the longest night of the year the cold and dusk came down at once, pressing in where the crisp afternoon should have been. University people, the archeos and their diggers, had been excavating David's hill and cave for weeks and were about to break the dig for Christmas. They had torn down the barn and dug pits in the earth, not quickly but with small trowels and brushes, painfully watching every lump turned over for treasure that might be locked within the dirt. They found more than they expected, and David had given permission for them to continue the whole of the following year, delaying his studio dream.

Peter came to stay with us that year for the holiday. David and I had walked up to the cave at dusk, and when we returned to the house, Peter had arrived, and was putting presents under a huge Christmas tree in the living room. A large stone fireplace, dry and empty, covered the far wall, and the others were lined with shelves of David's books. Two caramel-colored leather couches faced each other in the center of the room. A very old telescope in a wooden casing stood in the corner, pointing at a bookcase.

"This is a very romantic and glamorous story," Peter said to me.

"What is?" asked David.

"Why, you and Rosie." He stood up and thrust his chest forward and strode across the room toward me. He flung his arms wide. "A dramatic story. I love drama." He kissed me on both cheeks. "You know, I had a miserable time in New York and I need a celebration."

I held his hand. "We'll make you happy tonight." Peter was wearing a new, bright red sweater he had bought in New York, and his old fraying jacket over it.

"How did your filming go?" David asked.

"The shoot was fine, but I needed to get to Europe for some interviews and I couldn't. This court case is very frustrating. How long will it take to settle it? I feel like a prisoner."

"Just be patient, Peter," David said. "You have to believe that things are happening."

"Listen," I said, "we have a surprise. Well, a request, I guess. We would like you to live here with us."

Peter walked to the empty fireplace and leaned against the wide, carved mantle, his hands folded behind his back, his chest puffed like a European aristocrat posing for a portrait.

"How extraordinary. Why would you want that?"

"You're my friend," I said.

"Yes, but normal people don't set up house with all their friends."

David said, "I thought maybe we could develop some projects together. I've always been interested in movies."

Peter squinted. "But I don't really want to stay in California. My business is in New York. The beach is such a two-cheese sort of place, isn't it?" He opened his eyes wide and thrust his head forward until we laughed.

"It would make my life more normal if you were here," I said.

"Your life will never be normal, Rosie. You might think you are like everyone else, but you're not."

"Will you come?"

He paused a moment. "Who could say no to such an artistic community?"

"And the university people found something important."

"Important?"

"In the cave. First they took the stones, and now they found Chumash paintings on the cave walls. They'll be here next year, all year."

David came from the kitchen with glasses and champagne. He opened the bottle and passed the glasses to us.

"What did they find?" asked Peter. "Does this mean you can't start building your studio?"

"Some ancient drawings. There's only one other in Santa Barbara County. I figure my set-up can wait a while. This is ancient art."

Peter nodded and sat on the couch in front of the fireplace. He reached suddenly for his glass. "So this is the family?"

David glanced up at him and smiled as he swallowed. "This is it."

"Hmm. Certainly. Our family."

"James has invited us to a party on New Year's Eve. Of course, there are a couple others, the boss at my record company is having one and there's a big one at a club out at the beach."

Peter filled his own glass, and smiled at David. "So is that what we do together? Decide about parties?"

"Don't you want to go?" David asked.

"By all means. Yes, of course. There will be key people to meet who will be good for me, I'm sure. I'm just very depressed tonight. James doesn't think I'll get my travel papers before the case is settled."

"At least you're here with us," I said.

Peter folded his hands in his lap. "Yes, but no matter what we have, we always want more, don't we?"

"Let's build a fire," said David suddenly. "I'm freezing."

"We don't have fires in the desert, not where I come from," I said. "I have no idea how to start a fire."

"Well, we lived in the Toronto suburbs, and the maid always built our fires. So I'm not the guy for that job."

"In Hungary," said Peter, "we built fires out of the furniture. I will build it for you. Not with the furniture, of course."

He began to clean the fireplace with his hands, covering himself with ash and dust and long-forgotten trash. "When is the last time you had a fire here?"

"Never," said David.

"This is clear. You can tell a lot about people from their fireplaces." He pulled a dozen empty cigarette packets from the grate, and lifted a dead mouse by the tail and held it up for us to see. He said, "If there is one, there will be two. You will have to see to this problem. When I lived in New York we had mice in my basement. I used to track their movements, but essentially mice are quite boring creatures."

When the narrow flames began to catch the empty packets and touch the wood, he nodded to himself and stood back from it. He looked around the room to the bookshelves.

"Are these your books? Or do you buy them by the foot?"

"They're mine," said David smiling.

"You read a lot for a musician." He walked to the bookcase closest to him. "You have many books on psychology. Here you have more than a shelf. Is this what you studied at the university?"

"No, I didn't go to college. I didn't finish high school."

"Didn't I read an interview where you talked about being in college?"

David shrugged. "Not me," he said. "My stepfather is a shrink and I was always interested." He walked to where Peter stood, and stayed beside him. "These are organized alphabetically by subject, and you're in the psychology section there. The movie books are in F down at the other end."

"Ah," said Peter, raising his eyebrows. "An organized man. A gentleman's library." He pulled a large book from the shelf and read the title to us. "*The Zen of Horseriding*." He laughed loudly and asked, "And did you ever learn?"

"A little."

The shelves at the far side of the room formed an L-shape around electronic equipment, a tape deck, and turntable. David moved to the corner and took a reel-to-reel from its box, threading it onto the spool. "This will keep the animals off the hill," he said. The music was not his own, but a Zeppelin track, drums and wild guitar, and after it had run for a moment David lifted the volume even more.

Peter continued moving down the rows of books, occasionally slipping one from its place and reading. And all this time, David dogged behind him like a sentinel in fear of losing territory.

"Here is one in the wrong place," Peter said in a deep, clear voice that reached high over the music. "Isn't that strange? Not a book out of place but this one."

David didn't answer, but put his hand out to take the book, while Peter pretended he didn't see and continued leafing pages.

"What is it ?" I asked.

"Ballet notation theory. By Paletzine."

"Yes," said David, still standing before him with his hand in the air, willing the book back with his eyes closed.

"How strange," Peter said. "Ballet, dance, notation, father . . . it could be so many places. Why is it with the K's?"

David did not answer, and Peter began to fan the pages. "They use this system now, you know. Though he wrote it just before the War. He was far ahead of anyone else."

"I never did understand it," David said quickly, stumbling close to Peter, wheezing lightly and watching him over the back of the book.

"You don't like him much, do you?" Peter said.

"No. Do you like your father?"

"My father? He was an officer in the Hungarian army. Whether or not we like our fathers is fairly simplistic."

David was still holding his hand stubbornly in the air waiting for the book. His fingers, hovering so long, had moved closer and now touched the cover. "I'll take it now."

Peter looked up at him at last and slapped the book closed. "Certainly." He handed it to him, and as he did, a small photograph fell from the book. He stooped to pick it up, looking at it for a long while before he handed it back. On the back were tiny pinwheels of David's handwriting, and the front was an old photograph of his father as a young man, staged and in full costume.

"Your father is a genius."

"People keep saying that. But he's not a very nice person."

"Nice is not really a concern of genius."

David looked up from the book. His hands were shaking with a gentle and wild rhythm, like an alcoholic overspilling his memory.

"Did you ever live with him?" asked Peter.

"Only when I was very young. My mother and I left when I was five. We were in London then and she was still dancing, but Nikolai used to lock her in the closet when he got pissed off at her. Then when I was older we lived in Toronto and she sent me to visit him in the summer a couple of times. On his island. He made a heap of money working in movies in the '40s and he bought this tiny island off the Italian coast. It was a great place with an old, stone tower where I used to play. There was a legend about Ulysses even. But when my mother found out I was sleeping in my father's bed with him and his girlfriend she never let me go again."

Peter nodded, and put his big fingers on David's arm. "There is not a single one of us who can ever be saved from our parents," he whispered.

"No. You don't get it. When I was little my mother hated him, and I was where they fought it out."

I came beside them both, and could smell the heavy, sweet scent of Peter's Old Spice between them, and just a flush of ether and dust, a bruise marking all that had failed. I put my hands on their shoulders, knowing that I did not belong there. No memory from my desert had ever provoked such harm; what I had survived was the simplest of lives by comparison.

David looked over at me. He stood back, the wooden floorboards creaking as he did, and he slipped the book between others on the shelf. "Would you like to see the ranch? I'll show you the sights."

"In the dark?" asked Peter.

"Are you coming?" David asked. "We can have a midnight look at that cave."

* * *

The fog lay thick across the dark beach, so that as we walked the shore we could hear the thunder of the waves and could feel the sapped foam sloshing at our shoes, but could not see it. He led us along the sand and up a steep, dry path through low prickly shrubs to the edge of the cliff overlooking the sea. From there we moved inland, through a field of high weeds and past the stable where we could hear the moan and shudder of David's two unridden horses. We came eventually down a narrow path uneven and hardened by the cold, which led through the remains of an avenue of high eucalyptus, the sharp, bittersweet smell cutting through the fresh sea air like poison. When the avenue disappeared we were at the paddock.

"There is something out there," said Peter.

"No, the horses are stabled up for the night. Have to in this cold. A polecat, maybe," David said.

"No, I can hear something," said Peter, and in the center of the field a white light was playing on the grass, fluttering and brushing the dry field.

David climbed through the fence and walked toward it. A few yards from us he stopped and said, "It's a swan. An old whistler. Must have missed its flyway." He squatted before it, watching it, and slowly he began to curve his arms as though they were wings, straining to make them full and to lift them as the bird did, without violence and silently. He moved his leg forward slightly, and arched his body with the pretend grace of an animal. Then he fell backward, and lay on the invisible ground, laughing.

We left the swan scavenging in the middle of the field, and skirted the edge of the paddock until the fence veered away from us and we were climbing again through the crisp night over the hill to the site of the dig.

In the cave there was no moonlight, only a beacon set by the archeologists, a lamp casting a dirty yellow haze across the dank muddy ground. We stepped around the excavation pit, a deep hole now filled with mud-black rainwater. We sat against the rough, damp walls, and David and Peter lit cigarettes, warming a bit with the light and the smoke, staring out to the hovering light on the glistening pool at the cave entrance.

"There is a bird's nest up there," said Peter, straining his neck back to look straight above him.

Deep in the tomb-end of the cavern a cast of faint light reflected upon the wall paintings—twisted animal shapes drawn in blood-red and black. Peter walked to them and stood peering through a mesh cover at the brush of light on the walls.

"It's very warm back here," he said, although we could see him shivering. "The dead have their heaters on." He lifted the corner mesh and carefully peeled it back. He put his hand over one of the drawings, across the outline of a scarlet bull. He put both hands over the rough rock as though against a fire, breathing in the dank, warm air from the deep end of the ancient room.

"What are those figures at the top?" I asked.

"I don't know," said David. "They look human."

"Why don't you climb up and find out?" said Peter. "I can see ledges carved there."

I levered myself onto the first ledge, a huge flat one about four feet off the ground, which was just wide enough for me. I pressed and molded my body to the ridges of the wall, and reached up in the dim light to find grips for my next step. Two small, sharp outcroppings above my head became my handles, and I balanced the weight of my body by gripping fiercely with stinging, burning fingers, to the jagged rock.

I began to move one knee higher, feeling with my foot for a wider stone to lodge against. I could not see the human pictographs above my head, only the random, scarlet hashes upon the wall.

"Go higher!" called Peter. "Be careful, though. Go higher and be careful. Do you realize, we must be the first people to see these. Rosie, you will be the first since they were painted."

The moment I found a foothold and pressed my weight to hoist higher, I lost my balance and fell from the wall, flat across the thick muddy ground below, and the cave floor stung like a wooden board beating against me.

David came forward and lifted me, his hands gripping my shoulder and under my arm. "Are you all right?" he asked.

"Yeah," I said. "I can stand. You can let go."

"Nothing broken?" he asked. "I heard your back hit the ground." He paused. "I don't think I want to let go."

"Is that how you get your best shots?" asked Peter.

David said, "Let's get back to the house. Can you walk?"

"I'm fine. Just covered in mud and freezing."

We walked down the hill quickly, through the scrappy field of marguerites that led to the back door. Once inside, we stood before the fire in the living room, and Peter put large chunks of log on it, dry ones which had been lying in the log basket for months and which caught the flames immediately.

"You're ruining the carpet," Peter said to me. David laughed, and went to get towels. When he returned, he began wiping the mud away and trying to rub me warm.

"Maybe you should take your clothes off," David said, and took my hand in both of his, rubbing it hard and stroking through the spaces between my fingers. "Let's go have a shower," he said. He leaned over and kissed me, first my lips and then my throat.

Suddenly Peter asked, "Are you entirely certain you want me to live here?"

"Of course we do," said David. "This is the family. Zaca belongs to all of us."

PART TWO

THINGS THAT CAN'T BE MOVED

CHAPTER 7

In dreams I sometimes drive the old coast highway again, and although that road fell away years ago, I can remember every run and rise, every curve from Santa Barbara down to Santa Monica beach. To my right are the walls of white sea mansions dripping with magenta bougainvillea; golden canyon cliffs covered with ice plant, and rosemary weeds choked and fragrantly dying to my left. Now those warm coast hills crumble each winter in rain and sludge to the sea, smothering the cool Malibu houses that the music people and the movie people built so many years ago. The beaches turn to mud, the roads buckle and crack from the quakes, the hot, dry October winds bring fires that burn each year all the way to the water: for the life of me I cannot remember what made us think that we owned this place.

My dream is always of driving south to LA with the radio loud and the window down. That is how I want to remember it: the wind and the bright light coming off the ocean. I would pull out toward town, our LA town, down the eucalyptus drive from Zaca Creek, taking the slip road to meet the headland crest outlined sharp and dark against the sun. Once beyond the even palms of Santa Barbara, I would tear down the curving road past the beaches of Rincon and Ventura where surfers sat like shadowed rocks rising from the shallow sea-floor, waiting. The road swings sharply out then, around Point Mugu and past the navy firing range, slowing and easy, out to the rocks at Leo Carrillo and on to Zuma and LA. Today you can cut down quickly from the north valley and avoid LA altogether, but then it was quicker to drive the coast highway all the way down to Sunset, cutting inland past Black Fox where the rich Hollywood actors sent their boys to military school and past the frog farm which is now a wealthy yoga church.

Those canyonlands were tangled with nasturtium and sweet alyssum, down quiet roads covered with wild oaks and poisonous, pendulous piracantha berries hanging in the shade looking good enough to eat. The skies above those canyons were clean, and rabbits and coyotes still lived in the hills. Some old clapboard houses from the '20s were still wedged in the sage-covered clearings, and some of them had been abandoned decades before. My mother once told me of an antebellum mansion, half-rotted to the dirt, where she and the Hollywood tramp girls started production of their own gin on the broken mosaic floor of the great ballroom. She said they sailed down those dirt roads at dawn, clinging to the sideboards of a stolen milk truck, tanked on that poison gin, watching every bend for the cops. That old gin house was somewhere up at the top near Mulholland near the Gallas home.

On New Year's Eve in 1973, parts of those canyons were still wild places of broken houses and movie ghosts, but James Gallas lived at the very top of Coldwater, in a cul-de-sac that was forever immaculate. A fire tree marked the entry—huge, with crimson flowers clinging to smooth, gray bark. Over a hundred years before, James's grandfather and great uncle had brought this tree from the southern hemisphere on a schooner. They had sailed through storms and desolate landscapes while James's grandmother traveled across the American continent on a train, bound for the milk and honey of California. This tree had been part of the house since James's great-grandparents stole the land from the Spanish Californios. Old man Gallas fenced the boundaries of the canyon estate, the private road leading to it from the clear creek called Coldwater, and he and his wife set up their country retreat. Like any early settlers who left money for their children, old Gallas was a criminal, a thief who took this land and built a respectable Victorian home. My own people were never that sort, never had that kind of ruthless mettle or ingenuity. My family came out of the South, poor, ignorant scrappers from Louisiana with tiny dreams of the good life: a shack in the sun on the beach, a quiet corner of the beanfields lining Wilshire, a decent bottle of scotch.

I wore no jacket, only a silver backless dress made from thin, rubbery fabric that stuck to my tiny breasts, and I looked like a kid playing dress-up. We rushed up the white steps leading to the main entrance of the house just as a soft rain began to pelt the old red brick drive. Under the porch awning, David stopped and ran his hand through his damp hair, clearing it back from his face. The vibration from the bass line of distant music bounded at us and he looked over and smiled at me. "Whoever convinced you that rubber keeps you warm?" he asked and put his hand on my naked back.

Peter wore a black velvet jacket that David had given him for Christmas. His shoes were patent leather and his shirt was a deep burgundy color. He looked more like a lounge singer than a documentary director. We walked behind him, trying to keep up as he nervously maneuvered through the crowd. Finally, David took my hand and we moved forward into a rotunda with dark-stained oak beams lining the ceiling.

A dozen people gathered around us, reaching for him, greeting him, and promising him awards before the next year was over. Hands came at him, not grabbing but invading by pretending sincerity.

He stood rigidly, staring vacantly at each of them, and holding my hand tightly. A man in a brown bomber jacket came up suddenly from behind and spoke loudly in David's ear. He smiled again and nodded but did not move, even when the man's woman put herself between us and touched his waist. She wore brown leather as well, and her nails were long and hooked and painted dark red. David held himself perfectly still against the touch of those nails for what must have been two full minutes, closing down like a Mohawk on the forest floor in order to tolerate her red claws, waiting for her to unhook and leave him.

James was standing in a nearby doorway talking to two men I recognized to be city councilmen. When he saw us, he broke from the politicians and approached us urgently and tentatively.

"You look beautiful, Rosie," he said and put his arms around my waist. "That silver, I love that silver." He stared at my shoulders. "Does it itch?"

"Rosie always looks beautiful," said David. "Who are all these people, James?"

"Clients. Contributors to the campaign. The symphony people are expected any minute. That new Japanese conductor is coming and it's a major coup for him to choose my little party tonight."

"Hamoto?" asked Peter, suddenly radiating excitement. "You know Hamoto and he's coming? Of course, the Hungarians are not at all pleased that he got the job."

"But it's good for trade, don't you think?" asked James.

Peter shuffled back out of the light and the crowd. "I don't know. I guess I never think about trade," he muttered.

James nodded at him, freezing his host smile. "The rest of my guests are mostly politicos and lawyers, a few clients. Election year, hey? They all turn out. You understand it, don't you, David? After all, politics is just show business for ugly people. Come on, I want you to see my go-karts. The speedway is buzzing. And Peter," he leaned over, putting his arm across his shoulder. "I have some news. You have a court date. A hearing."

"They will want to deport me?"

"They will never deport you. You make too much money and you aren't a criminal. No, for sure they want to discuss your situation, hear your story, and in all likelihood, decide to make you an American resident. Sound good?"

"Yes, yes, of course," said Peter. "Tremendous."

"April 30th. My office will send you the details. We're almost home now." He grabbed Peter's shoulder, tugging quickly at him like a puppy. "Congratulations."

James turned suddenly to the doorway and his already-tired smile widened even more for the next guest.

"Matt, Matt, come in. Great to see you. Come meet some people. You know Rosie Kettle of course."

"Hi ya, Rosie, good to see you." Matt smiled quietly at me. He was a short and dark man with thick, luscious lips, dressed completely in white. He took my hand in both of his and held me between his warm, damp palms. "Hey, I saw that spread you did last month in New York—very, very good."

I had worked for Matt many times over the years since he had bought *New Rock City* from Peter.

"And this is David Wilderspin," said James.

"I guess I could recognize you anywhere. Pleasure to meet you," said Matt.

David, so much taller, leaned forward and smiled again easily.

Matt shook David's hand.

"And this," James said, "is the documentary director, Peter Varga."

"I know Peter. We go back a long way. Hello, Peter. It's good to see you." His voice was deep and casual.

"Oh really?" said James. "I had no idea."

"Peter founded *New Rock City*," he said generously, even though Peter had started a street rag in San Francisco, but Matt had built it into a multi-million dollar national magazine about contemporary culture.

"The truth is," said Matt, turning again to David, "I've been wanting to do a piece on you. We're getting hundreds of letters every week."

"So do it," David said. "I'm ready. I'll be in town for a while—until June."

"I hear you've got quite a spread up the coast. We could send somebody up next week." Matt moved forward to stand next to David. "Is this a deal?"

"Sure," said David. "And Rosie will do the shoot?"

"Naturally."

"Rosie shot me a *New Rock City* cover once before. Changed everything."

Matt grinned. "That's right. She brought you off the streets—straight into the noise and lights."

David had his hands on my shoulders and he was looking at me as though I might have been the only one in the conversation with him, but I knew he was starting to work Matt, that he had found the single most important contact at the party.

"I'm hungry," I said.

"Me too," said Peter. "Want to find the food with me?"

David lifted his hands from my shoulders. "You two go on. Matt and I will wander around on our own." His voice was controlled. He wanted to be alone with Matt to talk about music, about the business of his songs. They were both men who worked hard, paid taxes, and had opinions about the news long before the rest of the industry even looked up from the bar. They were both serious men who believed in playing by the rules.

He nearly touched my forehead with his lips but stopped, waiting and watching me. "Don't get into trouble."

"What do you mean by trouble?"

"Anything you can do without a camera, baby," he grinned.

Peter and I went to a room set with platforms of food spread down two sides of a hall, layers and bleachers of food on enormous tables—salmon and three kinds of meat and huge bowls of crab legs and vegetables and tureens of soup. Layers of bright-colored fruit, wedges of pineapple and watermelon and kiwi and cantaloupe so vibrant with that extra food coloring that good caterers bring with them. Bright gold bowls were filled with deep red strawberries, and huge rounds of brilliant orange cheeses chosen for their color lay on long golden platters.

Though the room was cavernous, we were warm from the heat of dozens of people milling together. Peter inhaled sharply as he stared at the tables, then stepped suddenly forward. He stood before a deep china basin overflowing with crab legs.

"I love crab," he said quietly, not looking away from the bowl. His breath was shallow and fast, and his hand, poised above the bowl, was shaking, his fingers vibrating with anticipation for it. "Oh, sweetie pops, now I am having fun. I want one of everything. Do you think I could have one of everything?"

"Have anything," said James, who had followed us. "Please." He grabbed an empty wicker basket and began filling it. "Come with me."

He took a bottle of champagne and led us through French-paned glass doors to the outside patio. We followed him down wide steps, down a soft slope hill to a den of tall pine trees. Peter slipped and skidded down the slick lawn, and when we came to rest against the wide, rough trunks, he squatted, exhausted, to the soft bed of pine needles beneath.

"I'm out of breath," said Peter. He took in the thick pine odor of the damp night. "Do you think I'm too old for all of this?"

"Peter, you are only just beginning," said James.

"Isn't that a tacky piano song?" Peter asked. "I should get up, you know. I can't help but think about the nobbly worms underneath."

James popped the cork of the bottle and handed it to me, pushing it against my lips. The froth spewed across my chin and neck, and the bubbles clipped, stinging my skin. "Drink some and you won't mind the rest, the rain or any of it." I took the bottle from him and tilted it toward the sky, gulping even while the burning scoured my throat. Peter stood up and watched me.

He smiled suddenly and grabbed my arm, pulling me away from James.

"Well, we can't eat in the rain," said James. "Come with me."

He moved quickly through his canyon glen, jumping over a tree stump, and at the end of a winding path he leaned against a huge fig tree. He wore tuxedo pants and had discarded his jacket. His shirt was damp, clinging to his muscle-rounded shoulders and his flat, surfer's belly, and as I emerged from the foliage he looked at us sternly like a schoolteacher watching naughty children. Peter was lagging behind, not hurrying, and humming as he ambled through the trees.

"You look so pretty," James said to me shyly. I could see a wooden ladder behind him, nailed to the tree trunk. "We'll be dry in my tree house. My great-grandparents brought this tree from Moreton Bay in Australia. It was planted a hundred years ago. Sturdy and safe." He leaned closer to me, and his lips touched my neck as he spoke. "I had hoped we would be here alone. I really want to talk to you." He helped push me up the steps, although he did it with such force that I lost my balance and lurched into the ladder, scraping my knee against the rough-wood slats. Finally, I pulled myself onto the platform, and sat at the edge of the porch, tucked into the uneven, jagged branches of this enormous tree.

"Talk to me about what?"

"What happened to your leg?" he asked, looking down at my knee where blood was trickling down my kneecap.

"You pushed me into the ladder," I said.

He put his hands gingerly on either side of my wound, leaning over and pressing his body down across my leg. At first I thought he was about to kiss my knee, like a father might, but instead he put his lips to the blood, sucking so gently across my skin so as not to sting the open flesh. "There," he sat up. He took a handkerchief from his pants pocket and tied it around my knee. I must have looked horrified, because he said, "It's clean, you know."

I put my hand on his arm. "I'm sure it is. But don't do that again."

"You probably won't ever give me the chance again."

"You're right. I'm living with David, and I'm in love with him. He's a client of yours."

"He's actually becoming my major client. I guess I'm taking quite a chance."

"James, I really do love him."

He sighed so loudly that I was immediately embarrassed. "Rosie, don't believe the songs. This stuff never stays the same.

Nothing stays the same except the law. Least of all, couples in your business. Don't you know you would have such an easy life with me? I want you to be safe."

"That's not what I'm looking for. Being safe isn't the point."

"It was the point for every generation and every country in history except ours. Why are we so different?"

I leaned back across the floor, and saw in the corner by the wall a cluster of dark pods of unborn worms, waiting in the damp for the spring. I touched a slender finger of this hardened flesh, and didn't answer him. He lay beside me and he smelled like the wild rosemary we had just walked through.

"Rosie, give me a chance."

"No. David is good to me. I would never leave him."

"He's a musician, for God's sake. Rocker love doesn't mean anything."

"Why don't you get it?" I sat up and turned around to him angrily. "It means something to me. You and I could never be together because believing this means nothing to you."

Peter called out to us from where he had been waiting at the bottom of the tree, "How far up is it? I can't see over the top."

James stared at me and finally whispered. "It does. I'm just not very good at explaining it." Then he stood up and shouted to Peter, "If you pass up the food first it will be easier to get up. Here, I'll come halfway down." He swung himself out on the branch directly below the platform, holding on with one hand like a great slender animal, his shaggy blond hair damp and clinging to his face. "Here, climb up halfway and I'll catch hold of it."

"I'm not sure I can climb halfway with one hand." Peter was already breathless from his walk.

"Sure you can. Just do it slowly. Only not too slowly, because I can't hang out here for too long." I watched him swing out wide as he must have done a thousand times as a child. He made faces in the rain at Peter and grunted, until Peter stopped his slow climb and craned his neck back gingerly to look at James.

"You are a very bad man," said Peter grinning.

He started climbing again, and I could hear him huffing with each rung, but he handed the basket to James just as he had been asked. James swung to grab it, stretching taut until I could see the outline of his back muscles, curved and hard like whalebone beneath his sodden shirt. As Peter climbed the rest of the way and hoisted himself to the platform, James swung out and pulled his whole body up by one arm only to reach the same level. They sat side by side, breathing hard together.

"Why didn't you just use the ladder?" asked Peter.

James laughed, stretching his arms out in front of him to release his cramping muscles. "Not as much fun."

Inside the tree house was one large room big enough for six or seven people sitting close together. The walls were painted blue, although the color had not been renewed for several years. The wood was warped and the paint was streaked with mold. The old, buckled cork floor was soft and warm as I lay across it. Peter and James came to sit beside me with the food basket and another bottle of champagne which we passed between us until we had drunk so much we could not stop laughing. I lay on the floor while James fed me little lumps of stuffing from a plate of baked mushrooms. Our arms and hips were touching, and he stroked my hair while the three of us talked.

"Will you take my passport photograph?" Peter asked.

"Sure."

"I will need one, won't I, James?"

"Yes, of course."

"I've never had a passport before."

"American passports are valuable," said James.

"Any passport. I've never had one. Is this really going to happen?"

"Without a doubt. From here on, it's routine. At my party next New Year's Eve, you will be an American."

Peter smiled. "That was a job well done, Jimmy," said Peter. "You were always someone with a passport and you never had to worry when you saw the police. You have no idea how important this is to me."

"I'm glad I could help. I guess I should go back to the party."

After he left Peter began to laugh.

"Don't laugh at him. He's kind. Not many people have that quality anymore."

"He is a full-blown tragic literary figure. I'm surprised he doesn't have tuberculosis as well. A young rich boy in this big place, all alone."

"How do you know that he's alone?"

"Because he did not introduce a hostess and because he came after you. What else are we doing up in this ridiculous tree?"

"James wanted a break, I think," I said. I put my hand on his arm. "You're my friend and you're supposed to trust me."

* * *

Late in the night the music could be heard in every part of the grounds. David and Matt had moved far away from the noise into hiding, and when I finally found them I did it unexpectedly, opening a door I thought might be a hallway and finding instead a small, white windowless room with only the two of them.

David stood in the center of a white carpet which was surrounded with deep, grey couches. He was looking straight at Matt while he spoke, holding his hands forward, cupping his tanned fingers together. He had worn a brand new black suit and black t-shirt which hung across his body as though they had been tailored for him. His hair reached a bit below his collar and shone a deep mahogany color beneath the glaring white room lights. But it was his heavy-lidded green eyes circled like a raccoon's with tired shadows and his high cheekbones that stopped me, and I stood in the doorway admiring him until he knew it and turned to look at me.

"Can I take your picture?" I asked and he smiled.

"Sure." He walked over to me and took my hand. "But you haven't got your camera." He held my fingers up in the air and put his own flat against them as though for a waltz. "You look beautiful."

"I look like a scrawny kid from the desert dressed up in silver rubber."

He grinned and put his arms around me. "Rosie, you really have no idea what you look like. Can I hang out with you for a while? I missed you."

Matt stood up from the couch. "Well, I've got some folks to catch up with. See you at the go-karts." He walked to the door and called over his shoulder, "Actually, I don't believe he really has go-karts. I'm sure it's just one of those LA legends."

When he had left, David said, "Old James is always good for a few tricks. When else would I get to spend an evening with one of the guys who invented rock and roll."

"*You* invented rock and roll. Matt just writes about it."

He sat on the couch and pulled me onto him. "Sit on my lap, Rosie." He put his arms around me. "You've been gone a couple of hours. Where have you been, anyway?"

"In a tree house."

"Your knee is bleeding. How did you skin your knee at a New Year's party in Beverly Hills?"

"James took us to his tree house."

"Great," he said without smiling. He put his hands at my waist and inched my dress up above my hips.

"Have you been good?" He put his hand on my hip and stroked it, and then kissed my neck. "Can I take your panties down? Should I spank you?"

"You're a horny old man."

"Come on, baby, move to the right a little bit and keep me happy."

I smiled at him, but didn't move.

"Rosie, you're a cold chick. I'm panting here."

I stood up and pulled at him to stand. He looked up at me. "You know, it's nearly midnight. Why don't we stay in here?

Baby, I just want to be here with you." He grinned slowly and leaned back against the couch, "You know, there've been three women in my life. My mother, of course. Then there was this chick in kindergarten, and that worked out pretty good. Then I met you. I've been chasing you since that bar with Robert Clay. You were it for me. You are it."

I sat across his legs, close to his body, and put my hand on his shoulder. "Is that a promise?" I asked. "I never wanted anything as much as I want to be with you." I put my face against his arm and I could smell the crisp, new fabric of his jacket, rough against my cheek.

"I don't know why you always pretend like I'm in charge here," he said. "You know damn well that I've been out of control for months."

* * *

The oval go-kart track had been cleared from an old oak wood. Between the two world wars as the California economy boomed, James's father had hired people to hack and strip the huge wild oaks to build covered bleachers, and to carve and polish more oaks into a long cocktail bar perched at the top of the stands. It was a lush and elegant, totally unnecessary building. Now, the track was surrounded with tall, full-growth eucalyptus, brought from Australia to block the wind. That night they were coated with light rain and smelling like cat urine through the damp night air. Down at the ground level the clearing had been landscaped, carved, and ornamented with tracks of Hawaiian flowers, hibiscus and gardenia and jasmine, displayed like bric-a-brac. Huge floods lit the course, hanging in arcs from high black poles like vultures circling the action and bringing it to near-daylight.

Four beautiful cars, not go-karts at all the way I remembered them from the desert, moved fast and smooth around the track as though on velvet air instead of wheels. The cars were low and narrow, barely large enough for an adult. We stood at the edge of the trees and could already hear the sound of metal slashing through the night, and when we finally came closer and saw the cars, metallic purple and blue and red and green, the colors slipped around the curves of the course, leaving blurring light behind. A lawyer I knew from his cocaine habit and a drummer who had once tried to make me in front of Peter, both wrenched around the oval.

David and I leaned over the rail waiting for the next race. A hundred people wandered in the bleachers behind us and James stood high in an announcer's box above the track at the top of the lights, shouting the winners. I shivered until David saw it and moved in behind me, closing his body over mine and wrapping his arms around me. I turned my face and put my lips against his clean black t-shirt.

"I'm going to make a bet," he said.

"A what?"

"Up at the bar, James set it up for betting."

"Isn't that illegal?"

"Here," he said laughing, "put my jacket on. Come on, let's go up and see what's happening."

Peter sat on a polished oak bench and caught me by the hand as David and I climbed up.

"Ho!" he said. "Ho there! You would fit."

He had taken off his velvet jacket and sat with the fine, crimped button-front of his burgundy shirt hanging open and limp in the night.

"What?" asked David, and let go of my hand as he turned.

"Rosie would fit. They need small people to drive small cars. You have to be skinny. Humiliating," he said. "I wouldn't have minded being too tall, but I am not skinny enough. I tried to get in but couldn't. In front of all these beautiful women. I was sure I would meet someone tonight, and now they all know the truth."

"Do you want to drive?" David asked me.

"No."

"Well, if you won you might get a prize," said Peter. "James might give you a kiss."

David looked quickly and sharply at him.

"Yes, you're right," said Peter. "I am good and drunk. It's almost midnight and I'm alone and drunk."

"You're not alone," said David.

"I appreciate the thought, but with me it is a state of mind." He stretched his neck back and looked up at the sky. "I think we are drying out." Peter was sweating from the alcohol he had drunk, and he quickly wiped his palm across his high forehead. "I have just seen your father."

"What?" asked David.

"Your father is with Hamoto. Up there by the bar."

David stood abruptly still; the suddenness of it was like violence in the harsh, bright night.

"How do you know it was him?" he asked. "What did he look like?"

Peter smiled. "For someone like me he is easily recognized. Anyway, I know him."

"You met him once," David said. "You only met him once."

"This is not a test," said Peter. His voice dropped and was suddenly sober. "If I give you a wrong answer it doesn't make me a liar. Your father will still be here, David."

"I thought he was in Italy. What is he doing here?"

"It's kind of scary when you end up at the same parties as your parents," I said, hoping he would laugh, but I saw that David's face had turned the color of used chalk, and he stood very still.

Peter said, "I expect you can never keep an itinerary for genius. But he is there, up at the top, drinking tea while Hamoto gets tanked. And he is with a pretty girl as well. Of course, when they saw I couldn't fit in the car, they laughed at me. Hamoto and your father took great pleasure in my little humiliation. Not the girl, though."

"He never told me he was back in California," David said, and began to light a cigarette. He touched one hand with the other, pressing them together around the flame to keep his fingers from shaking.

Suddenly, he grabbed my hand again and grinned fiercely.

"Time to climb," he said, and began vaulting in great strides to the top where the platform was crowded with people putting down bets on the next race. He moved quickly through them but stopped scarcely ten feet short of his father, and leaned casually across the counter. Around us the night was drying, and we were covered with the smell of rinsed lilac.

"I'll have a scotch," David said to the bartender. "What do you two want?"

Peter had been walking more slowly, and when he finally caught us he said, "He's over there at the table."

A painful sugar-blood taste covered my tongue as I waited for David to react.

"Is he?" David asked quietly, but looked carefully away, out to the track instead of at his father. The sky was perfect, vein-blue as though the night had stopped on a dime. "Here. Let's have some drinks. Are you sure you're not racing, Rosie?" Before I could answer, James's voice on the loudspeaker announced the close of bets, and a hundred people shoved around us, suddenly choking the bar before the next race. I saw Peter's lips move, but the noise of the crowd smothered his words. David perched against the bar for several minutes, still without looking at his father.

James called a warning for the beginning of the next race, and the crowd on the platform thinned. People climbed down the awkward bleachers to the track until the silence and the smell of mud and night-jasmine were all that was left.

"You're frightening me," I said.

Peter looked at me and put his hand on David's shoulder. "I'm afraid our Rosie has no room for our crazy terrain. To her, we are just nutburger valley. You know, we should go and greet your father." David shrugged like a sullen, dark-haired boy.

At the back of the table, far in the corner, sat Nikolai Paletzine, a man unconnected to his own son by name or experience, but someone who threatened him nevertheless. He was a tiny man, barely more than five feet tall, and he wore a black hat which all but covered his ghost-white face, and a thick, long scarf wrapped several times around his neck. Before he noticed David, his thin lips clamped together in scowling repose. When David stood in front of him, he looked carefully for a moment, a slow recognition, and then smiled.

"Nikolai," David said quietly. "It's good to see you."

"My son. But why are you here?" He raised his eyes to meet David's. His skin was mottled with large liver spots. His lashes were so long, framing deep green almond-shaped eyes the exact color of David's, and some black fire, a luminous blue-print drawn by blood, shone underneath his skin. He reached a hand towards David, his joints knotted with bone disease, but the shape of their fingers was the same, double-helixing as they clasped together.

"New Year's ritual," he said. "This is my lawyer's party."

"Your lawyer? Are you in trouble?"

"No. My business lawyer."

"Then you play music still."

"Yes."

"Do you write any?"

"Some."

"It is better to write than to play. It is a higher art."

"Nikolai, you didn't tell me you were coming."

"I'm not here for long. A few days. Do you know Marta?" He touched the young woman next to him, a silent, plump, dark-haired woman whose clothes pulled too tightly across her breasts and stomach. She wore her hair in short pigtails; her lipstick was faded, her eyeliner smudged at the creased corners of her eyes.

"Hello, Marta," David said.

"Marta is my notation advisor. We recently met in Florida at a Holiday Inn."

"I'm very happy to meet you," David said softly. "And this is Rosie, Nikolai. This is my girlfriend, Rosie Kettle."

The old man swept his hat off and held it to his chest while he offered me his hand. His hair was thick and full and dyed ink-black, the pasty black color of cheap shoe polish. He ran his hand through his hair, pushing it back from his forehead the way I had seen David do many times, his chin and head tilted up in unconscious, youthful vanity.

"Do you dance?" he asked.

"No," I said.

"You should. You have the body."

My eyes widened in astonishment when he spoke. I had not expected an elderly man to take the same license as the rocker boys I photographed.

"Rosie is an artist, a photographer," David said, and his father did not respond. "And you know Peter."

"Do I?" he asked, scrutinizing him. "From where?"

One of the Japanese stood forward and said, "Mr. Paletzine, is this your son, then? We had no idea David Wilderspin was your son."

Nikolai looked at David and nodded. "Of course. Can't you see he is a Paletzine? He took that other name because he had to, a remarriage is all. For expediency with his mother's new husband."

"Wilderspin is my stepfather's name. The man who raised me."

Hamoto nodded at David. "They are racing again. Coming then, Mr. Paletzine?"

Nikolai stood up slowly. He leaned lightly on his cane and began to step away from us. He did not reach to touch his son, but only backed away with Hamoto, tapping his hat back down across his forehead. As he moved toward the far crowd, he placed his gnarled fingers across Hamoto's forearm for balance. I looked over at David, and saw him staring at his father and this other man, squinting with a child's jealousy. David could never have the intimate access to his father that I had to mine, because Nikolai had chosen another universe where family meant nothing.

Suddenly, David asked, "Where are you staying?" Before Nikolai responded he continued, "Come to Santa Barbara with us. Stay with us on the ranch."

"I will be here until the fourth," Nikolai said. Marta stepped forward, and as she did the slightest scent of fallen pears lay across us. "It's possible."

"You will need to be asleep soon," she said to Nikolai.

He nodded to her.

"How long will it take to travel to Santa Barbara? Mr. Paletzine should be asleep by midnight."

David smiled. "Well, when we get there midnight will be long gone. But come on, we can leave now."

We followed him through the night, slowly down the bleachers. I could hear the crickets rising like a fever in the warm air. David stopped until we were all safely on the ground, then we moved on, first David leading between the giant, raw eucalyptus trunks; I followed, tottering still on thin silver shoe shanks; Marta came carefully, the soft olive color of her throat and arms ripening in the harsh light; Nikolai, hissing like prey down the bank slowly; and Peter finally, walking proudly, bending for the honeysuckle arch, then rising again like a swollen wave; all of us torn off in a single breath across a moss-silver meadow. Moments later we were on that coast highway toward home, all of us silent and tight in the car together. David drove carefully with his precious cargo, victorious that he had seduced his father to join us. And at midnight, the new year finally happened around us in the cool, quiet, the dark sea expanding out on our left and the hum of the car engine falling and rising with the turns in the road to Zaca Creek.

CHAPTER 8

I went out at dawn with my camera, climbing down the deep glade dank with the smell of half-rotted branches, through fallen oaks and wild nasturtium. At the bottom, the Zaca Creek splattered to the beach in a tiny fall over lime-rocks and I stood astride this water, holding my camera, waiting for the foreground to come alive with the angle of the light.

I walked the beach to the tide pools that puckered across huge rock slabs imbedded in the sand. I watched with my camera poised for the longest time while pink sea anemones floated in the clear, shallow water, but I could not see a picture among them. I could freeze the truth in a roomful of noise and movement, but after years of stalking musicians the brainless anthozoan were too serene for my eyes.

"You really are very odd," said Peter, moving quietly in behind me and speaking in a shattering tone for the beach dawn. "What are you doing, anyway?"

"I was trying to take an art picture, for a change."

"Ah." He opened his dark eyes so wide. "I might have known."

"Don't make fun of me." I sat in the cool morning sand, balancing my camera on my thighs.

"I wouldn't. Actually, I came to make a confession," Peter said.

I moved the camera around to face him and held it in front of my eyes while he watched me.

"This isn't a performance," he said.

"But I've never done your picture." I cracked the mechanical snap and wind of the buttons again and again over the soft, shuddering sound of the waves.

Peter waited patiently for a few moments. "This is very serious. I need to speak with you." He closed his eyes. "I'm in love and I don't know what to do. Please stop that and listen to me."

I lowered my camera, and reached for his hand. I led him like Hansel a few feet along the sand to a sheltered wrinkle in the immaculate lime cliff. We sat close together, our cool arms touching and our backs shoved up against the sea-carved rocks. I crossed my legs and cradled my camera like some country girl with fresh-picked apples in the skirt of her shift.

"Who are you in love with?" I asked.

He looked surprised. "Why, Marta. Paletzine's woman. Hopeless, isn't it? He is a genius. I have no chance with her. How could this happen? Of course, I haven't told David. I don't know what to do. If I get within ten feet of her I can't speak. I can't breathe. I shake and laugh out loud for no reason. I am an embarrassment. I think I should go away until they leave. Don't you? I can hardly keep my hands off her. Don't you think she's beautiful? Of course she will never look at me, but I should leave anyway. I'm bound to humiliate someone. What do you think, Rosie?"

"I don't understand how you can be in love. You only met her last night."

"I'm not asking you to evaluate my feelings. I already know how I feel. I'm asking what you think I should do."

"You aren't really thinking of leaving, are you?" I asked.

"Of course."

"But this is your home."

"It is a question of honor." As I watched him, a lizard on the wall behind began to move down, stirring tiny crumbles of lime dust. He turned to me. "This kind of honor does not exist here. Paletzine and I understand. These are European rules, men's rules, which must become public gestures. That is why I would leave."

"What are you talking about? This is your home. I don't even know why this man is here. David hates his father. Why did he invite him?"

"Between fathers and sons there is never a last chance."

"Do you really believe that?"

He nodded. "Between any two people at all there is rarely a last chance." Peter put his arm around me. "This is the most beautiful dawn I have ever seen. Smell this, my God, smell this ocean. Take your picture of it; you'll never see a better one."

"I can't. I'm not that kind of photographer. I haven't got the eye."

"Don't be a stupido. Of course you do."

"There's more to it than that, Peter. It's more complicated. There are a lot of things to think about."

"Take that picture. Take it now," he said hissing, "take it."

"You can't just take it. No one ever just takes a picture. You have to plan for it."

"That is where we are different. I would see it and simply take it."

I held my camera to my chest and stared at him.

"Rosie, you frighten me the way my schoolteachers used to. You remind me that I will end up with nothing." He slipped his hands into the sand until they were covered to his wrists. "This woman is very important to me."

Down the shore I could see David and Marta walking slowly across the hard-packed sand at the water-edge. They strolled barefoot, with their arms linked, as though they had known each other for years. Marta was talking quickly and looking at the surf as she walked, laughing and taking long, light, confident steps. She wore a thick, grey sweater and black fitted pants which were soaked to her thighs from the sea.

"I'm glad he is holding her," whispered Peter. "Otherwise it would be dangerous. I might do something silly. Here," he grabbed me, "hold my hand so it looks like I am a person who has close friends."

"But you are somebody with close friends."

"She doesn't know that."

I took his hand, and kissed his cheek.

He hissed at me. "What are you doing?"

"Showing what good friends we are."

"Don't kiss. No kissing. Now she will think we three play weird sex games." I began laughing, and he unbuttoned his shirt and pulled the end of his pants legs down over sock-bare ankles. He sat up very straight and leaned carefully back on the wall, waiting for them.

"Hello!" I called and they angled their path across the soft sand mounds toward us.

"Get any good shots?" David asked. They crouched and dripped seawater beside us.

"Our Rosie was trying to photograph sea invertebrates, but she says she's really only good at shooting your rockster invertebrates," said Peter.

Marta sat opposite us in the wet sand. She wore no makeup, yet any picture would have been of her copper-colored eyes set deep into clear, olive skin.

"Happy New Year," Peter said to her, scarcely looking up.

"Thank you." She lifted her arms over her head and began pulling her thick sweater off. Underneath she wore a tight and wrinkled pink t-shirt which gave her the look of a messy school-girl. Peter stared at her while she moved, but did not speak.

"What a great morning," David said. "This is so much better than Canada."

"Canada? Is that where you come from?" Marta asked.

"From Toronto. Right now the snow is a foot thick there and won't melt until April."

"In Cuba," said Marta, "there is so much sun, and the sea is perfect. Always." She was sitting up very straight. "In the jungle we have the most beautiful flowers. Tiny white orchids that fill the air with a heavy, sweet smell." Her fingers were delicate and slender and she drew them together to make this orchid. "We have these beautiful orchids and the ocean, but not much else."

"Marta was a dancer in Cuba," said David.

She turned to David. "Did Mr. Paletzine tell you I danced? He always does this."

"Is there a secret here?" asked Peter.

"Mr. Paletzine tells people I danced with Alonso before my family escaped, but you know I was only in the children's corps. Mainly, I grew up in Miami. My father worked as a dishwasher. Your father does not really like to tell that to people. Sometimes he says that I am a contessa. I waited tables and I taught Spanish at the community college, but I was never a real dancer." She laughed. "I am not a countess and I am not a ballerina, whatever Mr. Paletzine would like people to think."

"You are one of the most beautiful women I have seen," said Peter suddenly but not shyly.

"Then you have not seen many women," she said quietly.

David moved across the sand, and slipped his hand under the hem of my shift at the back, moving his fingers against my legs and hips. I put my arm around his shoulders and kissed his cheek.

"You two will have to stop doing that. You are embarrassing us," said Peter.

"It's a new year," David said. He pushed the neckline of my dress down below my shoulder blade, and put his lips to my skin. "I love you and it's a new year." He smelled like the fresh salt sea, and I was so close I could see the points of sweat across the back of his neck and hear the low, soft vibration of his voice against me.

"Go away," said Peter. "Go away and take care of those throbbing glands."

David laughed and turned around. "No secrets in my house, Marta."

Peter said. "Now go away and let us talk."

Hours later I stayed alone in our room, sleeping in the dimming winter sunlight, naked and sunken into the folds of the heavy soft duvet. From our corner bedroom we could see the headland and the sea, the ducks flying in before the early evening feed and the weed-covered train tracks from across the old two-lane highway. I awoke with sounds of the birds' wings scratching the air, and I stood by the window to catch the flash of several hundred of them as they flew to the field beyond the creek. I heard David's voice and Peter's on the porch below my window. A few seconds after, David came to our room.

"I made some plans," he said. "Dinner on the terrace. Around seven. And tomorrow we're all going to visit the mission in town. My father has never seen it. Is that okay with you?"

"Sure," I said.

"Peter and Marta were on the beach all day." He sat on the bed and leaned back. He wore an old pair of jeans and a white ivy league shirt, wrinkled and soft, hanging loose over his pants. His shirt cuffs were folded back, and from where I stood I could see part of the long scar which striped the tough muscle of his forearm. I stared at his arm and he stared at me, and as I stood naked in the dying afternoon light, I realized he would always be the more at risk of the two of us, because of all that he covered up.

"He has a crush on her, you know," I said. "What should we do?"

"Nothing. In two days she and Nikolai will be gone."

"What has your father been doing all day?"

"Sleeping, like you." He grinned. "But he sleeps because he's old." He came to stand beside me at the window. "Not because sex has wasted him." He put his hands on my shoulders and his mouth on my breast.

"You're calmer than last night," I said.

"I wonder why," he whispered. He moved his tongue across my nipple, sucking and holding, and suddenly he brought his teeth forward and held it firmly between them. He moved my breast in and out of his mouth, pausing at the hard brown tip of my nipple, almost biting but stopping short. "I want to eat it, but I can't."

"You're so bad. You already know I love you. You just want to hear it louder."

He put his hand at my crotch. "You're wet. Come here and help me."

Voices rose throughout the house, but at first we ignored them and I lay face down across the bed. He moved across me and grabbed my hands in his. But I heard those shrill voices, and they quickly rose to become words and distant crying. Finally they shouted across through the walls of our old house, and I heard the words "him" and "safe" clearly from Nikolai. With this, David stopped moving and lay quietly across me.

"I'm going to explode," I said.

We heard a crash against the wall, and Paletzine's voice came hard and loud, speaking with the premeditated strength of a performer's voice, burning through the house. "He will rape you!" David did not speak, but his body clenched when he heard this voice.

"Everyone argues, baby," I said and took his hand. "Don't worry." He rolled over and stared at me.

"You're out of your depth, Rosie. Do you think I invented those stories I told you about him?"

"Including your arm?" I asked quietly.

He put his head down on the pillow and whispered, "He didn't do that. My mother did. That's how smart he is."

"Do you want me to go check on them?"

"Of course not," he said sharply. "Do you think I would send you to deal with my own family?" He pulled his old jeans quickly up over his thighs and took a clean t-shirt from the chest of drawers.

"Don't talk to me like that. I'm trying to help."

"You can't help. You're not part of it, and you don't understand it."

He stood at the door with his hand on the knob, about to leave. Silence would have softened us, but it was just not in my repertoire then.

"I understand that he makes you crazy, but one day you have to stop letting him."

"Rosie, you know the worst thing about you is that you're so fucking self-righteous."

"Sometimes you're such a total asshole."

He lifted his arm suddenly, and brought it crashing down, slamming it against the wood. He folded his arms quickly across his chest, and I could see him rubbing his elbow from the pain.

"What's the matter with you?" I asked. "I've never seen you like this."

"There's a lot you've never seen," he said quietly.

* * *

I wandered by myself through the silent house down to the kitchen. Ginny, the folkie traveler woman from Zaca town who cleaned our house once a week, stood at the long counter, wrapping huge, cleaned trout into foil packets lined with almonds. Her thin, bony hands were covered with fish slime.

"Hello Rosie. You look pretty sharp." I wore a plain, white dress, cut square at the neck and falling loose and straight over my hips, the kind of dress you could find at Penney's on sale in any decade. In fact, I looked very plain.

"I don't, you know. I look like everyone else in the world."

"Thin people always look beautiful. That's all that really matters."

"So where is everyone?" I asked. "It's so quiet when this house is empty."

"Peter is out on the terrace. Your man is still out with the birds. I haven't heard any more from the other two."

"You were here for the argument?"

She nodded. "Gold-digging bitch."

I laughed. "Do you think David's father is rich enough to attract gold diggers?"

"He's a sweet old dear, very gentle. He listened to a song I'm working on and do you know what he said? He said to work with music is the highest art."

I uncorked a bottle of ice cold Sauvignon and handed her a glass. "You must have caught his attention. So what were they fighting about?"

"Peter."

"Peter? Why?"

"Because she spent the day with him on the beach when Mr. Paletzine needed her."

I sat at the table and helped seal the foil over the trout. "This looks really good."

"Thanks, Rosie. Do you mind taking this tray out to Peter while I get the trout in the oven?"

The terrace of the house extended off the kitchen and was built onto a bluff overlooking the sea. Away from the back door, suddenly what seemed like firm land became a huge and precarious shelf which might have been a lookout for ships when the house was originally built. David had reinforced it and laid large flagstone slabs. He had built a low stone wall and had run electric cables that provided light and music. He had also installed a powerful telescope on one side which gave access to the sky and the farthest part of the sea.

Peter stood on the terrace alone, leaning on the huge brass barrel of the telescope. The sound of oboes in a piece of Poulenc rose from the speakers in the warm, black night. I walked toward him, carrying Ginny's tray.

"Hungry?" I asked.

He turned suddenly, and stared at the tray. "Inedible flesh is still inedible even if it is placed on crackers. Not meaning to be unkind, of course, but Nikolai will care about this sort of thing. You look like a nun."

"Nuns wear black."

"In Budapest they sometimes wear white. Not all nuns are widows."

"Yes they are." I put the food tray beside him. "By definition."

"Well, what do I know? I am only a simple Jew. Do you like the music? I played the concerto in Paletzine's honor. I understand he is choreographing something to it."

I leaned to kiss his cheek and then stopped. "Is it okay if I kiss you?"

"Of course. It is much more than merely okay."

I came close to him and put my lips on his face. "You Hungarians are inconsistent."

"Consistency is the hobgoblin of the little American mind," he said, and we both laughed. "I was trying to look intellectual just then, in case she came out. Intellectual and tortured is attractive to women, isn't it?"

"You know, you already are intellectual and tortured, Peter. You don't have to pretend. You're acting so serious about this woman. She'll be gone day after tomorrow."

"No, she won't." He took a herring-slathered cracker off the tray and put the whole thing in his mouth. "Rosie, I am bewildered. Paletzine is a legend in Europe. He even danced with Pavlova. What am I doing? Do you think I am capable of being so dishonorable?" He ate another cracker and finally said, "I'm eating to calm myself. Do I have crumbs anywhere?" He breathed slowly for a while and then said, "Until now, I never understood what you and David have. What can I do? I must convince her to stay with me."

"Peter, what are you talking about?"

"Do you know what she said to me today? She said that for her to stay in California would be too perfect. Imagine! Too perfect." He smiled, then frowned, his facial muscles flickering like sprung triggers. "She thinks she doesn't deserve this. How different from the rest of us who think we deserve everything. I love her."

He clenched his hands into tight fists and rubbed his eyes, hard and frantically, his drunken love so concentrated and out of control that the symptoms were the same as madness. When he stopped, his skin had become dark and coppery, like the color of old pennies.

"Did you sleep with her?" I asked.

"Of course not. But I have made a promise to myself. Somehow I must act. And you must help me. This is the time to prove your friendship. After all, I saved your life."

His face glowed from the warmth of wearing too many clothes. He was always so unsure of how he should dress that on this night that really mattered to him he had decided to wear all his possibilities: a sleeveless white t-shirt, a dark blue polyester shirt and matching pants, an even darker blue tie, a heavy black cable-knit sweater and, topping all, a royal blue jacket. He was sweating from all these choices, but oblivious and focused.

"Do you want me to talk to her? Or to David?"

"How do I know? I don't know what will be needed, but you must be ready. You must believe in me. You must act blindly. Of course, it is not the American way, but you have to believe in me anyway."

He sat on the wide ledge holding one leg close to his chest, his eyes, clear and huge, and somehow he looked suddenly powerful.

"I believe you, Peter, and I'll do whatever you want me to."

He nodded. "Good."

When David and his father arrived, Nikolai stopped in the doorway, resting his hand on David's arm for balance. He looked directly at me and said in a deep, salacious voice, "This is an angel!"

Peter turned to him.

"The black sky, the white dress," Nikolai said. "Melodic."

Peter folded his hands together behind his back, thrust his chin toward the sky and said sarcastically, "I suppose the oboe helps." Nikolai did not answer and did not look at him.

David brought a chair for him to sit on by the sea-ledge and then returned to his father to lead him to it. They moved slowly across the terrace, Nikolai carrying a thick, wood cane, and, once sitting, leaned back, his arms stiff and straight. He wore the black hat and the same, soft black wool scarf wrapped around his throat, covering the bottom part of his mouth. He closed his eyes and sat motionless against the music in the night.

"Would you like a drink?" David asked his father. Nikolai nodded, but still did not open his eyes. "Peter and Rosie?" David walked toward the kitchen door, talking at us over his shoulder. "How about champagne? Where is Marta?"

"She will come," said Nikolai loudly. "She is late, but she will drink champagne with us."

David went into the kitchen and Peter walked across the flagstones to where Nikolai sat, tripping over an uneven stone edge as he approached. "What is your next project, Mr. Paletzine?"

"I return to Italy."

"Will you be choreographing there?" He stood next to him with his hand on the straight back of the wooden chair, hovering at Nikolai's shoulder.

"No, we go to the island until September. After, we go to London for a revival of the *Harlequin's Hat*."

"The Stravinsky in that is perfect," said Peter.

Nikolai opened his eyes and looked up. "Yes, it is. You are correct. You are a supporter of my work, then?"

"Yes, of course. You were a famous man in Hungary even when I was a child before the War."

"The War ruined us all," said Nikolai. "Anyone who wanted to make art was stopped. The War was the last time I danced. Not counting that ridiculous movie, which was not really dancing at all." He lifted his arm and placed his hand across Peter's fingers. "Being among friends and family is so important." Peter didn't move; his hand was trapped under the old man's fingers. He watched Nikolai silently, with alarm, as though he had been touched by a devil. "I have a new piece. Perhaps you can help me," said Nikolai. "A piece for ten dancers, with two principal women. Do you know who might buy this?"

"No," Peter said. "I'm afraid that the people who buy ballets are not my crowd." Nikolai moved his hand and allowed Peter to go free. "Funny," Peter asked, "is that how it works?" He backed away from the edge of the terrace. "It never occurred to me that you had to sell your own dances like turnips."

"Everyone is a salesman," Nikolai said. "You must be very strong to be an artist. In this new piece I am ahead of my time. It is hard to sell a dance with two women, particularly when they don't flap their arms. Two strong female bodies. This is not the way things are done now. But soon even the Europeans will want it. Marta is preparing a marketing plan and I will do interviews."

Ginny and David came out of the kitchen carrying trays of plates. "It's so warm tonight, David wants to eat out here. Al fresco."

"Unless you'll be too cold," David said to his father.

"No, the salt air is good for muscles."

"If y'all would just put the plates out," Ginny said, "I'll be right back." She scuttled into the kitchen like a Woolworth's counter girl. In fact, she had been a counter girl and still wore the pink peppermint-flavored lipstick she had bought at the Woolworth's in Santa Barbara when she worked there.

I walked over to Nikolai and asked, "What do you think Marta is doing?"

"She never likes being with new people. She is like a housecat." He began to push himself up from the chair, leaning heavily forward onto the cane. He struggled with painful breaths which I only half believed. Once standing, he came to my side. He was exactly my height, and surrounding him was the thick smell of perfume, an old woman's Guerlain of lilac and spice.

"Your parents are still alive?" he asked, and put his hand on my arm. His grip was like iron, but his arm was light like the weight of a slender, dry branch.

"My father."

"Only your father? You must be very brave, Rosamund. Families are so important. Does he live near to you?"

"In the desert."

He put his hand at the back of my head, stroking my hair. His fingers were curved like claws, and he continued rubbing them over me. "I think one day you and David will have children. Then you will know."

"Know what?"

"We begin by wanting the right thing. But you will see how dangerous it is to be a parent." He dropped his fingers to caress me and rested his hand like a thick clasp at the back.

"Here's the salad," said Ginny, blowing a lock of hair out of her face and licking the stark chalk-pink peppermint lipstick from her lips. David carried a huge, heavy tray decorated with thick iron scrollwork. His elbows were bent and his back taut. He put it noiselessly on the table and then watched as his father and I stood in the shadow by the low wall. He had dressed for dinner for Nikolai, wearing a crisp, grey linen shirt that Ginny had ironed for him that afternoon. The clean, perfect lines of the creases lay across his back, and even though it was not tight-fitting, the soft linen fell close around him and tucked into a pair of black wool pants. His waist was so slender it seemed adolescent.

"Hey," he whispered to me, although both Peter and Nikolai heard him speak. "Hey, come here."

I walked to his side.

"Dance with me? This is such a great night."

"You know I'm a terrible dancer. Your father is a professional. I could never stumble around like a cow in front of him."

He smiled and put his arm around my waist as though to lead me to an imaginary dance floor. "I'm the only one here. And I love everything you do." He put his face against me. "Your hair smells wonderful." He bent his hand and gently ran his knuckles across my cheek. "Can you love a dick-brain?"

"I don't know."

"Dance with me?" he asked again as he took my hand. He put his hips against mine and began to shift from side to side. "Do you forgive me? I would forgive you."

"I guess I do." I stretched up and kissed his cheek.

Peter had been standing beneath an upstairs window, half in bright light and half in shadow, watching us and grinning. At once, he straightened and frowned slightly, no longer smiling. I saw him press his head against the wall and I realized he was listening to a faint sound coming from the window.

He looked straight at me and asked, "Did you hear that?"

My hand was on David's shoulder, my fingers lying against his neck. I couldn't hear Peter's noises.

"What?" I asked.

"Listen," said Peter. "Now."

The music lifted over us out across the sea, but David did not relax. He looked at me and said, "I hear it. What is it?"

"Some knocking. Some kind of tapping," said Peter.

"And I can hear a voice," David said. "Crying or something." Then he stepped back from me and looked straight at his father, questioning. Nikolai had closed his eyes, his face hidden between the hat and the scarf.

Both David and Peter understood the noise at once, and they rushed suddenly for the door, throwing it open and lurching inside. I raced after them, and together we pounded quickly down the hall and up the stairs while Peter shouted Marta's name over and over. We sprinted up two flights to the guest rooms at the top of the house, and at the last landing, David rushed to the closed bathroom door. He pushed against it, but it was locked.

"Marta!" called Peter, and began to hammer frantically.

Marta's voice was so faint and choked with crying that we had to stand still in order to hear her.

"Please help me," she whispered.

"Get out of the way!" shouted David, as he stood back to kick through the worn wood. Peter screamed her name again, and as he did David's foot crashed at the door, cracking it and splitting it from the huge, iron hinges.

They lurched into the small room in front of me. Peter knelt on the cold, ivory tiles where she lay.

From her lips hung silver-colored duct tape, and her legs and hands were tied behind her. She had been trussed like a bird to be roasted, so she could not move or scream.

"Oh, dear god," Peter said, and sat beside her, pulling her close to his chest. Large shards of a broken glass lay about her on the tiles and tracks of blood were smeared across her skin and clothes.

David knelt down and began pushing the glass out of the way with his bare hands. When he had cleared the floor around us, he stood up and backed to the wall, standing helplessly apart.

Peter continued holding Marta, repeating, "Don't worry, don't worry," until at last she stopped whimpering.

"Marta, my god, what happened?" I asked, and grabbed a bandage box from the cabinet.

Peter said, "Hand me a cloth, will you?"

I sat next to them on the bloody floor, opening a bottle of disinfectant that filled the small room with that sudden, terrifying smell. Together we wiped her cuts, Peter touching the cloth to her skin so gently.

She explained that at first she lay still, amazed that she had allowed herself to be overpowered by the old man. Eventually, she knocked the glass to the floor with her loosened feet, so that large pieces of broken glass lay about her. Some of the glass slivers had cut her arms where she lay, and it was this blood that gave her the idea. Between two fingers she held one sharp and pointed piece of glass, and dragged this up and down the inside of her arms until she broke her skin in one, continuous split, hoping she would bleed to death.

"But then, I just didn't think of that anymore and I started to chew through the tape over my mouth." She called out many, many times before we came, and she pulled herself across the broken glass on the floor to kick at the door for our attention. She said that all this time she could hear the Poulenc that Peter had played in Nikolai's honor.

When she finished the story, I looked around and saw that David had left the bathroom.

The three of us stood up and Peter said, "I'm going to take Marta to my room." After they had left, David called to me from the small room at the end of the landing. When I reached him, he was sitting on the foot of his father's bed in the dark with the only light shining through from the hall. He looked up at me without moving. His face was damp from tears.

I flicked the light switch, and it was then I noticed his shirt. The soft, grey linen was smeared across his chest with wide tracks of blood.

"Are you all right?" I asked.

"I'm okay, but he's gotta go. I just don't think I can call the police on him."

"No," I whispered. "I know that."

He looked up at me like an animal about to take flight. "Will you help me pack his things? I have to get him out of here or Peter will kill him. Or maybe I will," he added quietly.

"Of course."

David sat quietly on the bed before me for a few moments. "You know, I think I'm going crazy."

"No. I know you're not. But right now, just worry about the things you can fix." I ran my hands over his blood-stained shirt.

"I guess Marta is stronger than my mother. A couple of times, Mom didn't have it in her to stop. Once she tried it in a hospital even. When we first got to Toronto, she did it at home. That time I was the one who found her."

I sat beside him with my arms around his shoulders; I moved closer and closer, touching him with every possible part of my body.

"You know," David said, "when I was a teenager, my step-father would tell me to sit quietly and think. He would tell me to process stuff like this first. He always said that intelligence is reasoned action, not just action." As he repeated those old words, he began crying again and struggled to speak.

"I love you so much," I said.

"I can't do it. I don't know where to start. My head is killing me. I'm losing it, Rosie."

"I will be your family," I whispered. He turned and kissed my cheek. I felt his face, damp and cool from the tears. "We can make our own family," I said. "In this house forever, we can make it perfect." I believed it when I said it, and so did he. Like every single generation of twenty-year-olds, love made us believe in evolution, that we could be smarter than our parents.

That night, I drove Nikolai to a hotel in town, and Marta stayed with us. It was many years before we saw him again, and strangely, when he left for Italy, Ginny disappeared. Later we heard from a neighbor that she had gone home with Nikolai to Positano. Apparently she stayed with him for a couple of years before vanishing into the Italian countryside.

CHAPTER 9

At the back of the house near the old carriage barn Peter found a patch of grass and weeds surrounded by a crumbling dry stone wall. Peter and Marta devoted themselves to rebuilding the wall and clearing the weed patch. In the mornings they would wake very late and spend the rest of the daylight poking at the ground, cracking rocks from discarded piles and building back that dry wall. Peter had picked up a pair of old flowered surfer shorts in a secondhand clothing store in Hollywood and he wore these with heavy brown leather Oxford shoes, marching, hoe in hand, in the crisp, faint February sunlight.

A rotting door frame still stood in the wall. Peter took Marta to comb the old junk shops in Goleta, and they returned with a post-war door, its green paint peeling. He hung it and then would lock it from the inside when they worked in the garden.

He spent several weeks planting, bringing petunias and geraniums from the nursery in southern Malibu, laying periwinkles like thick, bright paint around the borders of his garden. He left a clearing of old grass stubble in the center and bought a table and chairs for it. I often watched him in secret from my bedroom window. He wore a wide-brimmed cricket hat to shield his balding head from the sun, and he would sit at his rickety metal worktable, hammering away furiously on an old Olivetti typewriter, only pausing briefly to sip whisky from a glass tumbler he kept with the bottle beneath the table. Those late winter afternoons he would sit with Marta, reading his scripts to her and talking for hours until they were covered with the blue dusk-light.

Before, Peter and I had often climbed down the cliff path to the beach just to stare at the foggy horizon together, but after that January it never happened again. Where he and I had always been awake with the quiet of the morning, drinking coffee before dawn in the cool, unlit kitchen, now it became unnatural for him to spend those mornings without Marta. He brought her into his movie-making by teaching her to research, and so she became his partner, toiling with him in obscure libraries in Los Angeles and San Francisco. He had waited all those years for someone to love him, imagining what it would be like: now he knew exactly what to do. And she was grateful for a man who loved her utterly, who made her so happy.

David would not start tour rehearsals until May, and he told everyone at the label that he was taking some time off. In reality, he spent days and days sitting on the porch by himself with his guitars, or inside at the piano. After I finished my own work, I would come to sit with him, but usually he would say, "Rosie, baby, I'm just noodling around here. Give me a while and we'll go out." Mostly I left him alone, because I never wanted anyone watching me in a darkroom, either.

Sometimes he would invite Matt Rappaport to visit, and they would talk for hours, drinking brandy and philosophizing. He never called other musicians or his own band, and when his 'noodling' turned into a song, he would play it after dinner for me and Matt, or Peter and Marta.

In the late winter I had planted a garden of lemon mint and lavender by the front door, and as soon as the spring hit the coast these went wild with the sun, and often I would sit by myself in my garden, intoxicated by the heavy perfume of the stalks and the leaves rising in the heat.

By early spring, the record company sent a design team to take promotional pictures for the summer tour, and they came up the drive in Cadillacs and trucks, spreading diesel fumes in the heavy sunlight. A dozen of them got out of those cars, with their heavy black boxes of equipment, invading as though they owned our home, and in a depressing way, I suppose they did.

The art director spent an hour scouting the corners of Zaca, while the rest sat in our kitchen drinking coffee. Finally, he chose a spot in our living room to work, and they organized the scenes, using circus people they had hired as props. Two of them climbed to the top of David's bookshelves while the drummer lay on the floor beside the old telescope; a country singer wore a huge white hat and clown makeup, and sat holding an autoharp in her lap. In all, eight people I did not know were aligned in our living room like models for a surreal western folk painting. They staged this in a dozen configurations, while the photographer waited in the kitchen with me, talking about the old days of black and whites in cheap rehearsal rooms, the days when shots we missed had not been counted in dollars.

Eventually I escaped to the front porch and my lavender garden, and late that afternoon one of the circus acrobats came to join me. He sat on the bench beside me, and I could see that his tights were stained with scotch.

"Don't be afraid of us," he said, not unkindly.

"The only thing that makes me afraid is when you throw darts at our fireplace."

He chuckled without offense. "This is a sacred spot, you know. David is like a magician, like an Egyptian magician making wine from water."

"An Egyptian magician?"

"Jesus was Egyptian. He is like Jesus's son. And this is a magical place. That's why all the birds come here. The light is perfect, so bright. In Europe it is too gentle."

David had come quietly to the door behind us.

"The reason the ducks come here is because we feed them twice a day. And the creek. Pretty simple. They like the food and water."

The acrobat turned sharply to look at him. "You don't believe in magic?"

"No." David walked down to where we stood. He wore a white t-shirt and cut-off jeans, and he stretched as he came to us, like an animal in the sun. "They're doing another set-up for the shoot. You better go in," he said, and the man left immediately.

"You don't like this, do you?" I asked.

He shrugged. "It's not important." He rested his hand on my shoulder. "This is a great garden. You should take pictures here." He reached for my hand and held it. "You know, you always look beautiful, but lately, I don't know . . . you look like a painting. I'm almost afraid to touch you."

I had known for a day that I was pregnant, but had not yet told him. I should have chosen that moment, but so much of our lives belonged to him, and depended on him, that I convinced myself this one event, the baby, was mine, because it was inside me. I made myself believe that I could choose when and where to tell him, or if at all.

Late into the afternoon Peter and Marta came home. They had been in New York for two days looking unsuccessfully for a funder for a documentary Peter wanted to make about Stravinsky. I sat on the counter in the kitchen while they cooked for the houseful of people. "Where did all these people come from?" Peter asked.

I shrugged. "The record company. You don't have to cook, you know. They will send the catering truck."

"Maybe for me the cooking is therapeutic. But we're only making something simple. Caesar salad and chicken. You know, Marta makes a perfect Caesar salad. We ate our way around New York looking for the perfect Caesar salad, and then," he grinned broadly and touched her arm, "I found out. Hers is the perfect one!" He kissed her cheek with a loud smack and Marta shook her head, smiling.

"My darling, you need to stop talking to people about me like this."

"How did the money go?" I asked.

"Nothing," Peter said. "Not two pennies to rub together."

"The classics are unappreciated," Marta said.

"When the big bucks gentleman said no to us, we had one last meeting with the people at the National Endowment. I pitched the Stravinsky and of course they didn't care. So, thinking that perhaps Stravinsky was too modern, I began to pitch my old idea about Mahler. And do you know what she said, this dodo-ette from our national arts office? She said, 'Who's Mahler?'" He stared at me. "Well, what could I say after that? We were rotting our brains just being there."

David came to the kitchen door.

"Of course, Mr. Pop Culture here," said Peter, pointing at him, "I could get a million to film you."

"Don't scare me," said David. "You live with me—why would you want to film me?"

"Exactly," Peter said. "By the way, James is coming today. The real reason I'm cooking is that I invited him for dinner. And the immigration lawyer. You see, my hearing is very soon. He called and wanted to see me. This is it. Either they will have me or they will deport me."

"Oh, they'll have you," said David. "James says there's no question."

"You talked to him, too?" Peter asked.

"I talk to him all the time," David said.

"I suppose you knew he was coming for dinner?"

He looked at the floor. "Yeah."

"There aren't really any surprises for you in your house," said Peter.

"Not really. I'm sorry."

The caretaker had put three huge oak tables on the back terrace overlooking the sea. We spread a roll of red and white checked oilcloth across the length of them and piled the food and bottles of red wine down the middle. People wandered up from the basement, the living room, the front garden: like villagers at a fête, they dropped what they were doing to come and eat together. Peter and Marta sat at one end, passing down the platters of rosemary-grilled chicken. An Italian couple sat next to Marta, and had brought a baby with them, a child of about a year still in diapers who could sit but had not yet learned to walk. They put this child on the table in front of them, next to a huge bowl of Caesar salad.

The Italians and Marta sang a Tuscan folk song about a rabbit and a hunter and a deer, where the animals conspired against the hunter and won. They acted it out, using huge hand motions heavy in the air so that everyone at the table could understand. The child loved this song, and laughed until its face turned bright red when the adults put their hands like antlers on top of their heads.

We ate for hours, until the sun softened and the dark began to fall across the ocean. No one hurried back to making pictures, and after James and his lawyer friend had finished meeting with Peter and David, James came and sat beside me, staring out at the sea with his back to the table and the people.

"Aren't you hungry at all?" I asked.

"Not really. This is one hell of a view, Rosie. I can see why you love it here."

"The view and David. They're everything."

He sighed. "You've turned into such a love sap." He drank from his glass, nearly emptying it. He smiled broadly, and his eyes were that transparent crystal blue that always made him seem to be telling the truth. He was wearing a cream-colored suit, but now took off the jacket and sat with the ivory shirt sleeves rolled up to his elbows showing the wiry and tanned muscles of his forearms.

"What have you been doing all these hours?" I asked.

"Talking to Peter about the hearing. Are you going?"

"Of course."

"They're cute, aren't they?" he asked, and looked down the table to where Marta sat with her arm on Peter's shoulder. James turned around and put his legs under the table; he was facing the tiny child, who had his hands plunged into a bowl of oily lettuce. He stared at the baby. "This is total chaos, you know. Are you sure you're safe here?"

I put my hand on the soft space between his shoulder blades and stroked his back. "James, you're such a worrier. Is that what makes you a good lawyer?"

"How do you know I'm a good lawyer?"

"Because you're going to make Peter an American after all these years."

"Did you say warrior or worrier?" he asked, and grinned. Suddenly the child in front of him lifted the salad bowl and flung the greasy lettuce pieces across the table. "Oh my god," he said, but no one else at the table seemed to care. "How can you stand this?"

I smiled at him; James would always be a guy who needed to control the picture in front of him. "You just have to let it happen, and somehow figure out what's important. I'm taking good pictures and David is doing some great work these days."

"For god's sake, Rosie. He makes up songs; he doesn't work."

"That's a terrible thing to say."

"He would be the first to say it."

"He's written at least two songs that will stick forever."

He smiled at me for a moment. "You're lovesick. And most of what you like about him comes from his publicity people." He put his hand on the table, his fingers covering mine. "It takes a long time to really know someone."

"We have a lot of time ahead of us. I'm pregnant."

He leaned forward on his elbows, and as he moved I smelled the fresh sweat, faint and rising around him. "I had no idea," he said quietly. "Well, congratulations."

"Thank you."

"Are you going to keep it?"

"Of course. I've already named it."

He was still for a moment, staring down at the table.

"Aren't you going to ask me what?"

"Tell me," he said softly, raising his head.

"Sam, for my father."

"You mean Samuel. That was my grandfather's name. And what if it's a girl?"

"I think it will be a boy."

"Can you feel me falling apart here?" he asked and smiled quickly, the tiny muscles at the corners of his mouth twitching slightly. He cackled harshly above the fallen conversations around us, and nodded his head for no particular reason. "All this time, I was just waiting for you."

"I didn't mean to let you think we could be together."

"You didn't. But I always believed this thing with David would evaporate." He began shaking his head slowly. "I better get out of here." He stood up, lifting his briefcase from the table and held it over his chest, wrapping his arms around it.

"That's all? You're going?"

"Rosie, what did you think? That I would stay and party?"

"James, I'm sorry. Please be happy for me."

He kissed my cheek. "Who do I see about getting my car?"

I put my arm in his and walked with him through the quiet, empty house. He didn't speak, and as we passed the rooms of debris left by the company people who had dropped everything and run out to eat, I said, "It's kind of like Pompeii, isn't it," but he still didn't say a word.

Eventually we found his friend talking to David on the bench in my garden. His name was Charlie, a small, shy guy with thinning ginger-colored hair gone grey at his temples. He still wore his jacket with the fake academic patches at the elbows, and when he spoke it was with a soft, quick stutter. We stood in front of them and Charlie looked up at me.

"So will you be able to keep Peter safe?" I asked.

"Of course."

David's silly hat lay on the dirt where he had tossed it, and I picked it up and put it on the bench.

"Ready to take off?" James asked. "I have a dinner meeting in the city tonight, and I should get rolling." The headland sky was caught by then between purple and black, a clear and crisp night sky coming.

"Sure," Charlie said. "I'll just say goodbye to the Vargas."

"They aren't married, you know," David said.

"I know," he grinned. "The case would be even more fun if they were."

The three of us waited quietly for a moment when suddenly James shoved his hand out at David. "I should congratulate you. I hear you're going to be a father."

At first David said nothing. For so short an instant I knew that James didn't see it, David paused and glanced over at me, his face like a wall. Then quickly he smiled and held out his hand. He leaned forward and grabbed James by the shoulders. James put his arms around David; the two of them clutched at each other, holding there a few too many seconds until it began to seem like a farewell.

"Thanks, man."

"When will it happen?" James asked David.

"November," I said quickly, knowing that David had no idea. "Maybe even Thanksgiving."

"You two should think about getting married," James said, and they both smiled.

Even after they left, David was still holding that hollow smile. I remember him standing next to me as James drove his little white Mercedes down the long road to the highway; he was frozen with that smile long after no one but me could see his face.

"I'm sorry. I know I should have told you first. I only just found out for sure."

"It doesn't matter." He sat down on the bench.

"It does. It was stupid for me to tell him before I told you. I know it was embarrassing for you. You might not even want it."

Quickly, he looked over at me. "Embarrassing? You think that's it? You think I'm embarrassed?" He reached out and grabbed my hand. "Do you really think I'm such an asshole? Why would I mind if you told a friend of mine that you're pregnant?" he asked, suddenly raising his voice. "Unless for some weird reason you forgot to tell me." He pressed my hand harder and harder between his fingers. "But maybe it wasn't a weird reason. Maybe you needed to tell him because you got some other thing going on."

"Don't be ridiculous," I said. "He's not really your friend, is he?"

"No, he's my lawyer. He's your friend."

"I'm sorry, David. I'm so sorry you didn't find out the way you should have."

"You know, it kind of looks to me like you've been sleeping with him. Is that it?" Now it was dark around us, and however close I stood, I still couldn't see his eyes. I could hear a trickle of music in the night from the party behind the house, and the sharp tang of the lemon mint I had planted beside the lavender was beginning to rise around us.

"Don't say that." I waited silently like a small girl being punished. "You know I could never do that." Finally, he let go of my hand, and I reached over and grabbed a small branch of lemon leaves, rolling them between my fingers, bringing on the heavy, biting smell.

"You have to promise that you won't see him again. Otherwise I'd never be able to trust you."

"The only time I see him is with you. Who invited him here today? Not me."

David picked up his hat and put it on. "Just make this promise and don't be a smart ass."

"I didn't sleep with him. I don't understand why you would even think that."

He said quietly, "Whether you have already, or whether you might one day, there's not really much difference."

For him, there was no difference: love included intention; it included forever.

"Look, I will never sleep with James. I won't see him. I won't have lunch with him. I won't even talk to him on the phone. I promise. How's that?"

"Fine. You know, I can't even ask you to get married without it sounding like it's his idea," he mumbled.

"I had a plan about how I was going to tell you about the baby. This isn't it at all."

He shrugged. "I guess not." He patted the bench next to him. "Come sit down." I sat with him, stiffly aware that I was being forgiven. "Does this mean we're keeping it?" he asked gently.

"Why is that the first question people ask me?"

"Because what you want has a lot to do with what happens."

"It's your baby, too."

"Believe me, Rosie, I know that. I'm shaking here thinking you might want to get rid of it."

I turned to look at him. "So, it's okay?"

"Of course. Right now, I'm the proudest guy on the planet."

The lights had come on along the porch by then, the soft ivory shuddering across us. I put my head against his chest and wrapped my arms around his waist. "I love you so much."

As he closed me inside of his arms, I buried myself there, moving with his chest rising and falling. Finally, he said, "You're everything, Rosie." That cooling spring-night air had fallen across us, and he put his hand at my waist, and he spread his fingers over my stomach, covering it, pressing softly against the warmth of my body, just like my father must have done, just like guys have done forever when they finally, first understand what they are really capable of.

A breeze stumbled down about us, a flicker-flash of green behind the trees and that supple light entered me: the world swelled, suspended, like the headland woods filling with the smell of rain before it breaks. I opened my eyes and put my hand on the silky scar skin of David's forearm, the fingerprint of that lost family.

Within a week he had cleared the house of people, sent even the archeos packing back to the university. It was just the four of us, and Sam, until the tour started. David spent his days with Peter, learning the secrets of dry stone walls, and helping him build a small filmworks in the basement. And just after Peter's immigration hearing, I found out that David had fired James and hired a new law firm.

* * *

When I was nine years old my mother made me promise to get married only on the first of the month to make it easy to remember, and only in California because the community property laws were good for women there. When I became Wilderspin, I did it just as she had always asked, at the beginning of June in Santa Barbara, and the next day David and I left for the Asian dates of his tour.

That was the decisive summer of his career, when the company had made a significant investment in marketing him. Each day the publicist traveling with us brought a schedule that covered the moment David woke up until the time he was needed on stage. It was implicit that he had to do it all: the company had put serious sums of money on him and he knew they could foreclose at any moment.

By then, David had put out three albums, each turning a higher margin than the last, and the management team at the company used some obscure abacus to determine that David, of all the others, was the musical promise that summer. Each week they pouched to him an analysis of the gate returns, and in hotel rooms in every emerald metropolis in Asia, he would get up around lunchtime and read the numbers that made us all rich and that somehow became an indicator of his sanity.

We were somewhere in the north Pacific when he started spending big money. They called it investing instead of buying, and inevitably the things he acquired were ones that couldn't be moved. Over the phone he bought a racehorse and a small stable in Kentucky; he bought into some condos in Toronto. He and his new lawyer negotiated by wire and pouch the title on a new recording studio in the English countryside. And without realizing it, David started paying more attention to the things he owned than to the music. He began squeezing out sweet, clever songs that didn't dance. The more the kids crowded for him, the more he cold-cocked them with complicated arrangements of music that was too pretty for rock and roll.

By the end of July we had moved through the north Pacific to Tokyo, in and out of the humidity of the cities and the dryness of the hotel rooms and airplanes, and David's thirsty, tobacco-smothered voice was no longer exploding in the night. The company sent a doctor, but that was the '70s, when the medical answer was needles and pills. It didn't occur to us then that it was unnatural to move between so many borders so quickly, that screaming through the night and smoking three packs of cigarettes while consuming a quart of vodka, or cocaine chased by amphetamines, might cause irreversible damage. We just never believed that green vegetables, plenty of sleep, and exercise were, after all was said and done, the real remedies.

The sound people would tinker for days to find new ways to throw David's failing voice across the open air, to keep it from escaping into the night. Those technicians were magic to us, shaping the tired and drunk and broken voices into powerful, hurling calls in the dark; at the end of a long tour we worshipped the sound techs for lying to those crowds and saving the music.

During those months, wherever he played, David learned to say 'good evening' in the language. At first he did it as a joke, but somewhere on the Pacific Rim he became proud of himself for knowing so many languages, even though all he knew was 'good evening' and 'thank you.' The company publicist was mouthing to the press about all these languages and eventually David started believing his own riff. That is how I saw change; lies seeping across the truth and soaking it to the core, until we were expected to believe what had been invented, and that invention was what held the music together.

The kids took it wildly when he led off his concerts by speaking in their languages. In Osaka someone had painted enormous white banners with splashes of black ink like cranes flying, and with the first four chords of his opening song, the kids snapped, roared into an ocean, and the banners began to float out across the heads of the crowd with crazy clapping and chanting. He and the band would slam into the songs after that, stamping and jacking across the stage to the loping bass-sound splitting the air so easily, or to David furiously stroking and hashing the guitar. He would bend forward and skid out with his fingers feathering back and forth over the strings, bending them slowly sometimes or stopping cold and waiting, grinning. That was his best music, when the wheels stopped spinning and the chord flying off was a touch I recognized from some night in a hotel room. It all came from one kind of moment, when the muscles and his mind were terrifyingly synchronized; and when I traveled with him I would catch him trembling for it, sweating and trembling before thousands of kids, beating and longing for it.

The doctor insisted that I leave the tour in September. We had already done Hong Kong, Singapore, Korea, Australia, and Japan, and my skin was dry and cracking from the air conditioning night after night, and my hair had turned the color and texture of baked hay. I packed and unpacked and took planes, and though I had traveled on tours a dozen times before, I had no purpose on that one.

On the afternoon before the last Hawaiian concert, David was sitting silently on the floor of the hotel room, studying the pouch returns spread before him on the coffee table. I remember it was about four o'clock and we had not been awake long, but the sun was already melting toward the horizon, that pink light seeping across the black glass doors to our balcony. I still lay in the next room in bed, staring mindlessly at some daytime Hawaiian variety show on the television. I heard the hotel room door open suddenly, and I could see through the crack in the door that a white man in khaki pants and a bright green print shirt had come to stand in front of him. I recognized him from Japan, a frail little guy who worked for the Chicago promotions company that backed the dates. Shortly after, one of the label people came, and then the company lawyer. Each of them came into our room with their own keys. They stood around the coffee table, and the lawyer handed David a pale blue-bound packet of papers.

"We just need you to sign the last page," the promo guy said.

"I'll send it to my lawyer and get him to look at it," David replied.

The rest of them laughed when he said that, and shuffled over to the dining table to wait. David read through the pages, and finally got up off the floor. Slowly, he stacked the accounts in a neat pile at one end of the coffee table. Then he walked over to the men.

"You gotta be kidding," he said to them, and I could hear the anger and exhaustion come like an icy pull from his voice.

The promo guy stood up with his mouth open. David was so much taller and stronger, that he could have crushed his forehead between his hands.

"There is no kidding here, David," he said.

David came over to the door of our bedroom and closed it without speaking to me; maybe he didn't realize I was awake. He shut the door quietly, and I held my breath as though my heart had stopped, listening for the crashing violence to hurl into the room.

But what I heard was only his voice, crumbling in low, broken waves, as he began to beg. With the door closed I couldn't hear his words, only the sound of his voice, dissolving into humiliation. After several minutes I heard the outside door close. I found David alone on the balcony, twisting his neck from one side to the other until he could hear the crack of tension release. I shoved open the sliding glass door and stepped behind him, slipping my arms around his waist and moving as close as I could with my belly between us.

"What happened?" I asked.

He shrugged and left the balcony to make a phone call. "I'll be there," he said into the phone, and came back to me. "I have to go do the sound check. We can go out for dinner somewhere after. Where would you like to go? I'll take you someplace great, because this is the end for you, baby. Just you and me tonight. You choose."

"David, please tell me what happened."

"Rosie, it's just business. Don't worry." He laughed. "You're such an old lady, sometimes. Is that what motherhood does?"

He returned an hour later with the road manager, both of them laughing breathlessly, both of them flying. "Come on," he said, "come on, baby." He went to the closet and took my jacket off the hanger. "Here, you should put this on. The wind has come up. I'm starving. How about you?" He grabbed my arm and kissed the palm of my hand. "You know," he said, whispering in a soft frenzy, "sometimes I hear you singing in my sleep." His hands were hot and rough and he lumbered forward and put his tongue between my lips, sinking deep into my mouth. Just as suddenly, he withdrew and smiled at me. "You look beautiful. Let's go, okay?"

This was the rise, the start to every night, when he pushed the adrenalin hard, so that it shone from his skin, radiated from him like some violent fluorescent light. He went into the bathroom, still talking, and grabbed a bag from the counter. He took a bottle of red and white pills from it, amphetamine of the day, and gulped some water while he stared at the mirror.

"Okay, baby," he called to me. "Off we go, laughing and scratching!"

We ate at a Japanese grill with some of the guys in the band, sitting at a long plank table in a room with a vaulted, drafty ceiling, the air-conditioning blasting at us. David ordered for everyone, and when the sake was brought, he poured it into each glass. He gulped his own, refilled it, and then grabbed the black, laminated chopsticks in front of him. He held them both in one hand, clutched together, and cracked the sharp wood on the table, flipping his hand back and forth a dozen times.

I put my hand over his, and stopped the whack of the sticks on the wood.

"You think I'm a disaster, don't you?" he whispered.

"No," I said. "But you need to eat something."

He laughed then, cackling as loudly as he could with the voice that remained to him. When the food was served, he took those jet black chopsticks again and quickly lifted a thin slice of seared chicken between them. He held it inches from his mouth, let it steam in that cold room while the grill juice dripped from it. A moment later I noticed that he was still holding it, and was focused entirely on his hand and the chopsticks, staring in panic because his hand was trembling uncontrollably like a shortwave.

Later at the auditorium I waited alone with him for the five-minute call in a small, windowless dressing room. I sat on his lap with my arms around his neck, and he put his hands under my dress and over my stomach, cupping where the baby lay. By then he had collapsed into a dark, insulated space in his mind, and was absolutely silent. When they shouted for him, we walked quickly down a long, underground hall that was lit with bright white bulbs. At the end was a small, dark staircase leading up to a door.

He turned to me. "You look tired," he said, talking fast and breathing hard. His shirt was already soaked with sweat. "You don't have to stay for this. Why don't you go back to the hotel and rest?"

Before I could answer, one of the roadies put his hand on David's shoulder and was steering him forward. They went fast through the blackness, and we could hear the pounding and stamping from the crowd. He was gone then, and I stood for a moment hearing him suddenly surge into the music with the lights switching color and position and the sound of his poor voice shooting high and strong above our heads.

I went to bed before the show had finished, and woke in the hotel room around three AM, alone. I awoke speaking, asking for water, dreaming of languid pools and still rivers, of cliffs with sea that had no depth. I wore no clothes, and the heat was stifling me. I called for water again, opening my eyes in the darkness. I spoke out to a man I was sure was in the room, a one-legged, bald attorney from the city who had come to my dreams. I stumbled from the bed, and as I moved forward I remembered I was in a different place, Chicago, I thought, and I went to lower the heat control. I found myself in the tiny kitchen stroking the walls in the darkness for the dial that would lower the heat. The man said, "You aren't naked enough now," and stared at me from the darkened corner. I found a door and stepped into a brightly lit corridor, a cool corridor of marble walls with a carpet soft and thick. I remembered my baby, and knew it needed water too so I went into the cool tiled bathroom. I stepped into the shower and let the water run across me, to save this dry, dying baby, I let the cold water flush me, believing that, like a parched white rose, the drench of water on our skin would save us. When I stepped from the shower I did not dry myself, but sat on the velvet couch in the hot room and waited, trying to remember which city I was in, why I was there.

Eventually, David came and stood in the dark without seeing me. Very quickly he took off his watch and scarf, took the change from his pocket, and put all of these on the television. He flicked the TV on, and the blue light in the room cast across me.

"Rosie," he said quickly, startled, "what are you doing up?"

"The baby almost died. It was so thirsty."

"You're half asleep, Rosie. And you're cooking in here." He found the thermostat and lowered it. "You had the heat on." He sat across from me and smiled. "Come on, let's go to bed." He took my hands and stood up. "Let's go take care of that baby."

We lay in the huge bed together and he stroked my shoulder. Even if I hadn't been able to smell the reek of whisky on his skin and breath, I would have known that he had been drinking from the way his eyes tilted down at the corners. I took his hand from my shoulder and kissed his fingers, but I stopped suddenly because they smelled of gardenias and plumeria, and this aroma spread as though a bower had been laid around us. He began to whisper to me about love in hushed, clipped tones, and soon I just drifted back to sleep.

Chapter 10

The next day when we woke the coffee was in the room, and the newspapers were on our bed. I never got used to the thought that so many strangers had the keys to our rooms and could come like ghosts to us in our sleep, leaving us things they thought we needed.

David turned in bed to face me, and as he did the smell of gardenia perfume and sour alcohol rose from the sheets.

"You're going home," he smiled. "You're so lucky. Couple of days from now, you'll be in our own bed." He put his hand on my face. "That's the sweetest. I got two more months of this, and my throat is killing me. Did you hear me last night? I missed the whole top line. My throat was burning and I just stopped trying. The doc sprayed me for the pain. I'm so tired."

I was thinking about that smell of gardenias, but I didn't say that. I said: "You never seem to sleep."

"Can't."

"I'm sorry I'm leaving you." I turned to face him, putting my arm across his chest. "I love you so much. I'm not doing a very good job of taking care of you. I thought I could keep you safe."

He smiled. "Right now your job is taking care of that baby. Think you can hang on until I get home? I want to be there when it's born."

"Sure. I feel great. You'll be back for Thanksgiving, right?"

"We finish in Pittsburgh on the 14th. Then I'll be home." Somewhere in the room I could smell the sharpness of a fresh-cut orange, the sweetness bleeding out into the air. David's tall body was hidden beneath the rumpled sheet. He lifted his arm and put it across me, delicious in its touch on my skin.

"Come here," he said.

"Why were you so late last night?"

"I was drinking with the band. You know that."

"Do I?"

He looked at me quietly. "Don't worry, Rosie. You and I will be married forever. The smartest thing I ever did was to marry you. I don't need anything else."

I didn't answer him. Sam was six months inside of me, a key that had already been turned. Where do you go at that point if you lose your faith? I didn't know if he was screwing the girls around us or not, but I had too much riding on us then to believe it.

That afternoon was one of those last-drink moments, when the tight little squadron gets released from the job and five guys take five planes to five different places. Some bands were like families and some, like us, were like companies. However hard they worked or partied on tour, nobody ever went home together. We were sitting in the hotel lobby bar watching the coastline where a hard, hot rain had just fallen across the dark green mountains. We were surrounded by marble and huge overstuffed furniture made of dark missionary leather, and behind us the wall of the bar formed a huge tank filled with hundreds of brightly-colored fish. It was mid-afternoon and only the music people headed for the alcohol: the normal people were on that paradise beach, floating in soft turquoise waves. A group from our tour came toward us carrying little airplane bags, dressed to travel to other weather. One of them was our bass player and he took my hand and kissed my cheek.

"Well, we did it man." He stood beside his wife, leaning heavily on her shoulder. "At least we'll be in English from now on when we get to New York."

"Going someplace nice for your break?" David asked.

"We're catching a plane to Cincinnati in a few hours," said his wife. "Gonna go home and see my parents. What are you doing, Rosie?"

"Couple of days here. Some friends are coming to visit us. Then home."

Another of the group was our sound engineer, a young skinny guy not even twenty. He slumped into a leather chair, disappeared into it, and said, "What can I drink today?"

David raised his hand slightly and the cocktail waitress came to us.

"Why don't you try this special mai tai?" he asked. "They say if you have enough of these you can see a green flash across the horizon." David had been drinking them himself, and had stacked the glasses like a crystal engineering feat before him.

The other two from the tour, the road manager and a woman photographer, stood close to one another in front of the fish wall. The woman didn't hold a camera, but wore a beautiful dress and very high-heeled shoes.

"We're just about to catch the plane," said the manager. "Back to LA. What are you doing today?"

"Don't know yet," said David.

The photographer looked at me. "How's that baby? I'd love to take a picture of you. Like that, with the baby inside."

Once I saw a photograph in a magazine of a human embryo at seven weeks. The brain of it shone through its forehead, a cloudy halo of light, deep in the belly of its mother and breathing, the whole luminous mass beating and breathing and that brain driving the first thoughts through a fragile, silk-thin membrane. I always wondered what person had the privilege and the intelligence to take that picture, to intrude on life at its purest and most vulnerable moment.

"You haven't got your camera," I said quietly.

"No." She giggled a shrill-pitched sound. "Isn't that always the way?" David stared at her as she sat down alongside me; he was speaking to the road manager, but looking at her. Through the tour she had shot pictures of the guys backstage, big sensationalist ones of David with his arms around people and his mouth wide open and laughing, or of the bassman passed out in the corner of some Asian dressing room. I had invented that kind of picture, and it was eerie being the older woman on the tour when I was still under twenty-five.

Now she reached to put her hand on my stomach. She wore a petal-cut tropical dress of a violent turquoise color and as she touched me, the wrap of flowered cloth across her tanned breasts gaped open. As she leaned over me I could smell fresh gardenia on her skin. She wore a red hibiscus flower behind one ear and as she came close, her long, soft hair fell across my arm and that hibiscus dropped to my lap.

"Rosie is radiant, isn't she, David?" she said, and David abruptly stopped speaking to the roadie. He looked so ragged, glancing quickly at both of us, and I knew the alcohol had dazed him.

I lifted the flower from my lap and handed it back to her.

He took my hand carefully. "Yes, Rosie is always beautiful."

We stayed watching the horizon after the band had left, and eventually Peter and Marta were delivered to us by one of the bellmen.

"Thank you for that beautiful room, Mr. David," Marta said. "This is the most wonderful present." They both carried large wicker bags filled to the brims with beach supplies, and they dumped them heavily on the floor at our feet. "I'm so happy to be here."

David stood up and put his arms out to embrace them both. Seeing them was for him like being safe again, when so much of that tour had been unsafe. All the while the company or the manager or the publicist took us around purporting to protect David, but really they threw him in the path of harm day after day. They put drugs in his hands to keep him happy, they scheduled dates so close together that his downtime was spent on planes or in sound checks. They reported him to the company when he was tanked or tired or raw, and if he argued, they mentioned things like lawsuits or forfeits to keep him in line. When David saw Peter and Marta, he sank into them, as though they might be a safe harbor.

Peter was dressed as always in an old jacket and sandals with socks. He wore grey cotton shorts and a plaid shirt that hung loose over his thick waist. "I'm sure I knew you didn't need a passport for Hawaii," he said and turned to Marta. "Didn't I know that? Why didn't I believe them when they called the first time? I'm incredibly suspicious, aren't I?"

She put her arm around his waist. "Anyway, you're an American now. In another month you will have your real passport and can go anywhere in the world with nothing to worry about."

"Is it too late to go to the beach?" Peter asked. "Can pregnant women go to the beach?"

"Sure," I said. "We have a couple of hours of sun left."

"I know a better place than the beach," said David. "A secret place."

"Of course you do," said Peter, "of course you do. I was counting on that vast local knowledge. We have been reading astonishing things in our hometown papers about Mr. Wilder-spin here. It seems you have grown up in every country in Asia."

David stood behind me and put his hands on the back of my chair, leaning hard and unsteadily into it for support. He wore a pastel blue cotton shirt, and a dark, damp outline of sweat had begun to show around his armpits and across his back. "Don't believe everything you read."

"I don't," said Peter. "Do you?" He stared for a long time at the tank behind us, until a woman in a bikini dived in to feed the fish. "Look, my darling, a fish feeder. How extraordinary. Hawaii has everything."

David said, "Let's have a drink for the road."

"Don't you think you may have topped out on the drinking thing?" Peter pointed to the table.

I began to push myself up from that deep, cool chair, and David quickly put his hands out to help. "Here, baby. This is the part I like. Taking care of you."

We drove the slow Hawaiian coast, around those old deep lush bends framed by cliff waterfalls to the coves and over tiny wooden bridges that have since disappeared. Peter drove us up into the volcanic jungles, and when we got as high as we could go, David directed him to turn down a moist plantation track between banana trees heavy with bursting fruit. We drove and drove and I thought it would never end; the road was uneven, and we bounced along in this shiny car and every so often David would look at me and say, "Tell me if you need to stop."

We came to a ridge and a clearing in the thick fern growth. We could not drive on, so we climbed out of the car and David pulled a bag from the trunk. He slung it over his shoulder and led us across the smooth, cooled lava crust toward the horizon, toward the sound of crashing water. The hot, moist wind was belting around us and the clearing smelled of rotting carcasses and heavy orchid perfume where the fallen bony trunks lay on their sides, crumbling at last into soil. He took my arm to give me balance, and walked slowly so I could lean on him. Eventually, we could see the ocean in the distance, and around us the mist was rising like steam from the rich, dark soil and thick ferns. I removed my sandals and stepped into the sponge of the earth, my feet instantly covered with green juice and clay. Suddenly we were at an ancient lava shelf that had spilled down from the sea cliff. It had frozen there, forming a huge, deep pool which was nearly rectangular. Now we were out of the thick rainforest thatch, and the sun exploded across us in fistfuls of gold, lighting the clear, turquoise water and exposing hundreds of fish in neon yellow and purple and orange: trunkfish and snapper and hawkfish and butterflies.

"My God," said Peter, staring at this perfect place, the calm, clear pool and the mounds of dry, black lava crust bordered by the sea.

David undressed and dived into the water. He swam a couple of lengths, and came smiling to where I sat. "Come in. You can float with me." He pulled himself up, levering his body onto the wet shelf. He stood in the sun with the water streaming down his shoulders and thighs, reaching for me and helping me to stand and undress and enter his water. It was warm and smooth like an endless windowpane, and I moved my arms to begin slipping through the silence. A cluster of heat was rising in my throat and I could not speak. I breathed slowly and closed my eyes, sliding off David's wrists to guide myself. Sea blooms drifted around me, and Sam, warm inside of me, kept me afloat. I was rinsed alive by pleasure.

Then I heard David. "I'm sorry. I have to do this." Clouds hung like cocoons in the sky as he put his lips on my forehead.

The late afternoon wind was rising, sobering him at last, and he climbed from the pool and sat on the ledge. Marta swam over to him and lay flat upon the rocks in the sun, her olive-colored arms arched above her head, her breasts soft and ripe like spreading honey, and covered with droplets.

Peter floated to them. "If I get out do you promise I can go back in?"

Marta laughed, "I didn't mean to abandon you, my darling."

Peter scrambled from the water quickly, slipping on the rock-slime, and Marta put her hand to his palm. The three of them sat in a little cluster with the invisible pounding of the sea behind them, watching me drift through that lagoon.

I swam to their ledge and floated in the water beneath them, my hands on David's knees to anchor me. The copper afternoon light had begun to slant over us, and the warm breeze cut a river of busted glass across the surface of the pool.

"I don't think I can get out on my own." They stood quickly in the water beside me, their hands on my hips and arms in some strange birthing ritual, lifting and steadying me, helping me out.

David took my hand and lifted it to his lips, kissing the inside of my wrist and staring at the dark, deep blue vein-branches.

Marta said, "We brought your baby a present." She stood on the dry, hot stones and climbed across the ledge to her straw bag. She pulled out a small, black leather pouch, emptied it, and lay the contents carefully on top. "We were just in Taos. They say that nothing is random, that you choose the ones that have traveled with you in other lives." Across the soft leather lay a dozen small soapstone carvings of desert animals. "I believe if we put these around your bed while you are giving birth, the baby will be endowed with the earth's serenity."

"This may be crazy," said Peter, "but there really is no harm in trying, is there? It can't hurt?"

David took one of the carvings, cupping it in the palms of his hands and blowing on it. "They steam. Look, the surface steams like glass."

"I'm sure it's magic," said Peter.

"But it doesn't need to be," David said. "It could just be physics, couldn't it?" He looked over at me and grinned. "We've been wanting to ask both of you something. Rosie and I would like you to be the godparents for our child. Will you think about it? I know it's a big commitment."

"You know," said Marta, "once a long time ago my father gave me an old porcelain doll for my birthday. She had such long lashes and big innocent eyes. I always thought I would have a baby that looked like that. I thought I would have five babies and they would all be friends." She held the slick, black stones in her hands, and looked at my belly. "So I figured I could get old because I would have sons and daughters to take care of me. Now I look in the mirror and my skin looks dry and I am getting those old lady's wrinkles around my lips. And I haven't even got one child. I'm thirty-five; I waited too long. So giving me this, giving us this, is so generous."

"We may not have children, but we can be good parents," said Peter, staring down at the tufts of seaweed folded like cotton wadding over his feet. "It would be an honor for you to trust us with your child."

The riffling breeze soon became noisy; the sun had moved, leaving rust across the sky. Then two young Hawaiians pulled themselves over the lip of the lava to the calm of the secret pool. They nodded to us and put buckets on the ledge, disappearing again back into the sea. When they reappeared they carried spears and masks, and like us, wore nothing. Their muscular bodies were brown as berries.

They sat at the opposite side of the pool, laughing, rinsing their masks and fins, packing them into netting for the long walk home. When they had finished their work, they dived, one after another, into the pool and swam the length of it. Then I could see they were children, boys no more than fourteen, their bony shoulder blades lifting from the darkening water as they cut through it. They turned and shouted to each other, diving in some laughing, rough boys' game, and the water brimmed and pulsed with their bodies. They finished on their backs, floating and smiling at the sky, as though it and that perfect place belonged to them.

After a few moments of silence they climbed out and lay on the warm lava crust. One boy sat up and grabbed into the bucket at his catch, lifting up a fish that was the size of two thick hands, round and spiny-backed, and striped with indigo and bright gold.

He said to his friend, "Look, this one's not dead." He chuckled and held it in the air while its tail half-flapped furiously, until slowly, as we watched, the life went from it. He took his knife from the netting package and cut the head and tail off, flinging them into the sea. He lay the fish on a rock and sliced that bright-colored skin from it, carefully, like an artist separating paint. He put the pieces of pink flesh in his mouth and smiled. "I'm hungry."

"You eat anything," his friend said. "Even those butterfly fish that taste like shit. Your mom'd kill you if she found out you didn't cook it."

After he had finished, they both packed up again. Just before they left, they pulled swimming trunks from their bags and slipped them on.

"Bye!" they called to us like small children as they walked the path away from the sea, their spears and buckets clattering against the rocks.

David stood quietly and picked up the bag he had brought from the car. He climbed away from us up the ledge, and pulled his works out of the bag. He organized himself to shoot some heroin into a vein on his forearm, just a single pinch of heroin, pure enough to kick a mule's chest or to stop a heart on a bad day.

"What is he doing?" Peter asked.

"It's new," I said. "Heroin."

"Rosie, you know this is very serious."

"I've told him. You try."

Peter climbed to the top of the ridge.

"I can't get a light in this wind," said David. "Stand there, will you, and block it." Peter moved to shield him from the breeze, and as he did he cast a thick shadow across the rocks.

"You don't need this," said Peter. "Tell me one thing you want that you haven't got on this bloody cliff in Hawaii. Tell me one thing. I may not understand your hip rocker life, but I know that right now you are the biggest fool of the world."

David whispered, "Don't worry, Peter. Not everybody's a casualty, man."

"I thought you were smarter than this. All of a sudden you got stupid?"

"It just helps me relax. That's all. Don't worry." And he pierced his skin with the needle, a quick jab, a quick slide of the point into a roll of vein bulging from his arm; then release, his heart slackened, and the opium hum spread through him.

Peter watched him as I had watched him for a few days. David lay back on the lava and closed his eyes, and then what he shared with us, he shared alone.

"They are all free now," he said, and though he was talking to us, we had no idea what he saw.

"This will kill you," Peter said, but Marta held her hand up and he didn't speak again.

"Me? I'll save us all. Ask my lawyer. Ask the company. Hey, ask my mother, for that matter." Then he was silent, and when I looked around he might have been sleeping.

Peter walked back across the rocks to where I sat. "I should have joined the tour, but I could not get out of the country. I have no passport. I simply could not get out."

"I know that."

"Hawaii was the first place I could come to. What can we do? I don't know about these things."

"He's tired and scared. And he never understood how it would really be. He thought it would just be music all the time."

Marta climbed to the rocks next to where David lay and sat beside him, stroking his arm slowly and firmly, like she was spreading butter across his muscles.

"What about you?" asked Peter.

"I'm going home. I'm okay."

Peter scowled at me. "I don't believe you."

"Well, I wouldn't shoot myself up, if that's what you mean."

"I know that. But first he's drunk and now he's comatose and it's only our first day. Aren't you frightened?"

"He'll be all right."

"How can you get to 'all right' from this?"

"Peter, everything's changed. He sings, and then he has to manage the business. He gets phone calls all day from his lawyer and the corporados in Chicago. He changed managers this year because the last guy was a total loss, so now until there's a new one and he learns the ropes, it's all on David. The road is more fun when you have no place else to go and when there isn't so much money at stake. He'll be fine once the tour is finished."

* * *

That autumn I never wandered very far from the house. Those days are warm on the coast, but as I grew bigger I shadowed the buildings and was careful about walking on my own down the rocky path to the sea. By the end of October I became obsessed with the thought of falling and even imagined scenes of myself, hurt and alone, on paths in the woods or drowning in the rough water. I gave up wearing shoes and would walk barefoot to keep my balance through the powdery, dry dirt. Often at night I could not sleep, and so I set a permanent tripod on the back terrace. I bought extreme lenses and began taking pictures of the night sky over the sea. Sometimes in the deep night I would look for hours at the clear, black sky shredded with stars. I would sit like an old woman, with a sweater protecting my chest and arms from the chilled night, until I was too tired to keep my eyes open. When Sam first learned to talk he was fascinated with questions about heaven and planets, and when I allow myself to think about it, I often believe that he was destined to be an astronomer or an explorer of space, that his genius might have lain there. My first act as his mother was to reunite him with some ancient study of the sky, and I dreamed that one day I would burst with pride for him.

David called me every day in the early morning, as he was on his way to bed. By November it wasn't yet snowing in the East, but he was always sick from the cold, and I could hear his breath rattling in his throat. He would lie in bed in some hotel room, whispering into the phone about fights with the label execs and legal threats. He was out of his depth with no friends, and even the music had become a by-product of the money. Once he called before a show, standing in a corridor using a pay phone with the noise of equipment being hauled and banged around him. I could barely hear what he said, and he brought the mouthpiece much closer until the sound of his lips moving across the plastic was like a fuse snapping and dying in the night. He was drunk and tired, his voice slow and inarticulate as he tried to explain that the gate was so good the company wanted to add a couple of dates at the end of the tour.

"I'm sorry," he said.

"Don't worry." I tried to force a laugh, and started to tell him about Zaca, what it was like to be in my ninth month, how I felt, and who had visited, and the odd movement of another person inside of me.

He was quiet for so long. Finally, he said, "Rosie, I want to come home. I hate this. You're all that I need."

He couldn't come, though; he had legal commitments to the label, and Sam was born while he was in Pittsburgh. Peter and Marta were with me. I named the baby on my own, Samuel David Wilderspin. It's important to say that now, because I always thought it was a beautiful name that made me think of pioneers traveling across deep river valleys in early summer heat. When I called to tell him, I guess he told the guys on the tour, because by the time I returned home from the hospital there were some people from the LA papers trying to get in the gate at Zaca to see Sam.

David arrived a couple of weeks later, just before Thanksgiving. They helicoptered him in from the big LA airport to the one at Santa Barbara so he could get back to us quicker. He had been nominated for lots of awards that year, keeping the company guys in cocaine and gold limousines, so they would do anything for him. It was only two months since I had seen him, but when he pulled himself out of the car into the thin, late November sunlight, his skin looked like over-kneaded dough, slack and faded. He still wore his wedding ring, but on the smallest finger of his right hand he had a new ring, square and silver with a large, clear green stone. He wore an expensive Italian cotton shirt, a deep red color that brought out the ruddy alcohol patches on his cheeks. I could instantly see that he had lost an enormous amount of weight, thirty pounds it turned out, in those two months. But no matter how much of him had withered on that tour, when he got out of the car he held his arms out to us, grinning so innocently.

"Here we are." I stood on the porch holding Sam, smiling uncontrollably. "Here is Sam."

"I can't believe it," he said. We sat on the steps together and he took Sam easily in his arms, pulling him to his chest and feeling his son next to him. I was relieved at last to be watching them together. Even when I noticed the pinpoints across his skin, it didn't matter; I was still relieved to have him home.

He placed his hand over Sam's chest, feeling his lungs like tiny bellows rise and fall. "You did this," he said to me. "I've got so many presents for him. You have to see them. I have a few presents for you, too, baby." He took the ring off his little finger and held it in the palm of his hand. "Here," he said. "This is for you. Try it on. I got it in Virginia from an antique store. It was made during the Civil War by a guy in the Shenandoah Valley who worked with the underground railroad. Like it?"

"It's beautiful." I put it on my finger, rubbing the stone.

"It's an emerald. They even sold me an old photo of the woman who wore it first. I thought you'd like that." He was holding Sam, leaning toward me hesitantly. "I'm trying to say thank you for having our son, for doing it by yourself. I'm sorry you had to be on your own. Do you really like the ring?"

"I love it. I can't believe it's an emerald. It's huge. Can we afford it?"

"Rosie, we can afford anything. I'm a good hunter and gatherer, baby. Have you taken any pictures of our boy?"

"No. There's not really much time. You'll see. First you feed him, then you wash him, then you change him, then you do it all over again, all day long."

"Well, we need to hire someone to help. So you can start taking pictures again." Sam was opening and closing one of his hands and David put a finger into his tiny, translucent clasp.

"Happy?" I asked.

"You have no idea. I'm never going on the road again."

The next day he slept until noon, when he had an appointment to walk the ranch with the caretaker. I sat on the bed watching him try on pair after pair of jeans, all of them so huge over his hips they made him look ridiculous.

"Don't say anything," he said, laughing. Sam lay beside me, and David walked over and lifted him high into the air. He began singing to him, that circus song about a man flying in the air on a trapeze. "I feel better already." He sat on the pillows and leaned against me, his hair damp from the shower. "I started losing my hair while I was away. I guess I'm getting old."

"You know what it is, and it isn't age."

"Are you making a point here?" he asked without looking over.

"I am. I didn't really expect to be married to a junkie."

As soon as I said it, I knew that I had crossed a forbidden line in this homecoming. He paused, without moving, without speaking, every part of him suddenly tight. He held Sam's arm and stroked the tiny palm of his hand with immaculate control while he considered what to say.

"I guess you've seen a few," he said finally.

"What do you mean by that?"

"I mean we come from the same place, Rosie. We both used up our three wishes a long time ago." He moved his hand from Sam to touch me, closing his fingers across the ridge of my anklebone. His head was still bowed at our baby on the bed, but he looked up with a trace of hunger, this rough, impure anger teeming across him.

I could almost hear the rush of my own blood forcing through my inner ear. He moved his hand up my leg, almost a shadow shifting to my inner thigh. The top of his hand was bruised, his face gaunt, and his skin was darkened by tobacco and drugs and alcohol, and no sleep.

I said quietly, "Whatever chances we take now are so much bigger. We can't take any chances with Sam." He stared at me for a moment, then slowly he moved his hand away and let it rest on the coverlet. He began to breathe evenly, without tension, and his body softened. He glanced at the huge mirror across the room and watched his own reflection.

"I look like Frankenstein, don't I?" Then I felt the moment fold, and he put his hand back between my legs, gently this time, stroking my inner thighs with his fingertips.

"I'm not a junkie, baby. I can work it out if you'll stay with me. Give me a while, Rosie; I'll get back to normal."

I nodded. "It never occurred to me not to stay, David. We're a family now. That's forever."

PART THREE

SLIPPING OUT THE BACK DOOR

CHAPTER 11

David managed to stay off the road for a couple of years. When he understood that he had made enough money to keep us safe, he became interested in so many other things it was hard to remember the beginning times when music was all he wanted. In some bar in Santa Barbara he met an ornithologist from the university, a bald, soft-spoken Englishman who explained to him about bird migrations and the mudflats that lined the north shore of our property. He said in the old days most of California was spotted with lush marshland and thousands of snow geese would land at Zaca to feed on their flyway to South America. Of course, the ranchers who owned the land before us had destroyed the marsh and David took it as a personal challenge to re-establish the wetlands so that the geese would return. He read everything he could find, hired a gamekeeper to help him, and described to us the way it would look one day, a flock of soft white velvet bodies moving through the sky toward Zaca, the sound of five thousand pairs of wings beating through the air as they circled the sea cliffs for a landing.

Starting one spring, he worked for months shoveling mud and sand into low sloping banks, throwing seeds and protecting the struggling pipes of fresh plant growth. He rented an earthmover and learned how to drive it; he took a course one evening a week in weeding. He and the gamekeeper drew maps of the ponds based on the flight paths, then dug them, like they were painting across the landscape. He spent all the days outside and his skin turned ruddy brown, that healthy farmer red-brown.

Peter and Marta were writing proposals for a film they wanted to make on the birth of New York unions, and were still using the little, windowless room in the basement, because Zaca was too beautiful, they said, and they needed to stay away from distractions.

I had started taking pictures again, this time not of anything living but of the ancient cave paintings on our land. David and I went together out to the old Chumash settlement and I spent hours photographing the wall markings. I found a kneeling man and a boar surrounded by high forest. Each tree had five clean strokes of pigment, black seed juice crushed and preserved for a thousand years. I took the shots in color at a fast speed but printed them in black and white, sometimes in a sepia wash, so the images froze and cracked like ancient paintings themselves.

I desperately wanted to show them and got my agent working to find a gallery anywhere that would schedule me, but when he said my name all they wanted were my pictures of drunken boys and their guitars and finally I gave in to that idea. For months I felt like I was living in my own past, showing up and smiling at California openings of grainy, cynical black and whites of kids who had already been dead for years.

We had hired an old Russian woman to keep house and take care of Sam. She lived in Santa Barbara with her daughter and came to us through the Russian department at the university. David interviewed her three times before he would agree to hire her, and he checked five references from her. But he liked the idea of Sam learning Russian, and Peter, too, wanted to speak the Russian he had learned as a child, so Yana came to work for us.

On Yana's day off, I would sometimes take Sam for a picnic in the meadow overlooking our cliffs. We would lay a huge cotton-checked cloth out on the grass and Sam would make me laugh as he took such care and so much time placing our lunch on it. He had just learned to walk, and sometimes he would teeter over and fall onto the ground. Then he would lie on the clean, crisp red and white cloth, shaking with giggles and waving his arms and legs in the air. Sometimes we looked over the edge at his father driving the tractor down below, and Sam was always in awe when he saw David using such a huge piece of machinery.

Once we walked the path down to the beach and stood on the rock table, looking into the tide pools for sea creatures. David stopped working and came to us, squatting on the rock with Sam. I took my camera out and started to shoot them as David stood behind him, his big hands holding those small shoulders so carefully. Suddenly Sam turned his head to look at David's face. Seeing that his father's cheeks were smeared with mud spatters, Sam plunged both hands into the sand in front of him, scooped it into his fists, then spread it across his own tiny face, grinning. I took that picture of them standing over the tide pools with the sun glistening off the tiny ponds around them, both of my men covered with earth markings, staring at each other's faces, father and son, like stone-age carvings of gods.

When he came inside at evening-time David would bound up the stairs, grab Sam in his arms, lifting him onto his shoulders. That sound became part of me, his feet on the old wooden steps, four thumps every night, strong and sure, to reach us.

Most early evenings we gathered at a bar David had built into the stone ledge behind the house. Usually Peter would arrive first, make himself a cocktail, and then become bartender for the rest of us. He stocked the bar with European drinks like pastis and cassis syrup, and ordered an old French dice game from a friend of his in Paris. Every night we played this, Catso Vatay Uh, for hours, talking about our projects or politics or love. Later I realized Peter was saying the name in French, and that it was really called 421, a game where you had to end up with no chips, a part of Peter's romantic angst, that somehow to have nothing was to win.

During those times, David described the geese to us. Of course, he had only seen them in books, but he believed they would arrive one day like the dream of swallows at Capistrano. Peter laughed at him.

"You might be investing years in this digging for nothing."

David went to a chair and sat down with a sigh. "I'm so tired."

"That's exactly my point," said Peter. "You could be exhausting yourself for nothing."

"But it's a good kind of tired. Like when you know you did something useful."

Peter shrugged. "You might still be wasting your time, my friend."

"You miss a hundred percent of the shots you don't take. Rosie taught me that. And besides, I don't mind the work and I don't mind waiting."

"You said yourself it could take years."

"It could take ten years."

"Oh for god's sake," said Peter. "That's just ridiculous." He began laughing and then David did as well. "Are you in this game or not?" He began to rattle the dice in his hand, poised above the felt of the 421 board. "You, bird man. Come play, then."

"I can't. I can't move. I may never move again."

Marta carried a drink to him in his favorite glass, a crystal tumbler carved with diamonds. She put it in his hand and pressed his fingers around the glass. "There, Mr. David."

He looked up at her and smiled. "You are so good to me."

Yana brought Sam to us then, and he ran straight for Peter, who rocked back on unsteady feet as the breathless weight of my little boy pushed against his chest and both bodies fell backwards onto the ground, laughing, with their arms around each other.

"You are too young," Marta said, but it was clear she was speaking to Peter. She whispered to Sam, "He's an old man, Sammy, but he doesn't know it."

That warm, sun-roasted light fell across the wood planks at our feet.

"Oh, what the hell," said Peter at last. "You'll get your geese. I'm sure of it."

David sat in the sunlight with his eyes closed, sipping from his drink. I wandered over and sat in a chair alongside him. Eventually, he put his hand out and lay it softly across my arm.

"I think I'm gonna work tonight." Immediately, I knew he meant music.

"In LA?"

"No, just here. I've been playing around with the acoustic a little. I think I might try to get it down. Do you mind? Will you and Sam be okay?"

I lifted his hand to my face. His fingertips were cool and smelled faintly of anise. "Sure."

"You'll be making another album soon if you're not careful," said Peter.

David wrote and recorded at home by himself over the next eight weeks. The day we took the tapes down to the city, we left Sam with Yana, and went deep into West Hollywood, to the company's black and silver skyscraper on La Cienega. By then the old guys from the early '50s of rock and roll had been thrown out of those rich, hot jobs running huge Artists & Repertoire budgets. The people in control were just kids like us, sitting around in their offices ordering rum drinks from the company food service.

Nobody ever wore suits in those days, and we met with three executives who were dressed in bright silk shirts and jeans. We sat around a high-polished oak table near the top floor of the building with smoky, floor-to-ceiling windows, and looked out across the city.

The man sitting directly across from me was small and nervous, with dark fuzzy hair. He lurched forward with his arms spread out wide, like a small insect perched on a huge expanse of wood. He handed David's reels to his secretary and told her to have them copied. Then he sat back in his huge chair and poured scotch into a glass for himself. Alongside the scotch lay a square piece of glass with straight, long scratches criss-crossing it.

"What can I get you, David?"

"How good is your scotch?" asked David.

"They ship it to us direct from the Isle of Skye, so I think it's pretty damn good. Here, have some." He poured it for David, and asked, "Can you guess how happy we are to see you?" He paused nervously like an adolescent courting a girl. "After you gave us the final album two years ago, and then never returned our calls, well, the guys here have been pretty worried about you. At first we thought you were moving to another label. Then we heard a rumor that you had polio."

David shook his head and smiled suddenly. "Nope. Just some downtime. I'm back now, and these are some ideas. But I need a new band and some heavy rehearsal time before we get into the studio."

"Whatever you want. I got a hundred guys who would jump to be with you. And they're all good. Whatever you want. You want a flugel horn player, say it." He cackled loudly. "You get the best."

The secretary returned with the tapes and a new cassette, still warm from the machinery. The company guy grabbed it and slipped it into a player, "Can't wait to hear this." At first there came only a soft, tearing sound as the tape began to slide through the heads, but soon we could hear David's voice and his guitar, close and crisp through the system. No one in the room spoke. David folded his hands in front of him and looked at the table. After four songs, the guy stopped the tape.

"How much have you got?" he asked.

"Enough. About twenty-five songs, although some aren't really finished."

"You know what I think," the company man said. "I think you don't need anyone else. Forget the band and rehearsal. This is perfect. These are terrific. Personal. You don't even need to re-record them. We can use these. We can go to work and get them out right away. Don't you think, guys?"

His colleagues nodded, and one said, "We can market straight for the awards."

The first guy stood up and shoved his small, tanned hand at David. "You don't need me to tell you this is art. You win again." His loud, marketer's voice gave him away. He had spent years caressing guys like David, saying the same thing to so many cranky musicians that what was left now were compliments so crass they had became offensive.

But somewhere along the line David had learned grace. Without frustration or judgement, he turned his head slowly and smiled. "Thank you. I still got some work to do, though."

"Sure, of course. You're in control, David," he said and laughed. "We'll get the publicity up and start booking the tour. This is gonna make you rich all over again."

David was standing by the door, leaning on the wall as though he had been blown against it. I looked out of the window, but there was only yellow-grey sky cloaked with smog; no birds. When I looked back I was startled by David's eyes, huge and still.

He said, "But you should know from the start that I'm not taking it out."

"What?"

"That's the deal I'm offering. You can have the album, but I'm not taking it on the road."

"David, you're killing me," he said, his voice tight and whining.

"Look, we gotta get back to Zaca." He put his arm around my shoulders. "You think about it. Call me if you're interested."

* * *

Because it was acoustic the PR people were working overtime on the story that it was rock and roll art. They put it out to terrific reviews, and even though he had been digging mud ponds for the past two years, his album headed immediately up to the number four slot while David sat back thinking he had won. That was just before music television, and to crank the sales, you still had to do shows and interviews. After that first week with none of this, the record began to slip, and within a dozen days it had tanked. The company guys were livid and the presents stopped.

Even Matt Rappaport called. He invited us to a private club in the old part of Beverly Hills. We met on the street in front, all three of us dressed in the tacky bright fake fabrics of the '70s: Matt in a turquoise polyester Hawaiian shirt, David with his blue satin motorcycle jacket, and me in a painfully short, bright orange silk shift with brown stars plastered across it. At the beach or in West Hollywood we were in control, but in that sedate end of Beverly Hills, with quiet, slow traffic and old houses from the '20s, we were startlingly out of place.

The building was set far back from the street bordered by damp, dark-soil beds of orange California poppies and bright yellow daffodils. We entered through a heavy mahogany door, arched over with lavender wisteria blooms. We could have sat in the parlor or the library, the first a room filled with brocade-covered furniture and older men playing cards. As we passed, I saw the three of us in a slightly-tarnished mirror on the far wall, a huge antique one with swirling carved glass at the edges and flecks of black across our faces where the silver backing had disappeared. The light came hard through the parlor windows, washing us to grey in the old mirror, and suddenly the satin and the color baked to muddy black and white, like a ricochet shot to another time.

Matt decided to sit us in the library, dark and cool with big leather chairs and small-paned windows. The waiters were older men and ours, a sincere and soft-spoken gentleman, treated us with dignity even though we were hopelessly incongruous.

"This is a great place," I said.

"This is my club. I was the last open membership." He smiled proudly. Behind him, on top of a small oak table, lay the *Los Angeles Times*, fanned out in even sections, and next to it was a large silver tray holding several green-gold pears, heavy and ripe.

"You sure they won't try to throw you out once they figure out what you do for a living?" asked David.

"Who knows? But it's fun while it lasts."

A church bell began to sound in the distance, soft and full, for some old Beverly Hills congregation.

"So what's up?" David asked. "I'm sure you didn't invite us here to discuss a new cover. Did they ask you to come talk to me?"

"Of course not. Do you think I would do that?" He had a small, kind face, oval-shaped and tanned. "I'm only here to satisfy myself. I think you probably know what you're doing, but I wanted to be sure."

"I guess you saw the chart this week."

"You cold-cocked it, David. It's dead." He shrugged, holding his hands still in his lap. "I can say that. You're a good friend." Matt's essence was practical. He was neither embarrassed nor shy about what he wanted to say, and he continued to stare unwaveringly at David. He was the kind of man who had been born with both of his eyes starkly open, unafraid, planning.

"I'd like to move it back up the chart."

"If that's what you want, then you gotta take it on the road. There aren't thirty-seven other solutions."

David paused and took a drink from the glass of water in front of him, no color, no emotion, and then said tenuously, "The last time I went out I almost killed myself."

"Look, some people can do it and some people can't. I could name a hundred guys off the top of my head who were better musicians, greater songwriters, than anyone making records. The guys who stay at the top have never been the best, they just have the stomach for it. Do you need the cash?"

David looked up quickly at me and back to him. "No."

"Well, maybe you shouldn't care whether it stays on the chart, then."

"I do."

"I know you do, but maybe you shouldn't. Some people tour when they shouldn't. Some people just can't do it. Listen, in your business, you have to go on the road. That's the job. Do you still want to do this job? That's the real question."

"Of course. I've got a great lawyer now who put together a three-record deal for me before the label knew what hit 'em. I'm in this for the long haul. The company is committed and I am, too. I'm gonna make good music and sell records, I'm just gonna find a different way to do it. The awards may help, if they go my way."

"In my opinion, you're sure to win, and then of course your sales will spike for a while. But it won't save the album or your career. The decision you're making is not just about the road. You may have two more LP's in this deal, but if this one doesn't make the kind of money they budgeted, they won't put a dime into marketing the next one. They might even buy you out of the contract. Nobody gets carried anymore, David. This business has changed completely. I just want to make sure you know what you're really doing. You're getting out of the business. It's a pass out the back door. Is that what you want?"

The light in the room was bending away from David's face. He began to close down, making no extra movements, collapsing into a kind of waking sleep. I had seen him do this so many times, when survival meant turning off all the switches. Like an animal, his eyes became completely still, waiting in the silence of some damp forest floor.

"I respect you for this," said Matt. He looked at me and then said to David, "You're one of the heroes."

David said very quickly, "That's such crap."

Matt smiled. "You don't have to carry records to make music. There's other kinds of music besides rock and roll."

"Rock and roll is what I do. The company may be pissed at me, but it isn't the first time. They're still making money on me." Then suddenly he grinned, leaning forward and taking his glass. "I know I can stay off the road and keep making records. There's gotta be more than one way to do this job."

He smiled so easily, so assuredly, but I no longer believed it. You make a record; you go on the road. For as long as music has been selling revolution, our baby anarchists have always followed the rules of the business. I stood up and pulled at the hem of my dress, trying to drag it down across my bare thighs.

"I'll be back." I knew then that David had at last come full-blown into the fantasy that the company had made of him, and I moved away so he couldn't see this on my face.

I wandered through the rooms out onto a back patio and found an empty chair on the edge of a wide manicured lawn. This place had been built by farming and oil money from old Los Angeles, money that transformed outlaws into businessmen and their descendants into dilettantes for generations. Three of them, middle-aged men in all-white tennis clothes, sat at a table across from me, all three tanned and healthy with that even golden color that comes from the care of inherited affluence. Eventually, they began to glance over at me. My thin, orange silk was creased now, looking like a maid's housedress. The hem was so short that when I sat it bunched and crinkled up to expose my crotch, and I knew I was vulnerable and entirely beyond the boundaries of their society. I angled my body away from them and looked out across the putting green, to watch the distant men hunched over their golf-ball targets.

I felt a familiar hand on my shoulder, that gentle, confident pressure. David stood behind me, close to my chair and slipping his fingers softly through my hair, watching the golfers with me.

"Please don't worry about this. I'm not going to do anything stupid. I'm going to take care of you and Sam."

"I'm more worried about you than us."

He squatted in front of me then, and grinned with such ease, like a man in full control. "You're such a mother."

"You don't have to do any of this. We've been lucky in so many other ways. You can do anything you want."

"Only an American would say that," he said and took my hand from my lap, holding it between both of his. He glanced down at my short dress. "How did I let you out of the house in that get-up?" he asked, with amusement.

A honeysuckle fence alongside us was trembling with bees, the air bloated with the vibration.

"When I was a kid we had honeysuckle in our backyard. I don't know how they kept it growing in the desert."

David walked to the fence and put his hand into the blossoms, sliding it smoothly like a warm knife into butter, and pulled out a few bells of petal and nectar. He came back to me and held them out. "Come on, baby. Ready to go?"

He held my hand as we stood on the cool path at the front saying goodbye to Matt Rappaport. The border had been planted recently with bright yellow daffodils in diagonal rows, and a light breeze had come up, lifting tiny feathers of milkweed through the air across this geometric pattern.

Matt said, "Good luck with it, David. But remember to call me if it doesn't work out. I've got some ideas for you."

"Thanks." David stepped forward to extend his hand as his friend walked away. Suddenly he stopped, staring behind him, as James Gallas came through the club door down the path toward us. When he approached, David took my hand and squeezed my fingers possessively as he watched James come forward smiling. When they stood opposite each other, David reached out to shake James's hand and he, too, smiled.

"How have you been?"

"Great," James said. "The campaign's going just great."

"No hard feelings?" asked David.

"Of course not. Business is business."

"Yeah," David said, his voice rising strong. "Come on, baby. We better hit the road."

"Good to see you, Rosie." James moved abruptly past David, bending over near me and reaching for the daffodils. His straight, golden blonde hair fell forward over his face, and when he stood up he held out three yellow flowers. "To say congratulations on your marriage and your baby." He smiled sheepishly.

"That was so long ago, James. But thank you." I knew that this had surprised David and annoyed him, and now he walked toward us, determined. Quickly, I said, "But you shouldn't pick these flowers. They'll throw you out of the club." I didn't smile when I said it, although I had meant it as a joke.

He grinned broadly. "Not likely. My great-grandfather had them planted in the '20s when he founded this place."

David stood behind me and put his hands on my shoulders. "Let's go."

"Come on, Rosie. Smile for me," James said. "You must be really happy now."

"That's enough," David said, stepping between us. "You're way over the boundary, James."

Before either of them could speak again, I took David's hand and moved away with him, out to the sidewalk where the valet was waiting with the keys to our car. "There's enough to worry about without you imagining things. I am not interested in James. I love you," I said, trembling with anger. "Whenever you get what you want, you just want more."

"I could say the same thing about you." We climbed in the car, and he drove up to Sunset to start the winding drive to the beach. After a few minutes we came over the summit of the high cliffs and started the sweep down past lush glades to the wide, glassy afternoon calm of the surfer's bay. David reached over and touched my wrist. "I'm sorry. That wasn't your fault. It's between me and James. I just hate it when guys come on to you."

"He was only being nice."

"And you're being really naïve. But I'm still sorry, baby."

CHAPTER 12

David held off another week as we watched the album freefall down the charts. When it dropped below the one hundred spot, he called the label and told them he would take the record on the road, but only for interviews and small club appearances.

The night before he left in January we were going to have dinner at Zaca with Peter and Marta, who had just come home from a research trip to Brooklyn. David set out little votive candle lights all around the darkened dining room, and then came to sit next to me, his arm around my shoulders and his lips on my neck.

"I'll be away for your birthday, Rosie. I'm sorry." Then he smiled and asked, "How old are you this year? Nineteen again?"

"Always. I'll be nineteen forever."

"Weren't you nineteen when we met?"

I shimmied closer to him, calf, hip, touching him. He hadn't shaved all day and I put my face against the brown stubble on his jawline.

"What do you want for this birthday?"

"I don't know. A trunkful of chocolate."

"You're not pregnant again, are you?" he asked, grinning.

"No, baby. I'm not pregnant again."

He took a tiger lily from a vase on the table, tore the long stem off and tucked the bright orange flower behind my ear.

"If you could only see what I see." He leaned forward and kissed me.

When Peter and Marta arrived they brought gifts for me and for Sam.

Marta said, "I just realized, we have nothing for you, David. I'm so sorry."

"We're so rude," said Peter, grinning. "Why are we so rude, my darling? Anyway, you'll get some presents in New York. The *Times* is saying you will win an award or two this year."

The phone began to ring then, and Peter moved to answer it. "Don't," said David, holding his hand up. "Leave it." Peter let the receiver fall back onto the cradle, and David sat back against me, smiling.

"That's unlike you, Mr. Big Businessman," said Peter. "Have you started working on the next album yet?"

David sighed out loud. "Oh, God. I have two shit songs I just wrote. I promised them a new album right away. Somehow, I gotta come up with a dozen more songs now while I'm on the road."

"Why don't you just tell them you'll be a little late?"

"Can't anymore. I've done that already. The only thing I can do now is hunker down and write some more total shit and get into the studio."

Marta said, "This is art, David. You should never let it go unless you're proud of it."

"Maybe what you do is art, but this is barely music. I promised I'd deliver. If I don't come up with something now, we'll be in court. They got musicians booked, a great producer, an engineering team, studio time, not to mention the pressing plant is reserved, the paper for the jackets has been ordered, the art guys are waiting for the music and the title so they can start designing the cover, there's a photographer waiting to do the jacket shot and someone else ready to take the promo shots. And they're all waiting on me to come up with these songs. Man, I've gotta get into the studio as soon as I get back or they're gonna sue my ass."

"Why did you ever sign a contract that rushed you like that?" asked Marta. She reached over and put her hand on his brow. "Look at you, all worried and wrinkled."

He shook his head. "What a nightmare! Hey, this is the most boring thing we could talk about. Tell us what you're doing. Have some champagne."

Marta sat at the table and took our hands, smiling. "It's so good to be together."

Peter was wearing new glasses, and they cocked to one side. "We were very successful in New York. They gave us so much money for this film that we are rolling in it."

Marta said, "The research is going so well. You remember, it's the New York union idea." She leaned over and brushed a stray thread from Peter's jacket. "So tell me how our little boy is. And what pictures you're working on, Rosie. Still those historical things? We got the one you sent us. It was beautiful."

"She calls it archeological art," David said. "Making photographic paintings from ancient paintings. Now that really is art. I feel like I'm living with Cartier-Bresson."

I laughed. "I take Sam and wander out to the caves, shoot a little, and go back and play around with printing them. I love it. A couple of galleries have come to have a look. I think I may get a show together soon."

"And Sam?" asked Peter, putting his hand on David's shoulder.

"Sam is great," said David. "He's growing a lot. And he eats like a little horse."

Peter took a gulp of champagne and for a few moments no one spoke. I was thinking to myself, Here it is, the four of us now; this combination, each time we are together being born again instantly, wherever we are in the world, this feeling is always a stone's throw from us. These minutes were precious, and each of us knew it. We watched our faces in the flickering light, and Peter's faint, even wheezing was the only noise in the room.

Finally, Marta said, "Peter is afraid to tell you. But we really can't put it off any longer. This film is going to take a couple of years, you know. A long time. All of it is in New York. Research, writing, filming, everything. So we've taken an apartment there.

We need to be away from Zaca Creek for so long that we have decided to move to New York permanently."

"You have been so good to us," said Peter. "This was not easy to decide. And of course, being so far from Sam will be difficult."

"When?" asked David.

"Now. We're here to pack, but I think it's fair to say that we have already moved in spirit. Marta and I feel like New York people."

"I'm so sorry," said Marta.

"You know," Peter said, "I have never really thanked you."

"For what?" I asked.

"All of this. I was never even close to normal before I met you. You remember how it was in the old days, in San Francisco and Santa Monica. The depressed Peter. The bad Peter. I am different now and I want to thank you."

On the sill David had set a pulsing candle, like a jar of fireflies against the night. He got up and walked to it, blowing it to a blackened wick, and then moved around the room putting all the others out until we sat in darkness.

"Let's have dinner." He flicked the light switch, bursting the room open with electric light. "Anyway, you never know. Maybe now we'll fill the house with brothers and sisters for Sam." All of us smiled at his thought, but mostly I remember David in that candle junkyard, with the smell of wax surrounding us. He stood behind me, putting his arms around my shoulders gently, clasping his hands together like in a peasant's burning prayer.

* * *

While David was on the road I worked at the art department of the university, teaching a couple of workshops in beginning photography and an advanced one in reduced-lighting portraits. I worked three days a week with students who listened raptly to my stories about filters, and who wanted to learn what I knew about taking pictures fast in the dark. I was given a little office with an old wooden desk and an out-of-balance oak chair where teenaged kids would come and ask about how to do the chemistry in confined spaces.

I began to print my own pictures at school instead of at home. Even though at Zaca I had the best enlarger you could buy, and at the college I often had to wait to get on the equipment, somehow the smell of the fix and stop were better there. I would pass around the corner of the student dark room into the blackness. Like an oasis, that first sweet, sharp breath of the chemicals signaled that I was home safe. I would work for four or five hours without speaking, slipping filters and wheeling lenses like little moons of glass over my images that lay at first invisible on stark fiber paper. Printing up was my favorite, because that was the gratification. Working at the college, I began to find again what I had loved about this process, the excitement of watching a picture come slowly through the bath, watching while the images darken, never quite knowing when they would stop and whether or not I could finally coax the best out of the silver.

When I wasn't teaching or working I would sit with Sam in the late winter dusk, talking with him about spaceships and airplanes. Sometimes I would go to the college library and learn something new about the planets, just so I could surprise him with a wonderful fact.

David won a big award in New York in January, and his sales shot up. This caused the company to extend the tour on the east coast, and David secretly renamed it the Doomed Tour. At first he called every afternoon when he woke up from hotel room beds, and sometimes he would give me advice about school or Sam or the Creek, pretending to problem-solve from three thousand miles away. We had bought Sam a puppy that year, and every day David would ask me if I had remembered to feed it, as though he were somehow responsible for every detail of our lives. I don't know if he actually thought he was being helpful, but I always let him talk on till the very last, broken thought. Mostly, he would be high voltage, talking about the arguments of this new band, or the stupid hat that the drummer insisted on wearing which David somehow believed was the root of their problems. Sometimes he would stutter apologies to me about being away for so long, and I would listen and tell him not to worry. By the beginning of March he had stopped complaining and apologizing. He was as though washed down to bare, unpolished stone, and I knew he was depending on this heatless core to last him through until the spring and the big summer tour season.

I began making a list of all the moments at Zaca he had missed, like a lawyer building a case: my first real show in a no-name gallery in Santa Barbara, Mother's Day, Sam's first day at nursery school, a minor break-in when we lost some jewelry and equipment. I did it to chronicle my growing anger, but as Sam and I slowly became a different family, I finally just left the list in a drawer somewhere.

The first time I heard that strange tone of drug-induced lethargy in his voice again, I offered to fly out for the weekend with Sam.

"Why would you want to come now? It's still cold here."

"It was just a thought. I'd like to see you."

"Me too. Of course I would. I can hear birds singing behind you. Where are you sitting?"

"By the front window."

"It's cold here," he said again, and suddenly all energy ebbed from his voice and he had nothing left to say.

"Have you lost any weight this time?" I asked.

"Hey, out here even the birds are skinny. Wait until we get to Florida. Come then."

Sometimes we just lay in our beds with the receivers next to our ears, listening to the sounds of the other as we jacked off to the scars that were left between us. In the Southeast they ran into a violent early spring storm, and I didn't get a call for a couple of days. When he checked in again they were in Miami, and it was as though he had trailed off in a boat into the blinding sun, the hollowness in his voice stopping me like a high wall. I remember sitting with the phone at my ear, holding it in silence for minutes, because neither of us wanted to speak. I could taste his cigarette smoke on my tongue, as though he had pressed his thumb into it like a print.

"What's the matter?" I asked him.

"Nothing. I'm tired."

"It sounds like more than that. If you don't want to talk, let's hang up."

"Rosie, don't make a scene. I'm just tired. Trapped and tired."

"Can't you just come home to us? We need you here."

He didn't answer right away. I could hear him wheezing, his own choppy breath giving away a new illness. When at last he spoke to me, he fell into his words so heavily I knew he was drunk and dazed.

"No baby. I can't just come home. And you saying that just makes it all worse."

By the time he had opened the summer concert season in Texas our calls were only minutes long, and at some point I found a new photograph of him in a magazine taken by the photographer we had met on the old Asian tour. In the picture he wore a red shirt I did not recognize, and white jeans. He was tan, and stood barefoot on sugar-white sand with his back to a turquoise Florida lagoon. His head was cocked to one side, and he was not smiling. It was an overly-serious, posed shot that printed up not as the intended rock-boy's angst but as a picture of a debauched musician, his eyelids drooping from alcohol and the green irises clouded, a face gaunt and exhausted.

One afternoon in June while the sun was streaming into our kitchen, I put my hand under my t-shirt and pulled my breast from my bra, stroking my skin. It is soft skin, I thought; why doesn't it bring him home? It was July before finally I believed what was happening. I heard the rumors about heroin and women, and I asked David about his drugs, but never once mentioned the limp, over-handled photograph I had hidden in my studio, of him on that hot Florida beach, posing with a hungry, helpless look for that woman's camera.

Once as a small child I was given a psalm to memorize about green fields and still water, and however frightened I was, I could always recite it. That summer, just before the tour ended, I stood on the porch in a heavy coastal shower, watching a sloping field of mud, and I said that psalm out loud, my voice rising clearly like a wave. I could sing that damn song like I had written it myself, the irony of faith chewing quietly through the humid air.

After the last date in the East, David went back to New York and called me.

"I'm gonna stay here for a few weeks, Rosie."

I was sitting in the living room, and the smell of gardenia outside the open windows began to drift in.

"Stay there? What do you mean stay there?"

"I'm not coming home right away." He waited, and I did not even hear him breathe.

"Why not?"

I heard him move and sigh as though a muscle had twisted and cramped. Suddenly he said, "Baby, I better go. I'm at Peter and Marta's place and I'm using their phone again. Their bill is going to be astronomical."

I put my hand across my mouth and closed my eyes, waiting quietly until at last I understood that he was waiting for me.

"Well, I'll come to New York then."

"What about Sam?" As he spoke he began to cough, a deep wet sputter that rose in the back of his throat, the thick phlegm bubbling up from his chest. When his coughing subsided he sighed heavily, and I heard the click of his lighter and a swift suck of air as he inhaled again.

"Yana will stay with Sam."

"Yana?" he asked, as though he had forgotten the name.

"I'll come tomorrow."

"Rosie?" He said my name in a painful, hoarse effort that seemed to scrape across his throat.

"I'll see you tomorrow. David, I love you."

"Me, too," he said softly. When we hung up, I sat for a very long time trying to conjure up his face in my memory.

I think it was about two in the morning when finally I went to bed. I took my clothes off in front of the mirror in the downstairs room, that same room where I had awakened, lost, so many years ago. I went to our bedroom and pulled one of David's t-shirts out of a drawer. I put it over my head and let the worn cloth fall over my breasts. It was so old and so used, it would never come completely clean again, and I smelled him there, a faint clash of soap and cedar and evening sweat, still around me. I went to Sam's room and slipped into bed beside him. He awakened and called me, and I said, "It's okay, my love, don't worry, Mommy's here. Go back to sleep." He put his arms around my neck and his head on my chest and fell immediately back to dreaming. For the longest time I watched him, his soft, straight dark hair and the shape of his head, so like his father that I could lie there holding him and almost bring David home.

We woke with the daylight, and Sam moved close and kissed my cheek. He looked at me and started laughing and pointing at my face. He said, "Oh Mommy!" pretending to be the wiser of the two of us. I looked in the mirror on his dresser and saw that my eyes were circled with wide bands of mascara smudges, like clown makeup. I lifted him into my lap and told him a long story about the facts of women and cosmetics. He listened to it without squirming and minutes later when I had finished he nodded and said, "I'm hungry."

* * *

I arrived in Manhattan two days later, and took a taxi from the airport to Peter and Marta's apartment. From there we went to a tavern near Gramercy Park to meet David for dinner. He came alone and stood across from the old wooden booth where we sat. He waited without speaking, staring at me only, his eyes sunken back into darkened sockets. He smiled, and suddenly he lurched forward to slide in next to me, stumbling over the table legs and falling across my arms and chest.

"Oh, baby," he said, leaning close to look at me and then to kiss me, and the outline of his lips had melted into a greasy purple smear across his face. His eyes were watery, the lids were ringed with red shadows where he had rubbed the skin raw. His clothes smelled of soured milk and tobacco, and as he came near me he began to giggle. "Are you hungry, baby?" But before I could answer he said angrily, "You must be. Fucking airplane food. I've had enough of it to know."

He wore an old pair of black jeans, loose now on him, and an unpressed denim jacket even though this was a sweltering New York August night. He kissed Marta, and smiled at Peter with such childlike tenderness I thought he was about to cry.

"I'll be right back." He went to the bar and the toilet and returned, jittering back and forth like a current was leaping through him.

"David, sit down," Marta said.

"What? Sure. I'm sorry." He slipped into the booth next to me, and stared at the old wood plank table, carved over with rough hearts and initials like some Texas diner table. My hand was on the surface, and he covered it with his fingers and squeezed. Then he smiled at me. "I'm so happy you came, Rosie. We'll have a great time. I love New York, hey Peter? Don't you love New York?" David nodded quickly at his own statement, and added, "Some friends are coming by to eat with us. Okay?"

The waiter brought mugs of beer, and the sharp smell of the hops sloshed across the table.

"Catso vatay uh, anyone?" David asked, and suddenly we grinned at each other. Marta reached out carefully and put her hand across the fist David had made, opening his fingers and stroking his palm like you might a nervous child.

He smiled at her and she asked, "What friends, David?"

He struck a match, held it a moment, and cupped it to his face to light a cigarette. He took his jacket off and slung it over the plastic booth behind him, blinking as he did at the smoke that stung his eyes.

"Just some people I met a couple of weeks ago. That German filmmaker called Werther. He's here in town scouting locations for a movie he's making about Manhattan. And Ella Farrell. You remember her, Rosie? The photog who shot our first Asian tour."

"We'll need a bigger table," Peter said.

"That's okay, isn't it? You don't mind if they join us? Baby, you really need to eat something."

"David, you look so tired. Why don't we just go home?"

He didn't answer me right away, but stroked a small cut on the top of his arm, the reddened scabbed lips on either side of the wound opening again with a thin seep of blood.

"I'm okay now. The tour was pretty rough, but you know, I look at it as a wake-up call. I'm done. I'm outta the music business." He was scratching his fingernails across the table carvings. "Did I tell you that Werther wants me to be in a film he's casting? He thinks I can make it as an actor. I'll be in Munich for six months or so." He glanced up at me smiling.

I started to speak, but Peter put his hand on my wrist. "We really do need a bigger boat," Peter said.

"A what? A boat?" David laughed. "And you think I'm drunk!"

We sat together for a few moments, and eventually his new friends arrived. He introduced them, and the film director, Werther, put his hand on my shoulder.

"So your beautiful wife has come! How wonderful! I have always admired her work." He wore a long black shirt and a red silk scarf. He was completely bald, with huge frog eyes.

Peter spoke to him in German and the director shrugged and motioned to the waiter. When he got no response, Peter sighed and said, "I love New Yorkers. Even famous German directors are ignored. The only way we will get a bigger table is if David goes."

David nodded and stood, and as he did the photographer, Ella, moved into the booth next to me. Werther and David went to find the waiter, and she leaned across the table as though she were about to disclose a secret.

"Isn't it amazing that he wants to put David in his next work? Just amazing! Werther's films are so well received. You must be very proud." She spoke as though she knew us intimately, waving her hands, her long nails painted soft pink. She had full breasts and slender arms, and wore a dark green cotton dress that clung to her body. Peter watched her without comment, holding onto Marta's arm.

Ella looked at the two of them. "So what do you do?"

"We make documentaries. We're working on one now about the birth of the labor union movement in New York."

"Hmm. That's good. Can we eat? I'm starving."

The waiter had put new mugs of beer in front of us, and Ella reached for the menu. As she did, Marta leaned forward suddenly and grabbed her own beer. Somehow, this grab became a push and the entire pint went sprawling across the table over Ella's chest and into her lap.

"Oh my God!" Ella shouted. She stood up, covered in beer. "Why did you do that?"

"I'm sorry. It was an accident."

"I'll get a towel," Peter said.

"I smell like piss now. This dress is completely ruined." She looked at Marta. "I can't believe you did that. How clumsy can you be?"

Werther returned alone and stood beside Ella. "They are clearing a table for us. The best one in the restaurant."

"Well, we can't stay now," Ella said. "Look at me. Where's David?"

"He's in the bathroom," Werther replied, and suddenly looked at her in surprise. "Oh my, what happened to you? Here, I'll take you to my hotel to clean up."

He unwound the red silk scarf from his neck and put this meekly over her shoulders. He nodded quickly to us, and moved her towards the tavern door and out into the street.

When they had left, Marta looked up at Peter, expectant. "It was an accident."

He grinned at her. "Oh certainly. Anyone can see that."

"Where is David?" I asked.

"He will be a while," he said. "Sometimes when he gets like this he falls asleep and I have to go get him. Or someone does."

"He's disintegrating, isn't he?" I asked softly.

"It comes and goes," Marta said. "Sometimes he naps with a fistful of needles, and sometimes he's blazing with energy. Mostly though, talking to him is like walking on glass. On nights like this he may need a lot of help. If it weren't for you he might not come back at all."

When David appeared at our table he was luminous and smiling. He had washed his face, and had swept his damp, dark hair back from his forehead.

"Maybe you're right, baby. Maybe we should go. We can eat at the apartment, can't we?"

"Of course," Marta said. "Peter can make us all the new Manhattan omelette he invented this morning. I think it had green tea and rice in it."

"My darling, that was only an experiment." Peter led us into the hot, black streets, and began flailing his arms for a taxi to carry us home.

* * *

The room David slept in was Peter's office, although when he first showed up at their door, dazed and homeless, Peter had immediately removed the clutter from it. The walls were pale yellow, the color of rich cream, and the floor was made of bare, old hammered wood. David brought a couple of his guitars with him, and kept them out of their cases, propped on stands, although Marta told me that she never once heard him play. He had with him an old electric Strat and the acoustic he had used for his comeback album. He always traveled with a keyboard, and this lay on the floor beside the closet.

The bed was a big brass four-poster that Marta had bought years back in Santa Barbara, and as soon as I saw it, I dropped my coat and purse on the floor and crumpled onto the mattress.

"Rosie? Baby, what's up?" He lay beside me, kissing my throat so softly. He lifted my sweater and lay his palm on my stomach.

I had begun to cry, and he moved close and said, "Please don't. I'm sorry, baby. Thank you for coming."

Suddenly, he was calm, but he smelled, as though some part of his flesh was rotting with infection. As he lay with me breathing evenly, he began to sweat, and so he took off his jacket and walked to the window. He lifted it and lit a cigarette, carefully blowing the smoke into the night.

"So are you serious about the movie? Going to Munich?"

He threw the cigarette out the window and walked over to the bed.

"Yeah, I am. Max Werther is the real deal, the tops." He did not mention his own condition, only the aura of this new friend. I thought about all the things I could say in response to his pop boy's reasoning, about the harm and escape and turmoil that now surrounded him, but I kept thinking of myself, and of how for the first time I was afraid just by being near him. "It's a huge break," he added.

I nodded. "I haven't seen you in so long. I don't want you to go away again. I want you to come home to Zaca for a while."

He lifted his hand carefully, his nails torn and darkened, and passed his fingers through my hair. I could feel such tension it was as though he held a scrap of pure rage in his palm.

"You have no fucking idea, do you?" he asked, his tone loud.

"About what?"

"About what I've been through on this tour. You never did understand. I'm done with this business, Rosie. I couldn't do anything I wanted to do. I'm just a fucking failure."

"Don't make me the enemy, David. I just don't want you to leave again so soon. What about Sam?"

Everything about him seemed to move. He nodded his head quickly a dozen times, snapping his dirty fingers over and over while the sweat poured down his face and neck.

"What about Sam?" he shouted. "What about me? I can't even close my eyes anymore. Now that you're here, I can see my grave."

"Don't say that, David. You just need to be at home with your family."

"I'm not coming home," he said. "Ever." He stumbled forward and began to fall, but put his hand out to the guitar stand and steadied himself. He began to tremble, and suddenly his voice was deep, sliding away. "Rosie, don't you think I know what's happening to me?" His deep green eyes squinted as he strained to focus on his words. "I can't come home." He jerked his head up sharply and looked straight at me. "For Chrissakes, get your hooks out of me!"

Suddenly his fingers squeezed hard around the neck of the acoustic in the stand, and he wrenched it up and threw it on the floor. He jacked his foot high over the guitar and slammed it down, splintering the wood, smashing it again and again until he had shattered it, and the busted pieces and splinters lay strewn around him.

"You're crazy!" My voice was like a growl, so furious that my lips curled up over my teeth as I shouted at him. "Why are you doing this? You're just like the rest of them now, aren't you? Just another spoiled junkie."

"Fuck it," he said, "I don't care." He grabbed a small velvet bag from beside the bed and ripped it open. He squatted on the floor to cook, finally wrapping the rubber strip around his arm and pumping his fist as he watched for a clean, unsprung vein. He held the rubber between his teeth, and slapped his forearm at the same time. When at last he raised something, a dark worm across broken, mottled skin, he worked deftly and grabbed the silver-sheathed syringe, sliding the point into his flesh. He fell back then against the wall, spreading his long legs out before him on the dusty floor. He snapped the rubber knot free from his bruised arm and looked up at me, the needle drawing the anger out of him with drops of pure dew. "That's it," he mumbled and shut his eyes.

He lay like that for a long while, and I knelt beside him and watched. I slipped my arms around his waist, and he shifted to pull me close to him. I let myself sink into his arms again for that last moment, and eventually I pulled my body free. I found Marta and Peter in the kitchen, with undrunk cups of tea on the table in front of them.

"Tell us what you want to do," Marta said.

I shook my head and sat beside her. I tried to speak, but lay my head on the table and began to sob for a long time until every single muscle was exhausted.

"I want him to be well again."

"No," said Marta, "what do you want to do?"

I nodded, understanding the difference. "I think I should go home." And early the next morning without seeing David again, I returned to Sam and Zaca Creek on my own.

Chapter 13

David lived with Peter and Marta for weeks, and they would call me with news of him that was mostly filled with heroin and mornings that never started until the late afternoon. Somehow he managed to find a phone every week to call Sam and tell him good night. I tried not to answer between seven and eight, but once in a while I would forget and hear his voice on the other end. We never had a conversation, though; just hearing his voice would cause anger and longing to shoot through me like unguided missiles.

During that first month David dragged Peter to small clubs to hear the new music that was breaking through Manhattan then. Peter would tell me about going out at one or two in the morning to old warehouses to see guys who hadn't yet hit twenty screaming their own songs into cheap sound equipment. The places they played had no acoustics, but they were playing the ragged music of kids and the sound quality didn't matter. David was still under thirty, but already too old and too drugged to kick out that kind of bone-deep anger, and all he could do was sit back, covet their music, and beat off to the passion that had once belonged to him.

After a couple of months he moved into his own place down in SoHo. He still called Sam like clockwork once a week, but Peter and Marta rarely saw him. Occasionally I would catch a photo or a note on him in the trades, sometimes with a woman, and once Peter called me saying that he had seen David at a movie and that he looked 'trampled.' But that was it: suddenly he was no longer part of me and I heard the news accidentally, like everyone else.

My agent had booked another show for me at a big mid-Wilshire gallery in LA, and I was frantically working to finish printing the sepias I had made of the cave paintings. I had been invited by the college in Santa Barbara to take a full-time teaching job, and I had begun lesson planning and portfolio samples for the new classes. Sam and I spent the weekdays at Zaca learning to live by ourselves. He was so interested in the sky that I took night photographs of the constellations and attached them to his bedroom ceiling with their names labeled.

One by one I took down the photographs of David scattered around the house and slid them into a drawer, frames and all, in the empty bedroom on the top floor. There was one I couldn't bring myself to remove, though, an imperfect, muddy black and white I had taken of him before Sam was born. The trick with photography is combining perfect technique with anticipation, knowing the machine so well that the strokes of light and speed and focal point are exact, while at the same time knowing the object so well that you press the shutter before the moment. It is rare to get both; even with inanimate subjects, the look will change from second to second so that anticipation is just as important. I saved this picture not because it was perfect, but because it was the best example I ever took of the moment.

David sits on the edge of a stool against an ivy-covered wall, hunched over an old Paolo Soprani accordion. He's wearing a t-shirt and a thick leather wristband, and the veins of his forearm are splayed out. He's got a cigarette suspended from his lips and is looking sideways for a cue through eyes that are only slits. I remember he was holding for a count from the drummer, and under his breath he was counting himself, snapping a quick nod with each beat and keeping himself back until the others had caught up with him. The muscles of his face are clenched tight, but at the instant of the picture he is still, in the coil before the snap, focused on that single second when his music will begin and he will have another chance to bring out what he hears in his mind. There is no failure in that picture; that was the best of him. David never remembered me taking it, never even saw me watching him with the camera that day. I was squatting at the back of the yard, obscured by the noise and the people around him.

That fall Sam and I would play hide and seek, and I would always hide in the same place to make sure he could find me and wouldn't be afraid. I would go to the old coal shed, because the door looked pretty solid and safe to me. I used to hide in there teetering on the vestiges of uneven, crusty coal-rocks, waiting for Sam to scramble out to find me. That was where I always felt David watching me, thinking he was just outside and that what really separated us was this door and he was about to open it, to arrive from the East, to come home. By the early fall I understood that life is not changed by fantasy, only by practice, and what remained after all else was my son and my work.

Often in pictures I will see things I have stolen, angles or shadows I have seen in photographs by real artists that I have mimicked, hoping as I did that no one would notice. Once long ago in the Pinto desert I took a picture of my mother in a long jersey dress standing by a Ford Mustang, a black and white shot heavy with surface texture. I was covered with guilt when years later I realized that it was really an imitation of an Avedon I had seen in *Life* magazine. I don't know why I believed that taking a picture of my own mother could ever be bad, or why I thought that learning was somehow stealing. My mother would often stare at me for long moments and then suddenly tell me to be good to myself. It wasn't until that autumn that I began to understand any of this, the yin and yang of my childhood guilt.

Once she said to me: "When you're confused, stay away from churches and call a lawyer." James was the only lawyer I knew who didn't belong to David, and so one afternoon in November just before Sam's birthday, I left him with Yana and drove by myself south to Los Angeles. I sat in traffic on Pacific

Coast Highway for hours surrounded by smog and the hideous stark light bouncing off of metal, and by the time I got to the city it was long after five, and James's office was mostly deserted. I wandered past an empty reception desk, through odorless air conditioned rooms and halls until I reached his opened door. I stood by his desk in the empty room, watching the hot grey city through his huge plate-glass windows. James came at last, holding a heavy reference book, and stopped in the doorway staring at me.

"I was in the library," he said, closing the book and putting it under his arm. He wore gold-rimmed glasses that had fallen down the bridge of his nose. "Have you been waiting long?"

"I'm sorry I'm so late. I guess I held you up for hours."

He smiled and put the book on a chair. He walked over to me and put his hands on my shoulders. "Don't worry," he said. Still smiling with something like relief, he kissed my cheek and said. "You must know how happy I am to see you." His light blonde hair was shaved short up the sides, but he still wore the front long, glossy and falling across his eyes like a surfer-boy.

"I haven't seen you in years, James. I'm ashamed to be calling you now, but I need some help quick. Are you angry at me?"

He folded his arms across his chest. "Not anymore, Rosie. I never could stay mad at you."

"I heard you got engaged."

He shrugged and moved behind his desk. "That was last year."

"What happened?"

"She spent the summer in Italy and married a count." He grinned and his eyes were like cracked blue crystal. "And I'm only the count of the West Side."

"I'm sorry, James."

He shook his head. "I'm over it. I'm thirty this year, after all. I'm an adult now, and love just isn't the same."

"I always thought of you as the only grown-up we knew."

"I probably was, relatively speaking." His voice was deep and clear, and he leaned back in his chair. He wore a light blue, crisp cotton shirt, with small, pearled cufflinks. He said, "I'm sorry this has happened to you."

"You always said it would."

He stood up and came around the front of the desk. "Sit down." He leaned back, his tapered shirt baring lean swimmer's muscles under the cotton. "You realize I'm not a divorce lawyer."

"I know. I don't want a divorce, James. I just want Sam to be safe."

In that office there was no sound, no odor, no climate, not even an early summer moth. James was the only touch of a living thing, and he was filled with generosity and reason.

"I feel like I'm walking through quicksand. I'm not really sure of anything."

"David has a very heartless corner of him."

"I'm having a hard time imagining how it's going to be now. When I look at Sam, it breaks my heart that it's all changed for him." I looked down at my hands and noticed a smudge of oil across my palm. I guess it had come when I filled the car with gas in Ventura.

"Well, the important thing is to be protected financially. And lay the groundwork for custody of your son. Once we wire that down, you can figure out the future." He took a clean handkerchief from a drawer and handed it to me, watching as I wiped the oil from my skin. "I know that he will be back. It won't take him long to figure out how lucky he is. You need to be ready for it. You're out of his league. You're out of my league."

I smiled when he said that, but my arms and legs began to tremble. James came close and put his arm around me to stop my shaking.

"Have you eaten today?" he asked.

"I guess not."

"Let me feed you before you go back."

CHAPTER 14

Sam's birthday fell on the Saturday before Thanksgiving: he was five years old and had not seen his father for nearly a year. Often he would ask me when David was coming home, and I would only say that he was working in New York and had to stay there for a while. That morning when he asked, we were sitting on a bench in the garden, and behind Sam was a new silver sage bush I had planted, its smell cloaked by the early coastal mist. I pulled him close by my side, but he squirmed away and sat facing me.

"Why doesn't my dad live here?" he asked. The sage leaves were moving slightly in the breeze around him, panting like tongues behind his head.

"Because he's very busy. For a while he has to live in New York." I held his hand, scrawny and strong like the rest of him, but he pulled it away.

"But when is he coming?" The easy words were never good enough, and I never knew how to answer him without telling him the truth.

"He'll come as soon as he can." Somehow twisting the words in that way absolved me of my own role in keeping David from his son. I could not bring myself to release Sam to a man whose world had become so choked with drugs and harm.

"He's really strong. He's the strongest dad. Remember when I was little he took me in his tractor?"

"I do," I smiled.

"Okay," he said, and put his hand back to touch mine. "And you're the best mom." I hadn't meant to teach him to worry about me, but I knew from the way his fingers pressed around my palm that he did.

Later that morning, Peter and Marta arrived from Los Angeles, where they had been meeting with an independent bulk film supplier. Peter stood on the porch in a brand new, powder blue fisherman's sweater, his arms folded over his chest. Marta wore an identical sweater, but in purple. She reached out, tugging at his arm, and he quickly took hold of her hand. They seemed much older, and both wore clothes that didn't quite fit. They looked up at the portico that had been their bedroom window and neither their dowdy clothes nor how old they looked mattered.

"You can't buy bulk from anybody but the major brands," Peter said. "The quality is just not consistent. But we need the delivery by next week."

"You said it was the best deal," said Marta, smiling. "That's why we came. Actually, he just wanted an excuse to come see you." She leaned over and kissed my cheek.

"It's cold here," Peter said. "I don't remember it being cold." He walked into the house and drifted quietly from room to room, while Marta began disgorging a large shopping bag filled with gifts they had been collecting: finger puppets and a Lego astronaut and wind-up racing cars. "It's so hard not to buy things. There are so many things I think Sam would like. Where is he?"

"He went with James to Santa Barbara to choose a present and to pick up some friends for the party."

"You are seeing James, then?"

I nodded. "Sometimes."

"He always was good to Peter." She folded her hands over the porch railing. "It's so beautiful here, even in the mist."

"James doesn't think it's safe," I said.

"Why not?"

"He thinks I'm vulnerable here."

We found Peter in the kitchen, standing in the bleached light of the refrigerator, holding a drink he had already poured.

"Oh, Rosie," he said, "peppermint iced tea! I'm so impressed." He walked out onto the terrace and sat with his feet propped upon the stone ledge. "What pictures are you taking these days?"

"I had a pretty successful show in LA a few months ago. I sent you an invitation. People have started calling with commissions now. No more ancient history of rock and roll. The university hired me to work with them on an archeological thing. They found an eighteenth-century boat-wreck up the coast and I've been driving up every day to do a series on old wood as they bring it ashore."

He grinned at me. "You have to admit that it's kind of a specialist subject." I put my arm across his shoulders and kissed the top of his head.

"Maybe, but I've got a huge commission from a new history museum in San Francisco. They asked me to do a photographic fresco for their offices."

Marta sat next to us, her silvering hair held back loosely with snap-clips above her ears and frizzing into tiny curls at her scalp.

"We saw David last week," she said. "Really, he's the one who asked us to come. He wanted to be here for Sam's party, but he was afraid to ask you."

"David's never been afraid of anything."

"He's afraid of you now."

I thought suddenly about the bruises he had carried in the hollows of his arms, those failed vein blotches like shadows of tiny clouds on the land.

"How is he? Every time I hear anything about him, it sounds worse and worse. Somebody from a magazine called here last week wanting me to okay a story about a party David had in Greenwich Village where the police showed up because someone was shot."

"Why did they call you?" asked Marta.

"I don't know. Now that I'm a teacher I guess my number is easy to find."

"Well," said Peter, "the only thing that's not true about these stories is that David lives in SoHo, not Greenwich Village."

"That's not very comforting."

"He is desperate to see Sam," said Marta.

"You think I'm causing all this because I won't allow David to see his son? You think it's my fault?"

"Of course not," said Peter. "But I think it would help him to see Sam."

"He can see Sam anytime he can be clean." I sat on the ledge with the cold, open sea behind me, and I could feel my face suddenly get hot and red against the November mist. "Would you let your son go off with some guy teetering on the nickel?"

"He's not just 'some guy.' Maybe you could simply meet him somewhere."

"I don't want to meet him. I don't want to see his drugs or his women or the way he is now." Some of the decorations for Sam's party were straggling in the damp air; the crepe paper curls of orange and red hung limply from the kitchen door. I walked over to the wall and pressed them back up high by the light fixtures. "I'm not as angry as I sound," I said simply, although none of us believed it. "I'm sorry."

Peter came behind me, smelling heavily of Old Spice. He leaned against me as he lifted the crepe paper and re-attached it over the door, swaddling me from head to foot with his own body and the soft folds of his blue sweater.

"Last week we met him for a drink," he said.

"Do I really need to hear this?" I asked.

"Listen to me," said Peter sternly. "We can't let this happen to him. I think seeing Sam would help him. He told us that the last time they talked, the boy invited him here to his birthday party. We asked him to come with us. Do you know what he said? 'What would Rosie say?' He said he didn't think he was welcome."

"Well, he's not."

Peter sighed, cupping his chin in his hands. "Would you like to know what I think?"

He had finished his peppermint iced tea and without waiting for my answer, he walked back into the kitchen to fill his glass. Moments later he emerged onto the terrace and waited in the doorway, sipping.

"Go on. Tell me what you think."

"It's not complicated. Some people who love each other are a disaster when they get together and brilliant when they're apart. Some people are just the opposite. You and David are better people when you're together. That's all."

"I know that."

"Well then. Sometimes it's up to you to be bigger."

"You mean beg him to come home? I did that once."

"Well, you could keep him suffering, but normally you're not sadistic like that."

"Why should I humiliate myself again just to make it easy for him?"

Peter shrugged. "That's what being bigger is about."

PART FOUR

JIMMYFOOTING THE DEVIL

CHAPTER 15

My father died in March, at the beginning of the southern California spring. They told me he was standing in the kitchen late one night, pouring whisky at the counter, when he had a stroke and a heart attack. He collapsed on the floor and cracked his head on the tile as he fell.

Sam and I set off the next morning, driving first south along the glistening coast, then heading out around the northeast edge of LA, out toward the San Bernardino forest and then clear out to the old desert roads. Although we had gone regularly as a family to visit my father, I hadn't made that drive on my own in over a year. The familiar landmarks were finally gone; most every McDonald's or Foster's Freeze I remembered from high school had morphed into something new. Strip malls lined the new four-lane highway, filled with Chinese food places and nail salons where before it had just been burger joints for the military. Now, the towns seeped out onto the desert landscape with automotive supply stores and liquor stores and churches occupying former donut houses. The road through the reservation had become a tree-lined gleaming drive toward a casino, and as we drove it, the temperature was already over a hundred and I was lost.

I kept driving into the Pinto until finally Sam said, "You always get lost, Mom."

"I know, sweetie. I'm not very good at directions."

He giggled. "Turn here."

I looked in the rearview mirror, and saw that he was pointing at a filling station.

"Why?"

"Maybe they know where we are. Can I have a snow cone?"

Around us were a few streets of dilapidated old box-shaped houses from the '50s, a quick town that had been jerry-built to some developer's California dream. In the old days the desert spring was the best time, when the poppies bloomed and the faint barometric rise threw the fresh smell of desert plants across the horizon. Now, all I could smell was some old sulphuric factory rotting by the ancient lake bed, cracked and peeling and years-empty.

"Can I have the green flavor?" he asked, and I laughed. At old desert gas stations snow cones really didn't come in flavors, only colors.

He stood beside me sucking at the sweet, darkened ice shavings coating his teeth and tongue with the color of deep, moist moss. He listened to the directions from the mechanic, and as we walked back to the car he said confidently, "Okay. I'll remember." Although he had not seen his father in a year, he was still growing up to be that same kind of man.

We set off again, and this time we found the street where I had lived, lawn after lawn still edged with bright pink petunias that belonged in a lush, humid forest somewhere on the other side of the world. I pulled into the hot, cracked drive and brought the car to a stop under the lanai.

I dug into my purse to find the key to my father's house, my old key that now gave me ownership to this Pinto house, just as my father had promised.

We went in and I saw in the kitchen the smear of dried blood down the pale turquoise tiles, where my father must have hit his head as he collapsed to the ground the night of his death. I stared for a moment, and then took Sam's hand and led him out to the poolside chairs. His favorite place was the old trampoline, and he climbed on top of it now, crossing his legs and tapping a drummer's beat on the aluminum frame.

I leaned beside Sam, staring out at the clouding chlorine water.

"Can we go swimming?" Sam asked.

"It's almost five. We should go into town and get some dinner. Maybe when we come back."

We found a new Tiny Naylor's coffee shop in Pinto City, a place blasting ice cold air where the staff served endless cups of tawny-colored coffee water. We sat at an overstuffed Naugahyde booth, and a teenaged boy with shaggy hair brought us plastic menus that were covered with bright colored pictures of the food. Sam poured over the menu, struggling with the words but wanting to eat everything that had a photograph next to it.

When he had chosen, he looked up at me. "You're like me, huh?"

I smiled, by now used to random questions that followed some intense and silent train of thought. "I'm your mother. We're a lot alike."

"No, I mean you don't have any brothers or sisters."

"That's right. Why?"

He shrugged his small shoulders and pushed his hair off of his forehead. "Just wondering. We're a small family, aren't we? Now that grandpa is dead, it's just us."

"Well, don't forget your dad. And you do have another grandfather. Your dad's father. You know that. And another grandfather and grandmother in Canada. And Peter and Marta, of course."

"What's a cousin?" he asked.

"Mostly, it's the child of your aunt or uncle."

"All my friends have cousins. How come I don't?"

"Well, you can't have cousins if your dad and I don't have brothers and sisters."

"Why not?"

I sighed and looked around the restaurant. The waitress came toward us then carrying huge plates of food on the flat of her hands and balanced in the crook of her elbows. She put the food down on our table with a clatter. She wore a badge that said 'Amber,' and leaned over our booth for a moment to catch her breath.

"I think I went to high school with you," I said quietly. Amber cocked her head to one side, twisting her lips in a kind of inelegant chipmunk scrutiny.

"Yeah?" Her hair was a vivid orange, her nails were hot pink, and she put one hand carefully up to the high, tight, lacquered swirl of carrot-color. "What's your name?"

"Rosie. I used to be Rosie Kettle."

"No. I don't think so. I come from around here."

"So do I," I said, and she nodded and walked away. I looked over at Sam, shrugged, and glanced around the room. Half a dozen people with dried-out hair and squinty eyes were eating hot, gravy-covered dinners at booths like ours, and every one of their faces looked familiar to me.

"You don't like it here, do you?" Sam asked.

I raised my eyebrows at him and shook my head. "You're right about that, darling. I guess it's just too hot for me."

The next day Sam and I got up early and sat in the kitchen making a list of people we had to see. In addition to organizing the burial, I intended to get rid of the house as soon as possible so I would never have to return to the Pinto basin, the strangling heat, and the smell of wet-down creosote across the desert floor. We needed a realtor, a plumber to repair the leaking pipe that my father had forgotten about under the sink, a stonemason to finish the flagstone walk, a pool man to start coming regularly until the house sold, and we needed to visit the funeral parlor to plan the burial.

"We'll be here until the funeral," I said. "That's a couple of days, probably. Do you mind?"

"I like it here. Can we go to the restaurant for breakfast today?"

"You just had breakfast."

"Oops. I forgot," and he started giggling, and then I did. He squeezed himself into my lap, putting his skinny arms around my neck.

"I love you. You're the cutest kid in the whole world." I gave him a paper and pen. "Do you want to write the list?"

"Can I?" He grabbed the paper and held it down as though his life depended on it. "What's first?"

By the time we finished, it was eleven o'clock and both of us were still sitting in pajamas.

"I'm going to take a shower and get dressed. You go put your clothes on, and stay away from the pool. It's not safe until we get it cleaned."

"Okay. Can I wear my red shorts?"

"Sure. Good choice."

Later, when I came back into the heat I wore a cool, blue-checked cotton shift, sleeveless with a simple round collar that made me look like a schoolgirl. I stood in the kitchen calling Sam, and saw through the window that he was wading in the far end of the pool, laughing.

I shouted, "Sam, get out of the pool!" and went outside to grab him. I saw a huge clutch of enormous sunflowers, bright yellow on the faded green ping-pong table. Sam was not even looking at me but talking to someone, and then I saw David, sitting on the diving board, smiling broadly at his boy.

"Look!" shouted Sam when he saw me. "Look, Mom!"

I took a long, silent look. David jumped to his feet and said nervously, "Sam, you better get out of the water." Immediately, our son climbed onto the concrete edge.

David turned to face me. "I'm sorry I didn't call. I couldn't find the number. Are you okay?" He wore a grey t-shirt and old black, bleach-mottled jeans, clothes that were ironed and that smelled faintly of fresh laundry. He stood with one hand slung in his front pocket and the other reaching out to the side, holding it there, waiting for Sam to take it. "I figured there would be something I could do to help. I know your father never trusted me, but I thought at least maybe I could sing a hymn at the funeral." He crossed his arms, brown and glistening from the rising heat. "I'm sorry, Rosie. Was he sick?"

"No, just old. And lonely." I moved a step toward them and sat on the rough diving board.

"Let's go," said Sam. "We can take Dad to the restaurant, can't we?"

David waited, staring up at me through the harsh sunlight, his head cocked to avoid the glare, the sharp line of his jaw so familiar that the palest of hungers lifted in me. "Sam says you have a lot to do today."

I nodded again, "I want to get this house ready to sell. So I don't have to come back."

"I'd like to help if you don't mind." Sam crept behind him and climbed onto his shoulders, and David smiled. He put his arms behind his back like a cradle, holding Sam close and lifting him. "Rosie, you look really beautiful."

"Are you alone?"

He stared at me in the sun-scorched blast of the absolutely empty sky. A few backyards away some kid began to gun his car engine to life, but no other sounds closed around us. I could see him considering all the possible answers he might give, and at last he said only, "Yeah, I am."

After lunch, the three of us went together to run those errands, to see the plumber and the pool man, and the funeral parlor. David stood beside me as the mortician showed me my father laid out on a table underground, and he held my hand as I chose a coffin that would hold my dad through the rest of history. When it was all finished we drove out past the empty bullpen to Berdoo Canyon where the spring flowers grew. The last rain had come late that year, and the purple lupine still lay in March meadows and the ocotillo sprouted salmon-colored blossoms across the cracked, brown desert. We parked the car and hiked out to the Cottonwood Wash, far beyond the edge of Pinto City where the colors had reclaimed the land and threw a bouquet of golden poppies and Canterbury bells around us. David took Sam in his lap, wrapping his arms around him, and Sam automatically leaned back against him to touch his head on his father's chest.

"You know," David said, "there are lizards and snakes out here."

"Where?"

"Out there. You have to be quiet to see them." David was whispering with his lips so close they were touching the lobe of Sam's ear.

"You don't see with your ears," Sam said.

"You're right. But the things that move are little and always the same color as the ground. You have to concentrate to see them. You can't run and shout and see the snakes at the same time."

"Okay," he said. He leaned forward to watch and put his hands on David's knees.

So easily I became only a mother again, tumbling toward that relief as it washed around me. The memory of the last year ruptured apart inside of me, all those hard months of learning how to be alone, to be the only adult, without any needs and responsible for everything. I fumbled through the pain, confessing now to what I had wanted all along. I began to cry, quietly and where no one could see, smearing tears across my face with my fingers.

After a while, David called over his shoulder, "Hey, what happened to you?" He lifted Sam to his feet and got up. "We better go. It'll take a while to get back. Here, Sammy, drink before we start." He handed the water bottle to Sam. I stood behind David and put my hand on his shoulder as we watched Sam drink furiously. He lifted his other hand across to cover mine and we stood together, mended for a moment while we looked at our son.

In the desert, the night comes so quickly. It presses a deep blue down upon a cloudless sky, hollow and clear like the color of the sea. By the time we reached the car, the far hills were purple from the dying light, and David was carrying Sam on his shoulders, both of them quiet, tired, and content. At my father's house the cold came over the ridge fast, and we stayed inside to eat, at last putting Sam to sleep in my childhood bedroom. David and I sat for a while in the living room, watching the television news about some tribal battle in the mountains in eastern Europe. When the news dissolved into a game show, David flicked the sound off and turned to me.

"I spent Christmas with Matt Rappaport. Did you know that? He said to say hi to you."

"You were in LA for Christmas?"

We sat side by side in the large armchairs that my parents had used for decades, and in front of us were television tables from the '60s, old metal ones with dark swirls of roses painted across them.

"No, we were back East. He's moving the magazine to New York, and he called me while he was in town, so we had dinner together. You know, Werther still wants me to do that part in his movie and I asked Matt what he thought of the idea." David was spinning a penny across the little table, propelling it over and over until he could keep it edge-hopping for several seconds. "I told him I needed a new career. Lost my voice, couldn't write. I told him the business was literally killing me." He smiled and reached over to put the penny down on my table. "Well, I didn't have to tell him that. Anyone could see what was happening to me then. But he really surprised me, Rosie. He said that he spent his career trying to be like me, and that when he heard what I did to myself he didn't believe it. And the funny thing is, he said the reason he respected me had nothing to do with my music. He said I always showed up on time and paid my bills. Had a nice family. Didn't take what wasn't mine. He told me I should step out of the way and let the demons rush past."

"What?"

"Stop fighting it all. Stop throwing myself in front of it. Get back to music."

"He's a smart guy."

"Yeah, he is. You know, I'm better now. I'm clean, I mean. And I'm moving back to LA. I have a lot of old debts to pay off, so Matt got me a job writing some movie music." He shrugged. "Not very exciting, is it?" I smiled and didn't answer. He pushed the little table to the side and stood up. "I guess I better go."

"You don't have to."

"Are you sure? I can always get a room at the motel."

"There's no need. I'll sleep in my parents' room and you can have the guest room, the one he made you stay in the year before we got married."

David grinned. "Okay, if you really don't mind."

My first dream that night was about damp London streets and the imprints left in empty, wooden rooms by murdered women. I opened my eyes in the dark, and immediately fell back to sleep. My second dream was about a robin picking off fat wing-lice and eating them, but it woke me up and I left my bed around 2 AM to check on Sam. I went barefoot down the hall and stopped in the shadows when I saw David at Sam's open door. He stood with his hands at his sides, wearing no clothes. He turned suddenly, "He's fine," he whispered. "I just wanted to watch for a while."

"Come talk to me."

"You should go back to sleep. There's a lot to do today. What time does Sam get up these days?"

"It's okay. He keeps musicians' hours," I said and he laughed. We slipped into my father's bedroom, and I sat cross-legged on the bed, my white cotton nightdress curled in shadows and bunches across my thighs. Just then we heard a shudder outside like light rain falling, an impossible sound in the spring desert, and we listened for a moment, curiously.

"Oh," I whispered, and put my hand on his arm, just a slight touch on his warm skin. "It's the sprinklers. They're on a timer." The smell of moist, rich soil began to rise in the dry night.

He crossed his legs and looked over at me. His face was hunched in shadows, and he watched me for a long time. "Rosie, I'm sorry." He swallowed nervously. "I fucked it all up." Slowly he brought his hand to the lace edging at my shoulder. He held the tiny petals between his fingers, careful not to touch my skin. "I'm sorry."

I leaned over and kissed his cheek, and he touched my face. My throat began to burn, and I held my breath as the cool tips of his fingers touched my jaw. Finally he turned his face to kiss me. I lay back when I felt his tongue, new again to me, come between my lips. He pushed my gown up and lay his hand flat on my stomach, looking at my skin and stroking with his thumb as though he were searching for old fingerprints.

"You feel like silk," he whispered. What I wanted was so clear. I slipped across his lap to face him, lifting my nightdress over my head, dropping it onto the floor.

"Come on," I said, and he put his mouth to my breasts and began to kiss me again. I felt his fingertips slip across my back, searching for the trace of my spine. "I don't want to wait," I said. He smiled and lifted me up, then setting me down so that he could move deep inside of me.

I began to make a sound like a thick, low chime, and he opened his eyes to watch me. When I saw this, I spoke to him in that same low ache, only my words were stupid, like an angry child more desirous of harm than pleasure. "Is this what you do with the other women?"

He continued to watch, moving so smoothly, and at last said, "Go on, say it again." He grabbed my shoulders, arching hard to make sure I felt him. "This is what I do with you. Or did you forget?" He caught my wrists and pushed them above my head, lurching forward so hard I was pushed back to the board. He rocked into me gently, and asked at last, "How is this, baby?"

He whispered, "You're gonna forget I ever left." He began then to finish it, finding the angle that paralyzed me, beating through it perfectly, so fast and sure that within seconds I exploded, and a moment later he did. We lay for a long time in that immaculate space between sleep and exhaustion, and finally David opened his eyes, "Are you okay?" He pulled the cool sheet across our bodies. "I thought about this for months," he whispered, "but I gotta tell you, I never pictured doing it in your parents' bed." We both started to giggle, and he took my hand in the warmth under the sheet. I looked across the room to the dresser where I had put the sunflowers he had brought. Their huge shapes glowed like golden lions' faces, and when he caught me looking at them he asked, "Do you remember that time at Zaca before Sam was born when you planted sunflowers?"

"Sure. You sat on a rock and heckled me."

He grimaced. "I was watching, because you had on that pink shirt that used to drive me crazy. Anyway, you were so determined. I never believed you would get them going."

"Everything grows at Zaca." I started to move my hand from under the sheet, and he took it again in both of his, holding it against his chest. All around me was the familiar taste of salted sweat on his skin, and a thick, sweet smell, like heated amber.

"Did you get sunflowers this year?"

"Of course. I put some hollyhocks in, too. Outside the glass doors off the kitchen."

"You know, you really turned into an old-fashioned girl. And here I always thought I married the fastest chick in town."

"You thought I was fast?"

"Well, maybe not fast. But you had a pretty hot reputation."

"You're so full of shit," I said.

"It's true," he said. "When we got together in the parking lot I'd heard some stories."

"You remember the parking lot?"

"Baby, I remember everything."

"You were a pretty bad boy back then, yourself. You needed to be reined in."

He put his head back against the pillow and laughed. "You're tough with me," he whispered.

We watched while the morning came up against the windows, our shapes like cocoons wrapped in the sheets.

"How did you know about my father?"

He sighed and sat up, his goofy smile dissolving quickly. He began to tap his fingers against the pillow, thrumming between his thumb and forefinger. "I was on my way to Zaca to see you, and Yana told me what happened. I was coming anyway."

"Why?"

"Okay. Here's the thing." He waited for a moment, watching me. "This is hard to get out. You kind of frighten me, you know."

"Good."

"Rosie, give me a break here. It's hard to beg." He took a drink out of my glass of water next to the bed. "Okay, what I want is to come home. That's it. I love you. I want a chance to be good to you again. I love you." He sat cross-legged, pretending calm but betrayed by arms and hands that were clenched so tightly his skin glowed white at the joints.

"I don't want a drugger husband."

"I'm not a junkie," he said very quickly. "I have been, but I'm not now." There was no sound, no birds like at Zaca because there are no songbirds in a desert morning. I got up from the bed, grabbed my nightgown off the floor and slipped into it, starting for the door. He reached out and grabbed my arm. "Look at me," he said, his voice trembling.

"Let go of me."

"No. I want you to tell me what you want. What I need to do."

I told him sharply, looking straight into his eyes. "I don't want a drugger. I don't want a liar. I want a husband who doesn't screw around and doesn't give up. You want to know what I really want? I want a man who is a lot braver than you were."

The day began, the windows glittering with the sunlight that crackled through the sprinkler drops still clinging to the glass. "I know I hurt both of you. I made stupid, selfish decisions. I understand how badly I fucked up."

"No, you don't. You have no idea what it's been like," and then my chest pulled tight, my stomach and arms and throat cramped and I began to cry in front of him, groaning deeply and unable to stop, like any piece of trailer trash, like my own mother lost in the desert.

"Oh God," he whispered, and put his arms around me.

"You told me you would love me forever. I still hate you for that." I said this to him, and all the while I let him hold me.

At last he said, "Am I asking for too much, here?"

The shabby little room had come to light, revealing that old house of my father with plaster cracks running like rivers on a map. My school pictures sat in cheap frames on the dresser. My mother cleaned and dusted this room once a week for decades, arranged his cufflinks in the little tray and put his lunch in a brown paper bag every morning. I watched it all, every minute of it, and still had no idea how to survive. I shrugged and sat next to him. I could see he was afraid to speak again. He folded his arms together across his chest, his scar glowing like a damp fossil in the dim light.

"Do you remember when you said we'd be married forever?" I asked.

"Rosie, I know that you're gonna be angry at me for a long time. I'm not asking you to stop being angry. Just let me come home. I won't hurt you again."

And so I agreed, and together we sorted the house out, and the funeral, and at the end of the week we drove from the desert to the Santa Ynez hills, all of Zaca ranch pulsing in a prism of late winter sunlight reflected off the sea. All the way up the Pacific Coast Highway on the stretch from LA, Sam sat in the back pointing at palm trees or old buildings or coves where we had walked, asking, "Do you remember that, Dad?" And each time David laughed unabashedly, washed by Sam's eagerness as though it were a bath of champagne.

* * *

Our first night back, Sam climbed into bed with us and refused to leave. He lay between us, holding onto our arms, burrowing into the warmth, and we fell to an easy sleep that lasted until dawn. I awoke in the early morning alone in the bed with him, both of us covered with pale, white light rising against the window through the coastal fog. His puffy infant face had begun to disappear, and I could see even then that he would have those high Slavic cheekbones that so marked his father's face.

I found David in the kitchen at the huge oak table.

"Did I wake you up?" he asked. He sat on the bench, holding a coffee cup with his elbows propped like a tripod in front of him. He wore old grey sweats, and a thick red winter sweater. "It's freezing here. I put the heat on a minute ago. Come here, baby. I want to kiss you good morning." I leaned over to him and he put his hand around the back of my head, bringing my face close. I sat next to him on the bench and put my arms around his chest. "I found this in the refrigerator." He pointed to a huge bowl of fresh blueberries next to him. "Where did you get blueberries this time of year?"

"Yana brings them. She's always bringing us food."

"These look so good. And I found some cream, too."

"Yana," I said again. He poured the pitcher of thick cream over the entire bowl of blueberries, drowning them.

"I haven't had blueberries and cream since I was a kid. Maybe it's a Russian thing." He put a huge tablespoon into the bowl and brought the fruit to me. "Here, have some before I eat it all."

"What do you want to do today?"

"I don't know. Unpack and look around. Spend time with you and Sam. Maybe you could take some pictures of us." He was talking and chewing at the same time, shoveling the blueberries into his mouth, cold and sweet and bursting indigo into the cream. "That was amazing. Food tastes completely different when you're not sweating out junk."

"How long has it been?" I asked, and put my hand on his shoulder, rubbing it.

"Long enough. I'll do it. Don't worry. Matt took me down to a place in the Bahamas. I slept through most of it. Pretty lucky, huh?" Sam's dog was curled at our feet next to the heater vent. His eyes were closed, but I could tell he was waiting to jump at the first sign of morning food.

"I better feed Joe," I said.

David grabbed my shoulders. "Wait. I love you." He put his face against my neck and began kissing me, and I could feel his lips, cool and damp from the cream, brushing across my skin. "I have to talk to you," he whispered. "I need to ask you something."

"What is it?"

He took a ring out of his pocket and put it on the table. He took a drink from his coffee cup and watched me. "I was looking on the dresser for that St. Christopher medal my father gave me." His finger rested on the edge of the ring, a thick silver band with onyx laid in, a man's ring, an old one. "I found this." He looked at me and put his hand on my thigh.

"It belongs to James. He must have left it here." I watched as the flash of color spread up his cheeks and I waited.

"Okay," he said carefully. "Now what?"

"I'll give it back to him and explain what's happened. That's all. There's no question, David."

He nodded, and took the blueberry bowl in both hands, lifting it to his mouth and drinking what was left of the cream. He leaned back against the wall into paled morning shadows, and wiped his mouth with the back of his hand.

"How about this. How about if I give it back to him?"

"No. I need to talk to him."

He held the ring in the cradle of his hand, rattling and rocking it there while he thought about what to say next. "This isn't easy, is it?" he asked at last and clattered the ring suddenly across the table. "You know, I understand that I have no rights here. But it's still fucking hard to swallow." He stood and went to the door. "I'm gonna go walk this off. I'll be back in a while."

Out on the far north corner of Zaca was an enormous pond perched high on a mesa above the sea, with a border of old oak growth shading and protecting it. Back in the eighteenth century it had been named Dos Pueblos by the priests at Santa Barbara mission, a place where two small Chumash villages came together for market. We seldom went there, because I always thought of it as a creepy place and it was such a difficult climb to get to it, up a hillside field of prickly teasel stalks and raspberry vines. That afternoon when the fog burned off and David returned, Sam asked if we could go out to that far pond for a picnic.

"It's too late for a picnic," I said. "It's almost dinnertime."

David smiled at me and said to Sam, "Your mother's so rigid. She thinks picnics are only lunch."

"They can be anything, Mom. Please."

"Yeah," said David. "They can be anything, Mom." He was laughing and relaxed again. He grabbed Sam and lifted him to his shoulders. "Come on. Let's get the food."

We marched up the steep ridge with our supplies, and I took as well an easy, little camera for quick pictures. David spread a huge blanket across the damp ground alongside the water. Sam immediately tore off all his clothing and took a running cannonball jump into the pond, screaming like a banshee as he catapulted through the air. His father followed him and they swam together, pushing and dunking each other into that black water until they were tired out and hungry. They climbed up and stood dripping and naked in the moss, silver flashing around their feet from the afternoon sunlight.

"Sit there," I said. "Let me take your picture." David lay back in the water's edge, and pulled Sam on top of him, their ribcages stretched and touching, both lying flat looking at each other and smiling. I went through a couple of rolls of film while David held Sam and talked to him.

"You're a good swimmer, Sammy. All the Paletzine men are good swimmers."

"What's a paletzine?" asked Sam, and David paused.

"It's our name. We are Paletzines. It's a blood thing."

"I thought I was Sam Wilderspin."

Then David began to explain to him about families and stepfamilies, a long tribal history of prideful Russian men that I had never heard. He told him about cousins he had in

St. Petersburg and Sam grinned when he heard this. I knew he was thinking that finally, with his father back, he measured up to his friends because he now had cousins. At the end David grabbed his jeans and pulled a little silver St. Christopher medal out of the pocket. "Here. This was my father's and now it's yours. It will protect you wherever you go."

Sam was staring at his father intently. "Can I keep it?" he asked quietly as he took the chain in his fingers.

"Yeah. But it belongs to the family. The family goes on forever. When you have a son, you have to give it to him, just like I'm doing now."

"Okay," said Sam. "I'll do that," and before I had really understood what was happening, the agreement passed between them, a Paletzine family ceremony, my little boy and his father like men in some damaged bloodline. A cuff of wasps circled the rotting leaves by the water, and without thinking I waved them away to protect Sam and watched him put the chain and medallion around his neck, tying him to a family of which I knew so little.

Chapter 16

By January, Sam had started his first school year and David had picked up a couple of new movie scoring jobs. He would get up early and drive Sam to the local elementary school, then work the ponds and shoreline for the rest of the morning until the damp coast air had exhausted him. In the afternoons he would settle in front of the piano and work until the early winter dark closed in.

I remember it rained solidly that season until the road up to Zaca was a sodden marsh of sliding mud. Once during an electrical storm it rained so hard that I had to abandon the car halfway up the hill and walk through the mud on the unlit path. This was in the darkest part of the year, and that night the rain pelted hard and relentlessly, in water sheets cast violet by the moon. I carried my wool coat in my arms, because it had soaked through. I slipped a couple of times on the way up the road, and cut my hand on a thorn branch I had grabbed for balance. By the time I reached the porch of the house I was drenched and dirty, and my palm was bleeding.

As I neared the door I heard the huge, thick pound of percussion coming from the house, so loud it overpowered the rain and thunder. Through the windowpanes I could see a gold fireglow rising up in the darkened room and when I stepped inside, the heat from the full blazing fire was suffocating. I recognized the violent music from "The Planets Suite," the voice of Mars that David had always loved, and I dropped my wet belongings in the doorway.

They sat facing the fireplace with their backs to me. Sam was holding a Coke in his hands and watching the fire, not saying a word nor moving, but listening intently to the music. As I neared them David turned to me. His face was flushed from the heat and he wore a kind of dazed expression from the noise, but he stood when he saw me and moved across the room to turn the music down.

"Mom!" shouted Sam, and ran over to me. "We didn't know where you were. Why didn't you call?"

I lifted him up and held him against my chest. "I couldn't honey. It's a really bad storm." I turned to David and added, "I got stuck in the mud and had to leave the car down the hill."

"You're soaked. You should go have a hot bath. Sam and I made dinner."

"We made dinner," Sam repeated.

"Scary," I grinned. "Where's Yana?"

"I told her to go home before the rain got bad." He lifted Sam from my arms. "Go on upstairs. I bet you're freezing." David was holding Sam but watching me and when Sam started to squirm he looked over and said suddenly to him, "You have blood on your shoulder. Look, Sam's bleeding."

"What?" I asked, and then touched his shirt where it was smeared with blood. "No, that's me. I grabbed onto some brambles to keep from falling and cut my hand."

He put Sam down and took my hand to look. "You tore your palm open, Rosie. This is pretty deep. Come on." He put his arm around my shoulders. "Let's go clean it up."

We sat in the bathroom upstairs, and Sam squatted on the floor beside us, while David disinfected the mud and silt grains from my hand. When he finished he turned on the bath. "That was a bad storm to get caught in. You relax now. Get warm."

"I can hear the phone," said Sam. "Can I answer it?"

"No, I'll get it," David said. "That's the gatehouse line." When he returned he said, "That was the police. They're coming up. There's some problem at the Cooley's farm."

"They won't be able to get up the road."

He smiled at me like I was a child trying to comment on nuclear physics. "This is the sheriff, baby. They have four-wheel drive." He put his hand around the back of my neck.

"You're shivering. Why don't you take Sam and go have your bath?"

"I will later. I want to know what's happening."

"I guess you're never gonna do as you're told, are you?"

"They don't make us like that anymore," I said.

A sheriff arrived on our porch in a huge oilskin raincoat, dripping puddles on the darkened wood boards, and carrying a swing handle flashlight.

"Come in," David said.

"Thank you, no sir. Not much time. I'm going to need your help, Mr. Wilderspin. Someone opened the gate on the Cooley cattle and the whole herd is moving toward the north mesa. In this rain they'll be over your cliff at Dos Pueblos in about half an hour. We're trying to block the turn at the west corner of your property. We asked for officers from Santa Barbara, but it'll be a while. So I need everyone who's willing to help."

David did not even look my way. Immediately he said, "I'll get my coat," and grabbed it off the banister in the hallway.

I was holding Sam's hand and watching the sheriff, but I must have looked frightened because he said to me, "Don't worry, m'am. He'll be all right."

"My wife worries about everything."

"What about the fire department?" I asked.

"They were called out to a couple of human emergencies this evening. There's some flooding to the south and one of your neighbors lost half their house over the cliff. Cattle are pretty low on the Fire Department priority list."

"I'll get my caretaker," David said. "Would that help?"

"That'd be good. Much appreciated by the department and the Cooleys."

"I can come, too," I said, but David looked swiftly over at me as though I had disobeyed him.

"You can't. There's no one to stay with Sam."

"The fact is, Mr. Wilderspin, we have some child care organized at the Cooley house." He shrugged. "I'm sorry, sir. We need every person we can get."

I sat in the back of the jeep with Sam strapped in beside me, and we drove down the hill through the rain, sliding through the mud that had spread across the road. Sam wore his new little yellow rain parka with the bright hood. When we reached the bottom of the hill, the car bounced forward into a ditch and stayed, lurching back and forth as the tires ground further down into the sop. The sheriff shoved the stick into four-wheel drive and slowly through that cold, pelting rain, we lifted out of the mud like on a magic carpet and rolled forward onto the paved road. Sam reached to touch me, and I took hold of him and put my arm around his shoulders, pulling him very close.

"It's all right. We're with the sheriff."

David heard me, and looked over his shoulder to us. He grinned so broadly and said, "Hey, Mr. Sam, this is going to be a wild night, huh?"

When we got to the Cooley farmhouse, I took Sam around the back to the kitchen door. About six other children were sitting at the old pine table, drawing pictures and laughing while Brenda Cooley handed out potato chips. Two of the boys were from Sam's school and he sat with them easily like a ringleader, and the three immediately began shoving each other until they fell giggling into a heap on the floor.

"Sam!" I shouted, but he didn't look up.

"Leave us to it," said Mrs. Cooley. "We'll be fine." She was about thirty-five and had her blonde hair pulled back in a ponytail. Her skin was mottled with red from the sun or from alcohol, but her eyes were green and clear. "Thank you for doing this. We just can't lose the herd. There'd be nothing left." She had a voice hoarse from cigarettes and a tired, hard expression on her face. "The Guardinos lost their roof tonight. Just caved in on them. I never saw rain like this before in the Santa Ynez."

We drove straight over our land to Dos Pueblos, up that teasel hill, crushing down the last of the stalks. After one final grind of power over the crest, we came to rest at the top of the mesa behind the overflowing pond boiling with stabs of rain, a hundred yards from the cliff. About fifty people sheltered under the oaks, holding flashlamps.

The sheriff stepped behind us, shouting to be heard above the violent rain. "I'm sorry, we're already on your land. We moved down here when we couldn't stop the herd on Cooley land."

"Of course," David yelled. We waited in the open field while he pulled flashlights from the jeep and almost immediately the force of the storm winds and the water soaked through my coat and clothes, cutting the cold across my bones. "What do you want us to do?" he asked.

The sheriff put his arms around our shoulders to bring us out of the pounding noise. "It's pretty simple. Stand hand-to-hand along the path as the cattle pass and keep them from the cliff. A human chain will turn them back. They won't break through, and as long as people don't move suddenly, they'll just follow the leader."

We ran through the mud to the crowd, and we huddled against the trees with the others, listening once more as the sheriffs shouted out the directions over the thunder and rain. We splayed out along the ridge behind Dos Pueblos, the women placed at the top, safer spots, and the men down toward the cliff. The sheriffs took their places about ten yards in from the edge, where the momentum of the cattle and the drop of the cliff was greatest. All of us stood at this weird attention, arms, chests, and fingers held taut, neighbor to neighbor, nearly touching in the driving, freezing rain.

As the cows came down the Cooley crest, they moved slowly in a wave of dumb flesh, pulling close together. I heard no sound from them, but the ground began to hum with their weight and the air was swollen with vibration. Slowly they pushed past and began the straight path down the hill beneath us, intent without thought, force without motive gathering speed and strength as they neared the cliff.

The men stood linked against them in a line knocked by the constant gale, ten yards back from the mudface that dropped to the sea. As the herd rumbled toward the spot that marked the turn away from the cliff, I heard the hum of the earth grow and flatten, and finally turn into a soft, slicing sound. Some of the women began to shout suddenly, men jumped back from the mesa and fell across the drenched meadow, sliding and grabbing out. And through that wild darkness I heard a noise so loud that the night might have swung to a stop upon that sound. We heard a whistling rise up, the earth groaning, and suddenly part of the cliff gave way, crashing onto the beach. We ran then, all of us, through the spongy field, stopping short at the edge of the cliff. The sheriffs began shouting to us to fall into our line again, and the men who had fallen in the grass at the first tear of the cliff leapt up and formed that line in the rain, all black with mud.

"Over here! Over here!" one of the sheriffs shouted again and again, frantically waving, setting each of us to run to a place until we had lined the path the cattle would take to safety. We stood again, stretching like electrified scarecrows in the deluge, sheets of rain pitching against us until finally the herd moved beyond us, and Cooley and his ranch hands led them back toward the farm gates.

Out of fifty neighbors, we had no idea if any men were over the cliff, and I couldn't find David. At last, I saw a slender man about six feet tall standing alone near the edge, and I ran to him, grabbing his jacket sleeve.

"Come on, ma'am," he said, and it was a sheriff. "We need your light on the beach now."

We shone our flashlights across the shore, concentrating together on the waves brought close by the tides and the crest of beach that now held part of the hill. On the sand lay two cows that had gone over, huge animals unable to stand, their backs or legs broken and partly covered in sand and mud.

"I don't see any men," said the sheriff. "Is there still a path down there?"

"Over there." I pointed to the far oak circle. "Behind the trees." Two of the police began the trudge through the deep mud to the path.

"I'll go with you," I heard David say, and I turned and saw he was standing behind me.

I put my arms around his waist, and he held me for a moment, and then he and the other men set off toward the path.

I must have stood with the other women on that cliff for half an hour watching. We could hear the cows groaning through the rain and the waves, crying against the roar of the sea, until at last they just gave in and lay there on the wet sand, still breathing but released from will. One of the sheriffs took his gun and shot them both. Eventually, we walked back to the cars to wait, and when David appeared at the jeep window with the sheriff who had brought us, he did not open the door, but tapped on the glass for me to roll it down.

"I'm going to stay here a while and make sure things are secure. Dan here will drive you back to get Sam. You have a bath and go to bed." He put his hand behind my neck and his face close against mine. "And I want you to do it this time," he whispered.

David didn't return until long after midnight. I lay in bed in the dark, and behind the still-thunderous rain I could hear the engine of a car, his voice outside below me talking to other men, and his footsteps on the porch. The door opened and closed, and then the house was silent. Finally, I left our bed and wandered down through our empty rooms, finding David sitting on the floor by the dying fire like a drunken shepherd, his sodden shirt stripped off, a glass and a bottle of scotch next to him.

I put my hand on his shoulder.

"Are you okay?"

He smiled at me easily, with a look of relief.

"Yeah. Just tired and cold."

"I was pretty worried."

"The house will be okay. It's been here for a hundred and fifty years."

"No, I mean about you. I'm not very good at waiting."

"I guess you'd never make it as a peasant wife out on the steppes." I put the tip of my tongue deeply into his mouth, gulping at him as though he had been gone for a decade.

"You're dreaming," he whispered.

"Maybe."

He put his arms around me. "The sheriff said the rain will clear by morning, and we'll have some sun."

"He's an optimist."

"It's hard to believe. It was like a horror movie tonight. But we did okay. We did the job." He lay back calmly and put his arms above his head on the warm wood floor. "How did Sam take it all? Was he worried?"

"No, he's like you. He just gets on with what's in front of him."

"Sam's a great kid because of you. I tell everyone what a good mother you are." He brushed the hair out of my eyes. "Last year when I left, Sam never knew anything about what really happened, did he? You didn't let him hate me." I put my hand on his chest and he took it and lifted my fingers to his mouth, sinking them one by one between his parted lips. He sat up in the warm, copper-soaked air and lifted the poker to the fire again. "You know, I didn't realize when I bought Zaca what it would be. The town, the way people are here. It's good to be part of it. Do you mind not being in LA or New York?"

"No."

"Cooley invited us to a party tomorrow, if the rain stops. Out at Nojoqui Falls, that old restaurant by the airfield. Want to go?"

"Sure."

"He invited everyone who was out there tonight. And all their families. I thought we could take Yana, too." After a minute he suddenly said, "Hey, let's have a dozen kids, Rosie," and we both laughed. He drew me closer to him. "I'm serious. And here's the other thing. I want to call my father."

"In Canada?"

"No. I mean Nikolai. He's never even seen Sam. It's been over six years since he was here."

I had only that one violent memory of his real father, those night pictures that clung always to the edges of our lives at Zaca, of David crying in the dark when he forced his father to leave. "Do you think he's changed?" I asked.

"I don't know. Everybody changes in six years. I'd like to see him. Maybe have him visit."

Until then, I had believed that part of David had collapsed, but I could see now that he still harbored the dream of his family. "How would we ever explain it to Peter and Marta?" I whispered.

"So you don't want me to?"

"It's not about me." But suddenly it was about me, and I was begging him, my voice out of control like an animal digging in to fight. "All I remember is that night, and the way you fell apart when you saw him. And your stories about how he hurt your mother. How could you forgive him for all that?"

He nodded his head slowly. "I don't know, but I think I should try. He's getting so old, and I don't want him to die without seeing Sam. He's a genius. I want Sam to be proud of that, at least."

That very week he phoned his father while Sam and I sat beside him. He passed the phone to each of us like a collection plate; even Yana was called upon, and she talked to Nikolai for several minutes in Russian, smiling and laughing like a little girl. David finally took the phone again, and said that he wanted Nikolai to meet Sam, inviting him to come to us whenever he could and for however long he wanted. When it was over he hoisted Sam onto his shoulders and took him to Peter's old secret garden. I watched them from our bedroom window, as years before I had watched Peter. David squatted on the flagstones cracked open now from weeds, and touched Sam's shoulder. I never knew what they said. I could see their lips moving, and sometimes they smiled, but I never knew what passed between them.

By the spring we had fallen easily into a rhythm that was built around my teaching, David's composing, and Sam's school.

Our days began at seven and ended at ten, and unlike in his rocker life, we slept with the dark and rose with the light. Every Sunday lunchtime we joined our neighbors at the Nojoqui airfield restaurant, run by an old World War II flyer-turned-farmer. The kitchen operated out of the old control shack, and the place was a web of willow-wood tables and old planes that he had hammered together and laid out across the disused landing strips and hangars. His working farm surrounded it, and the runway was bordered by a forgotten apple orchard with trees so old and twisted they never gave fruit, only blossoms that crumbled and fell. It was only open on Sunday, and because it was hidden in private farmland, only the community knew about it. There we were suddenly safe, and our faces were familiar. David could discuss crops and his quest for geese, and all of us could complain or laugh about our children.

It was at the airfield that Sam and his friends first invented the game "Cows on the Beach," where one team would form a child-chain and the other team would pretend to be cows lurching for the sea. In this way, the children began to carve it into county legend, and I once heard Sam, like a shaman, telling a wild story of that night to a four-year-old. By then David had erected a barbed wire fence across the cliff-edge at Dos Pueblos to keep the livestock and the children out. Sam always asked to go up there again to see the carcasses, but of course we had burned them until only a black powder scar of carbon was left across the sand, and even that disappeared after a couple of days.

David spent the spring digging a huge pond close to the house, and Cooley came over to help him fill it with reeds and mallow that would attract dragonflies, which would in turn attract frogs and guarantee the health of the pond. Not one snow goose had come to the shoreline mudflats he had constructed, so the pond was a substitute, a smaller, controlled environment where he could plan the wildlife and be sure.

In September Cooley came over to see the finished pond and casually mentioned to David that with a little work a couple of swans might nest there. They began to redesign it then, re-digging the pond edging to make it easier for the swans. They built a small island in the center and in the shallow water surrounding it they planted sago and pondweed, white water buttercups and muskgrass. They brought a couple of large stones from the cave and put them on the island like a kind of yeast starter for the mud and grasses. One day they drove off in Cooley's truck and came back with a pair of wild swans. These birds were huge and strong, with wingspreads of four feet at full flight, and it took both David and his new farmer friend most of the day to get them to remain on the pond. He helped David mix a kind of feed that would keep the birds coming back, and he and David banded their legs, so that wherever they flew in their migrations over the years, news would be sent back to Zaca by birders up through Canada and down as far as the Mexican border.

Over the weeks leading to winter, they managed to get those swans to stay with us. By the end of October the pond lilies had gone, but the swans remained, and every morning I awoke to the sound of them flying low home to us through the darkened dawn. I remember lying in bed on my own listening to the graze of their huge wings against the air, that sound falling from the sky as they brushed through the morning circling the flat meadow. These were fiercely loyal birds, and David never hesitated to say to his friends that swans mate for life, just like the Wilderspins.

One early morning in November Peter called to invite us, finally, to the first night of his union documentary.

"Did I wake you?" he asked.

"No," said David. "I've been up for hours feeding the birds."

"You got your geese at last?"

"Not yet. Another year maybe."

Peter laughed so hard I could hear his bellowing through the phone. "I believe you. Marta and I have the champagne ready for when they come. But listen, I'm calling to tell you we're finally finished."

"What do you mean?" David asked.

"The film. We finished it. I know it took much longer than we thought, but now it's done. We're showing it for the first time and Marta and I would love for you and Rosie to come. Of course, it's not a glamorous event. Our main funder was a public television station in Los Angeles, so they organized the showing at UCLA in the film school. There's only a little reception afterward. No big names except the two of you."

David laughed, and he said to me, "Peter says they finished the documentary." He stretched his arm out to touch me.

"It isn't a Hollywood moment," Peter said.

"Well, we're pretty boring people, you know," David said. "Ma and Pa Wilderspin, that's all. When is it?"

"In December. The tenth."

"We'll be there. How long will you be in town for? You'll come stay with us?"

"We come in on the Thursday morning and leave on Monday. We were hoping we could come up to see you on Saturday and Sunday."

"That's great."

When he hung up the phone he was grinning. It was so early he hadn't shaved yet, and the stubble spreading across his jaw was beginning to show sprinkles of grey. I put my palm over it, just skimming the prickly ends, brushing softly back and forth over the frosted growth.

"How old are you this year?" I asked.

"What? Thirty-two. You know that."

"I forgot." I took the dead phone from his hand and put it on the table, and began to massage his shoulders, pressing my fingers deep between his shoulder blades until he groaned out loud as his muscles relaxed.

"We have to get Sam ready for school," he said. "We can't do this now."

"You're so tense."

"I'm not tense. You're just horny."

"Thirty-two. That's an old guy."

"Thank you, dear," he whispered, pulling me around to sit next to him, and slipping his warm hands under my shirt.

"I'm still under thirty, you know," I said, smiling.

"Barely." He put his lips over mine and kissed me. I remember that picture so crisply, the two of us alone in the quiet for those few moments before the day started, our son upstairs asleep, and us making some silly joke with each other about growing old. "Come on. I'll get Sam ready for school and we can all drive together." Then he paused, staring out the window at a movement on the sea, a boat darkening against the rising daylight, and for a moment his eyes opened wide like a stag lost in a headlight.

* * *

On that Friday evening in December we left Sam with Yana and drove down the coast to LA to see Peter and Marta again. What began as a heavy mist out of Santa Barbara became pelting rain by the time we got to Westwood. We parked in the middle of the campus, and stood at the overhang of the parking lot watching the downpour.

"Well, we could get the umbrella. Or we could run like crazy through the rain." He grinned at me when he said it and added, "I'll race you."

"But I don't know where we're going."

"You can follow me."

"Well, how is that a race, then?"

He laughed and took my hand, pulling me out into the pouring rain. We dashed up the hill to the open quad outside the theater, shouting at each other like children as we ran. The wind had come up by then, cold and furious through the whistle-way of the passage, and the terracotta slabs around had darkened to deep red from the fallen rain. We stopped there for a moment, and huddled close to each other.

"We're older than we thought," he said, laughing.

Then from across the archway came Peter's loud voice, "Oh my!" he shouted, and rushed to meet us. He threw his big arms around us and Marta came behind, doing the same. And for such a long time we stood together, holding hands, washed to the bone by the cold rain.

They led us to the front entrance of the old auditorium, to the huge, thick mahogany doors of the theater. Several hundred people attended that night, because over the years of their New York lives, Peter and Marta had become famous as scholars on early labor union development. Many progressive politicians were in the crowd, shaking their hands and praising the film. We all drank wine in a reception room in Royce Hall, and at one point a US Senator was brought over to meet Peter.

She clinked her champagne glass to his and said, "Mr. Varga, that was a brilliant film. It needed to be made, and you are a great American for doing it."

Marta smiled hollowly and was about to speak, but Peter sighed and said quickly, "How very kind of you." When she had moved away from us, Peter looked at David and said to him, "Only now am I beginning to understand you."

"You're not gonna crack up on me, are you Peter?" David laughed.

"We both miss you so much," Marta said.

Early on Saturday morning they drove up to Zaca Creek in their little rented car, bringing a satchel of belated birthday presents for Sam. We sat on the floor of Sam's bedroom and watched him open these, while the rain drizzled against the windowpanes behind us. Their gifts were always the best he received, not toys but mostly curious objects they would find as they traveled, and David and I were just as excited as Sam was to see what would emerge after the wrapping paper was torn away. They had spent a week in Maine that summer, and brought him a miniature lobster pot. Since Sam had never seen a lobster, Marta took his crayons and drew a picture of one, while Peter made up a story about the noble Avenging Lobster that protects the sea and all of its creatures.

When they had finished, Sam looked at Marta's drawing and asked, "So lobsters are the same as crabs?"

She had in fact drawn a picture of a crab, and the four of us burst out laughing.

"Well, what do I know?" she asked. "I live in Manhattan."

"We have crabs down at the beach. Maybe we could catch crabs in my lobster pot."

"Sure," I said. "I bet you could."

"Who wants to go?" Sam called out, as though he were rallying his friends around a new adventure.

"We all do, Sammy," Peter said. "This is your birthday all over again." Sam smiled then, that slow honest smile that looked so much like David's.

Peter made a sign for Sam's bedroom door that said, 'Gone Crabbing,' and the five of us hiked down to the beach together, wearing old yellow rain slickers and carrying buckets for the crabs. We squatted at the tide pools for an hour, while the rain subsided and the new sun burned off the mist. Sam dipped his little lobster pot in and out of the shifting water, but of course, the crabs evaded him, and finally Marta bent over the pools to help him.

Late in the morning, David decided to go back to the house and Peter and I went with him.

"I'll stay with Sam," said Marta. "We've almost figured this out, I think."

"We'll make lunch," David said.

"Can we have crab?" asked Sam, and David leaned over to his son and lifted him high in the air, grinning. "Of course, kiddo."

Up at the house Yana had already made a huge meal of fried potatoes with onions and pork, and the rich smell of the grease lingered in the kitchen. She had uncorked a bottle of Napa Cabernet, and the sweet, thick smell filled the room.

We waited until the early afternoon for Sam and Marta, but finally Peter said he was too hungry to wait any longer and the three of us ate on the terrace at the back so we could watch the sea together.

When we had finished David said, "You know, I think we should get Sam back now. He needs to eat something."

"He never changes, does he?" asked Peter grinning at us. "Still an overprotective father."

David stood from the table and put his hand on Peter's shoulder. "That's me. I'll be back in a couple minutes."

After a while we heard Yana talking in the front of the house in loud Russian.

"There they are," I said. "They probably spilled seawater on the carpet or something."

Yana came through the door then, chattering and smiling. She wore a dark brown polyester skirt and she held the fabric bunched together in her fist, swinging it back and forth as she walked like a young village girl. She was not alone, but when I saw that she came with David's father, I must have gasped aloud, because Peter looked over immediately. The two of them walked with their arms linked together in sudden friendship. Nikolai carried a grey coat over one arm, and held his black hat between thick fingers that were misshapen from arthritis.

"Look who I found!" Nikolai smiled at her.

I remember the look of astonishment on Peter's face, stiffened as though it had been frozen there. He shoved his chair back from the table immediately.

"What do you want?" he asked.

As though Nikolai had not heard, he held out his arms to me saying, "Oh, my Rosamund, how are you? I am happy to be in your home again." He moved forward to embrace me, but as he neared I stood up and moved out of his reach.

"What are you doing here?" Peter asked again, his voice suddenly swelling like a great wound pumping out blood.

"I have come to visit my son and his family," Nikolai replied.

"You need to go," Peter said. "Go on!" His face was covered with sweat and his jawline pulled back hard like a gargoyle. The exhumed rage broke across him like electricity and quickly he raised his huge hands. He stepped toward Nikolai, and stopped, his shoulders and chest shaking uncontrollably. "You monster! You dare come to this house again?"

Yana hissed and let go of Nikolai's arm, and the little man cocked his head back in a sweep of theatrical arrogance. Peter lurched forward and grabbed Nikolai's shoulder. He shoved him hard to the ground, and raised his fists over Nikolai's face.

I shouted out and ran toward them, but felt someone push me out of the way. I looked around and saw David rush past, and behind him stood Marta, Yana, and Sam, against a corner of the wall, each of them gaping and terrified.

David seized Peter's wrists and yanked him up hard off of Nikolai. He shouted, "What are you doing?"

Peter did not move. He asked in a shrill voice, "What is he doing here?"

David turned away without answering, and leaned over his father, offering his hand to help him up from the flagstones where he lay.

"Are you okay? Did you break anything?" He led him through the house and out the front door to a seat on the porch. When he returned, he said to Yana, "Take Sam outside to play," and then he came over to Peter.

"You fucking idiot," he said hoarsely. His eyes were perfectly clear, his cheek muscles hard, his lips tight.

Marta walked to them and put her arms around Peter. "It's all right, my love. It's all right." Her eyes were ringed with tears and they both stared at David.

"What is he doing here?" asked Peter. His voice had turned into a muzzled pain that slipped from him in soft cries.

David said, "I invited him."

I could see the look of betrayal in Peter's eyes. "We didn't know he was coming today," I said. I sat on the low stone wall at the edge of the terrace, and pulled my knees to my ribs. "It wasn't like that."

And then David turned toward me and said angrily, "This is our house and he's my father and we don't have to make any excuses."

"What?"

"You heard me."

Peter grabbed Marta's hand quickly. "We are leaving now."

"David, this house belongs to all of us. We are family," I said.

He began to shake his head then, and moved forward toward Peter and Marta, jabbing his finger at them. "Don't make me choose between my father and you."

They stared at him for a very long time, and finally Marta put her hand out to touch him. The terrace was covered by a cold, blue dusk light, and I could see David shiver when he felt her fingertips.

"You don't have to choose," she said. David stared at her and backed away, quiet suddenly as though her calm had infected him.

"My darling," said Peter, "you don't have to stay here with that demon."

"Yes, I do. We are going to stay with our friends and with Sam."

David lifted his head and said, "I'm sorry. I didn't plan for him to come now while you two were here." He walked to her and touched her cheek. "Look at you. You're crying."

She nodded and swept the tears from her face. "I cry very easily. You know that."

"I bet Peter never made you cry," he said softly. "Marta, I would never expect you to be here with him. But whatever happened before, it's important for Sam to know Nikolai."

"I know," she said. Peter stood behind her, his arm wrapped around her waist.

"I'm sorry, Peter," said David.

Peter nodded without speaking.

"I'll go get him into the hotel in town," David said simply. He turned away from us and walked into the kitchen.

It was only seconds before I heard David shout. His voice came from the front of the house, thick and hard like a pulse of fear. Even before I understood his words, my heart jump-started from the terror in his cry and we ran through the open doors to the front porch by the pond.

Nikolai sat silently on my bench in the falling light. His black hat was perched on his head, and his eyes were hard and focused as he watched the cob swan that was splashing furiously with its huge wings.

"Sam!" David screamed, as he lurched through the water toward the center of the pond. Sam lay face down by the island, his lobster pot floating next to him, while the swan lifted its muscled wings and beat at his head and back with all its terrified force.

Marta, Peter, and I raced in after David. We saw him reach the island, and hurl himself at the swan, his voice hammering like a thunderbolt until the cob retreated. He lifted Sam up and when I was close enough, I could see a smear of blood across Sam's forehead where he had fallen against one of the rocks.

The cry I released came from every part of me, deep and terrified, but David did not even look at me. He grabbed Sam's unconscious body and carried him to the pond edge, kneeling alongside him on the bank. He propped his head back to breathe into his mouth, while we sat in the mud around him.

"How long was he in there?" Peter snapped at Nikolai. When the old man did not answer him, Peter shouted at him. "Why didn't you call us? You are God's own devil!"

Nikolai glanced at Peter and shrugged. "It was too late," he said, "by the time I saw what was happening to him."

Marta went instantly to the phone to call an ambulance and David tried for many minutes to give Sam breath, persisting until the torment rose up in him like a hook in his heart.

What I saw then, I will always see. The darkened pond silted from the rain, tin-colored leaves, ash across the soil, soft mud stirring deep: all pictures of my boy's grave.

We held him between us without moving until the ambulance arrived. They took Sam, and then it was Marta who finally drove Nikolai out of our lives, without any of us knowing whether he caused Sam's death, or allowed it, or simply could not stop it.

* * *

We buried Sam in Santa Barbara. David and I remained together at Zaca for a few months, pretending we could find strength in each other, but really only stunned to silence. One day in February I was supposed to meet him after school in town for dinner and I forgot. I stayed at the studio, working through until ten that night. When I arrived at Zaca he was waiting for me in the kitchen, furious. I remember him moving across the room toward me shouting, his hand in the air. He swung hard and hit me in the face and I felt his fingers across my cheek stinging like broken glass on my hot skin. I was so shocked I didn't move immediately, and he pushed me against the counter and hit me again.

"Tell me who you were with!" he shouted, but by then I had run for the door. I made it to my car and drove away, drove to Los Angeles and stayed in a hotel while I thought about what I could do.

Eventually, I went back to San Francisco, and found a teaching job, leaving my clothes and furniture and pictures, everything I had owned, behind in Santa Barbara.

David stayed at Zaca Creek. He killed the swans and filled up the pond, and lived like a hermit for years on that headland. I imagined he held the birds under his arm, one at a time, grabbing them and slitting through their necks with a knife, their muscle-bound bodies pulsing between his arm and chest.

CHAPTER 17

When I arrived in northern California I found a small house out on the ocean side of the San Francisco peninsula, out where civilization ends. I lived there on my own for many years, in the cheap avenues that are always covered in sea-fog. My neighborhood was down on the flats, made of row after row of small, identical houses built in the late '40s for longshoremen. When I moved in it had become a transient rental place, and my neighbors were white trash, people like me, with untended, salt-swept gardens and little nothing jobs. For eight years I lived in a small, yellow clapboard house on a funny, nowhere street across from the beach. I owned this house, or rather, David and I did: although we had not spoken to each other for many years, neither of us ever bothered to complete the divorce.

From my window I could see huge tufts of pampas grass growing in the dunes, and beyond that, the grey horizon that was sometimes broken by the afternoon sun encasing the dark water like polished gunmetal. My street was normally so cold and the surf so rough that the long, wide shore was only good for dogs and wet-suit surfers, for a tai chi class on the sand or a person in deep contemplation.

I would awake at six to the sound of waves pounding across the hard-packed beach, and I would make my coffee, put on my sweats, and sit in the early chill on my front porch. At that time of the morning only the surfing boys were out. On days when the water was not too toxic, they arrived in old jeeps and parked across from my house. They stood barefoot in the street and slowly, methodically pulled on the heavy, black rubber leggings and tops, bending and stretching to pull those second skins into place. They grabbed their boards and sometimes nodded to me, then walked to the sea, paddling out into the rising morning surf and waiting in the cold, without speaking to each other, watching the dim horizon that was dusted with dawn sunlight, while they waited for the elusive true and perfect wave.

My house was not always yellow. It began life as a cheap shack after the war, slapped with white paint and edged with green like somebody's lost dream of Cape Cod. The salt spray and winds on the coast corrode everything, and when I found the house, the paint was the color of pale green mold, peeling in large sheets off the rotting sideboards. I painted it yellow and put the flowers in the front and the bougainvillea in the back.

Marta, Peter, and I remained friends, and often when they came to this coast we would eat together at strange little restaurants in the city that Peter had heard of. They came in the hot week at the beginning of last September, and we walked along the beach for a couple of miles to a new place right across from the ocean, a huge old building covered with that veil of dried salt, and tucked back at the end of Golden Gate Park. It was a warm Indian summer evening, but by the time we reached the Beach Chalet the wind had come up and started to churn off the top of the sea into whitecaps.

"This breeze feels good," said Peter, and he walked in long steps with his hands clasped behind his back.

"You never did like the heat," I said.

"Well, I guess I'll have to get used to it now."

"What do you mean?"

"We finally got the funding for the Stravinsky film. We're moving back to LA for a few months to do some interviews. There are only a handful of artists still alive who actually worked closely with him, and it turns out that most of them are sitting on the beach in southern California." He laughed loudly. "We Europeans are such sybarites. That's where we're heading tomorrow."

"Oh my God." I grinned at them. "You're coming back? I can't believe it."

"We'll be so close again," Marta said, putting her arm around my waist.

"Well, not forever," said Peter, "just for a few months."

"That's what you said when you went to New York. But people always come back to California. It's God's country."

Peter laughed at me. "I'm starving. I hear they have amazing mussels here. And they brew their own beer."

"How do you find out about these places?" I asked, "when you live so far away?"

He shrugged. "I get around," and the weight of his Hungarian accent lay just as heavily across his words as it always had.

We sat at a table on the wide, wooden terrace and drank cool ale while we watched the deep, clear outline of the Farallon Islands turn purple and darken before us. The waiter came with oversized thick ceramic bowls and a steaming tureen filled with mussels in garlic broth. He returned a few moments later carrying a platter of crisp shoestring potatoes, piled high like a mountain of spun golden glass.

"Oh, this is too beautiful," said Peter. He plucked the top nest of potatoes in his fingers and slipped them into his mouth. "Ah, they melt. This is perfect. You may not want to know this," he said without looking at me. "But I thought I should tell you. We saw David."

"I know that you keep in touch. It's okay. My lawyer talks to his lawyer all the time."

"No," said Marta, and she lay her hand across Peter's. "Peter means that we saw him today. A couple of hours ago. He's here."

"Where?" I asked.

"In San Francisco. He comes up here to work sometimes. We've asked him to do the music for our last little film, and we were with him at a sound studio downtown."

"I didn't know he ever left Zaca. I thought he had become a hermit. He's never called me." I was staring at the mussel shells floating in brine before us, cracked open, brittle-black, porous, and I could feel my breath shorten.

"Did you really think he would? Rosie, look at me. He could meet us here. He's flying home later tonight; this is on the way out to the airport. I could call him. Only if you want, of course."

"You mean he's waiting somewhere?"

"Sort of," Marta said.

All the pictures I had ever taken of him swelled up suddenly, all the light I had ever chased around his face. I folded my hands together and noticed a couple of brown spots across the backs, splitting open a lost memory of my mother at her desk, talking secretively on the phone to my father. In some small place beneath, I understood that David and I had never unearthed any answers, neither together nor alone. I could see that like a target in a sight, burning into the horizon.

"I guess a decade is long enough," I said at last, and both of them grinned at me, immediately and like children.

"Well, all right then," said Peter. "This is so exciting."

"Don't make me any more nervous than I already am. I might change my mind."

When he came at last I had moved beyond anxiety, sitting quietly with my arms crossed over my chest. I was facing the sea and could not see him approach the table, but when I saw Marta lift her head slightly and her mouth drop open to a smile, I knew that he stood behind me.

"Hi there," she said. "Sit down, David."

An empty chair was across from me, and he moved behind it, waiting. His hair was shorter, and flecked with grey at the temples; his face was tanned and the shine from the terrace lights fell across his forehead and cheekbones to make that picture I had taken so many times, so many years ago. He watched me for a moment without moving, then asked, "Do you mind if I sit with you?" His voice was so familiar that it ripped me open silently while I smiled at him. He wore jeans and a white button-down shirt under a soft grey suede jacket. "You look great," he said, but I don't even remember what I was wearing. He slipped his arms out of the jacket and slung it across the chair, and I could see that his waist had thickened only a little in ten years; in his white shirt against the wide, indigo night sky, everything about him seemed strong and bright and gentle.

Peter dropped a spoon on the floor, and David leaned to retrieve it. When he resurfaced, he looked first at me, grinning like a young boy with a secret. He lay the spoon next to Peter's arm, and I could see that the backs of his hands were suntanned and that he still wore his wedding ring. He caught me staring at it, wondering, and he shrugged silently. I knew then he was thinking that we had never been divorced, that legally we were still married; I could hear him thinking that so clearly he might have spoken it.

"I guess you're right," I said quietly.

"Right about what?" asked Peter.

"Nothing," said David, and we both laughed. He looked at me, and put his hand across the table alongside mine.

"How long are you here for?" I asked.

"Half an hour, and then I have to get to the airport to get a flight back."

"Are you hungry?" asked Marta.

"Not really. I only have a few minutes. Coffee would be great, though." He looked over my shoulder to catch the eye of the waiter, and asked me, "Do you want anything?" as though he had been caring for me without a break for all these past years. The offshore breeze had come up then, laying a clean smell of salt spray over the terrace. I wrapped my arms around my body against the cold. "Here," he said and handed me his jacket. I put it around my shoulders, the silk lining slick against my chilled skin. After he ordered he looked at me again. "I hear you're teaching at the College of Arts and Crafts. That's pretty impressive."

"Thanks. I've had a couple of shows up here, and things seem to be going pretty well."

"I know. I saw them."

"You saw them?" I asked, but he didn't answer.

Peter began talking then about the film they were making, telling some joke about old white Russians hobbling along the Santa Monica pier to find rock candy. All the while I watched David, hunched forward over his coffee, smiling nervously, and once when he looked up to catch my gaze in the light of the restaurant's yellow neon, my breathing stopped instantly.

He gulped the last of his coffee. "You know, I have to leave. I'm sorry."

"Do you need a ride to the airport?" asked Peter.

"No, I've got a rental, thanks." He stood up, looking down over me, his hand on the back of my chair. "Walk me out?" he asked.

We strolled across the wide, dirty lot without speaking, to where he had parked adjacent to the sea. The warm, salt-smelling wind was blowing hard, pressing my thin dress around me.

"Here, I should give you your jacket back."

He nodded his head. "I'm glad you agreed to see me tonight."

"It was time. I've always missed you."

He stood against the car door and said, "I can see why you like it here. It's like home." He was slouching, his hands shoved deep in his pockets, and when he talked about Zaca looking at me, I could feel my heart pumping loose and hard.

"For me, this is home." Suddenly, silently, my face was burning and sweating in the cold beach wind; although I was hidden in the dark, I was scared.

"I should have come to get you," he said softly. "I should never have left you alone."

"Maybe. Who knows now?" A night fisherman climbed out of a van not far from us then, carrying tackle and rods, and moved toward the dark water. For a while we could hear the sound of his footsteps slapping the pavement, brushing across the sand-spit lot. We were quiet for a moment while he passed, as though we were saving our secret from strangers. "Will you phone me sometime when you come?" I asked.

"Sure." He quickly took his keys from his pocket. "I guess I better go." He fumbled for a moment and then suddenly turned back to me. "I'll be up again next week. Could we have dinner?" I put my hand on his white cotton sleeve, damp and bright in the warm night. He looked down at my fingers, and put his hand over them.

* * *

He came a few times that fall, gingerly carrying plans into town. Once he arrived early from a meeting south of Market, and he sat in the big, white sunlit chair in my living room pretending to choose a radio channel but instead watching me in the mirror while I put lipstick on. Another time I was waiting for him one evening. I remember standing at the base of the staircase in the darkened living room, noticing a shadow on the porch against the crooked screen door. He was there, quietly staring at my empty room with the evening mist dissolving around him. The week of Sam's birthday, David called to cancel a date he had made, but that was the only time he let me down. In January I asked him to come up specially on the weekend before my birthday for a party at my house that some friends had organized. I remember that night he was so shy, an armful of awkwardness like a scarecrow stuffed with hay.

He stayed after the others left, and when I found him, he was in the kitchen washing glasses. I waited at the open door watching him until he glanced over his shoulder and grinned broadly at me.

"Come over here." I walked to him. "Sit down. I think we should talk." I sat in the chair across from him. "If I asked you how many men have been here with you, would you tell me the truth?" he asked.

I had drunk a lot of the bottle of birthday whisky that my students had given me, and I giggled very loudly. "Absolutely not."

"I'd like to know," he said, "I mean if you're seeing anyone now. I'm only curious."

"That's a different question."

"You don't have any music here, do you?"

"Of course I do. Over by the bookshelf there are a whole lot of CD's."

"No, I mean you don't have a piano or guitar or anything."

"Well, I was never the musician, remember."

"Not even a wind chime."

"No. No wind chime." I reached over the table and flicked off the stark overhead light. "You know, I'm really not that drunk. And just so you understand, I'm not seeing anyone who could get in your way." He stood up and moved over to me. The bottom buttons of his shirt were open so that my cheek pressed against his stomach. I began to open the other buttons, and put my hands on his warm skin, moving my fingers across the soft, dark chest hairs speckled grey now. Putting my lips on his ribs one by one, I felt him inhale sharply. He pulled my shirt up over my head, and then slipped the hooks and straps of my bra free, exposing my body to the dim amber light. Looking now at my breasts, he touched one of my nipples with dampened fingers, stroking it so it tingled with the cool air. I let him touch me; his green eyes were huge, his pupils swollen black.

"You know there's no one else here," he said, standing back to look at me. I felt his hands, weathered and rough, slip under my skirt, trailing up the inner line of my thighs.

"Don't you ever get lonely here?" he asked, putting his mouth on my throat. I unbuttoned his fly and as I did his penis pressed out, huge and full and hard, and he stood up and pulled his jeans off. I leaned forward and pulled him into my mouth. He groaned so deeply I could feel the sound rise from his stomach, and he grabbed my hair in his fist.

"Stop it. I want to come in you. I wanted that for years. I even dreamed it."

"I hate it when you look at me now," I said. "I'm old now. I'm embarrassed." As though he hadn't heard me, he led me to the couch in the living room. The front door was still open and the salt wind blew against the screen, scraping the uneven frame with a clattering thump. He pulled me down alongside him, both of us stretching across the soft, sage-colored pillows.

"I love you," he whispered. And like a voice across an ocean of ether vapor, suspended in it and saved by it, too, he said, "I waited ten years to get you back." He stroked my hair and my forehead, staring at my face.

I saw that on his shoulder something had scraped the skin, leaving a trail of ruptured blood drops in a thick line down his bicep. I ran my tongue along them, and it tasted sweet like the dark juice of a desert pomegranate. "Making love to me will never get anything back," I said. "We lost all that."

"We lost nothing. If you forgive me, then we lost nothing." He put his hand down to my crotch and slid his fingers up into me. He flipped on top and as he lurched into me, he was trembling. At last he released a thin cry, and rolled off, lying for a few minutes with his eyes closed. His skin was covered with sweat, his arm still swirled with some blood that smeared across his skin like a tattoo of granted prayer.

Finally he said, "I didn't take you with me."

"No, but it's okay." He took my nipple between his thumb and index finger and began to roll and squeeze it until my gut and crotch were pulsing again. "If you don't stop you're gonna have to do it all over again."

"I could." He opened his eyes. "I'm not that old, baby." I turned on my stomach beside him, and he spread his hand across the base of my spine, absently rubbing his fingers along the sweat-dampened space between bone and hip-flesh.

I moved his hand away and sat up. My skin had chilled at last as the deep coast night fell across the house. "No, it really is okay. Let's go upstairs to bed."

I led him up to my own room and we lay holding each other.

After a few minutes, he asked, "Do you remember the night you left Zaca?"

"Of course I do."

"I hurt you. I know I hit you really hard." He said it so quietly I could barely hear him. I could remember my swollen face again and the way he had bruised it to dark purple.

"You were so angry because you thought I was with someone else. But you know, that night I just forgot. There wasn't anyone else. You fought with me for nothing." I said it calmly, but I had been waiting a decade to tell him. "I never really understood why you did that."

"It was good you left, because I just wanted to keep hurting you." Tears began to slip down his cheeks. "Rosie, we don't have to talk about this if you don't want to. Maybe I shouldn't tell you this at all."

"It's okay. I guess we have to talk about it sometime."

"After that night, most of what I did around there was to hurt you." His voice dropped like a wave suddenly collapsing. "I'm sorry. I even destroyed your garden."

"David, that night was a long time ago. I already forgave you."

"How could you? You don't even know why I did it."

"I've always been afraid of you," he looked away. "You were the only one who could punish me," he said slowly. "That night I tore out your garden and I started to burn everything else that meant something to you. None of your things are left, Rosie." He paused and looked at me, measuring the shadows around my face, my hair, my skin, whatever was folded into me. "When I hit you I understood how good it felt to hurt you. And I never came for you because I knew that nobody could forgive that."

Neither of us breathed; the house and the sea swallowed us in the drifting smell of the salt air.

"Forgiving somebody isn't really about them," I said. The pink cotton sheets beneath us had soaked through, and I stood up out of the bed in a rush. "I'm suffocating. I'm going downstairs," and as I watched him I came to understand why I had never fallen in love with anyone else. What I missed in him all those years was his courage, and now I saw it again, the mettle he had that I had always wanted for myself.

The next day he got up early and drove to the hardware store, and when I awoke he was on the front porch wearing only his jeans in the thin winter sunlight, lifting the screen door into place.

"Those hinges were rusted shut." He released the door into its slots and picked up the old hinges. "Look at this. This is why you could never get it closed. I guess you never weathered it, did you? This house needs a lot of work, Rosie. That bougainvillea out back is gonna collapse the fence soon." I walked over to him and put my arms around his bare chest. "I'm starving," he said. "Will you make me breakfast?" He picked his shirt off the porch and put it on. "Do you mind that I did that?"

"Of course not. It's actually your house, too."

He laughed, "This is not my house. Nothing I own is in this bad shape. You keep it painted yellow, baby, but that's about it."

We ate in the backyard, sitting opposite each other at an old picnic table. He told me about some changes at Zaca, grinning and saying, "I've become a farmer. You'd be surprised at what I've learned to do." He was eating a huge omelet filled with mushrooms and cheese, and guzzling a pot of black, bitter coffee. "When you own land, there's something new you gotta do every day."

He came around and stood behind me, putting his hands on my shoulders. I could feel his belt buckle pressing on my back. "I have to catch a plane soon," he said.

Later, I stood with him in front of my house, saying goodbye and watching him put his things in the car. As he leaned over to kiss me, he asked suddenly, "Would you ever come visit me at Zaca?" I must have looked frightened, because he said almost immediately, "It doesn't matter, baby. I will always come to you." He held his hand and touched my cheek so softly like it was a warm vapor moving darkly across my skin.

"I guess I should," I whispered. "I know I should do it. I just always wanted to believe I didn't need to."

"Well, it's winter now," he said quickly. "The Creek was never very good in the winter. Maybe you should wait till next spring."

"I'm just a coward. You've been living there all these years, facing it." I was a coward even with the word I chose, such a small word, an otherwise insignificant pronoun, but as though I had turned a key when I spoke, everything about Sam held there for a decade tumbled out between us.

"Both of us face it," he said. "I think of Sam every day, and I know you do, too."

It had been years since I had heard his name. We stood without moving for a very long time, faithful to it, stained with it.

"It never gets better, baby," he said to me, "it doesn't mean you can't survive."

"I don't want you to think I'm hiding."

"I don't. What happened to our family isn't something anyone can hide from." He wrapped his arms around me, and I could see the veins of his forearms raised like silver light. "But if you want to come to Zaca one day, it will always belong to you."

CHAPTER 18

We continued like that through the late winter; he would fly in despite heavy rain or thick fog, sometimes waiting for hours in airports for the sky to clear enough to get a plane up from the southern coast. Twice during those months he came with Peter and Marta straight from LA. They all stayed in my little beachside cottage, and Peter would make a fire while Marta walked on the cold-swept beach by herself. Peter always had a sad or funny story about his old Russian émigrés, the ancient, arthritic ballerina talking about the time Nijinsky had dropped her on her ass, or the interview he did at Zucky's Deli when the now white-haired violinist first discovered the joy of hot apple pie with melted cheddar cheese.

In late February they visited again, and the morning before they left, Peter and I sat by ourselves at my kitchen table, drinking coffee and waiting for David and Marta to wake. David had thrown his overnight bag in the corner of the kitchen the night before and it lay there still, closed and unused.

Peter saw it out of the corner of his eye and nodded toward it. "I don't know why he bothers to bring a bag these days. Our Mr. David has now installed all essential items at your house. The question on all of our lips, of course, is when will you return the favor?"

"What?"

His skin was pale, and his eyes were big and black. "If you want to be saved like a princess, you have to act like one, and not like a mistress."

"What do you mean?"

He reached for the coffee pot and filled his cup again. His voice had become suddenly sharp, and he took a spoon and shoveled sugar into his drink, clattering it around the cup. "I mean this is easy for you." He waved the spoon through the air in wide circles. "This whole out-of-towner thing that you let him do."

"He doesn't mind."

"No, of course he doesn't. But how long are you planning to let him do it? Aren't you wanting anything else with him?" He lay the spoon on the bare table and shrugged. "I'll stop. I turn to stone if I tell the truth, anyway."

"I don't know why you think it's easy. It's not easy watching him leave each time." I crossed my arms over my chest. "Why are you all of a sudden attacking me about it, anyway?"

"Never mind."

"No, tell me. I'm sorry. Say what you were saying."

Peter's wallet lay behind him on the counter, and now he reached for it. "Every single day I look at this." He flipped it open and pushed the cheap, faded leather across the tabletop. I saw it at once, the top photograph behind plastic frosted with dirt and wear, a small picture of Sam I had taken when he was five years old. The glare from the overhead light fell across my son's face, obscuring his eyes, and although I remembered his expression from the day I printed the picture, slowly I drew it out of the plastic sleeve and held it.

"Look at him," I whispered into the silent room. Sam's grin glowed faintly under my fingernail. The shape of it looked so much like my own smile that it startled me.

"He was the image of you," said Peter, his shoulders shaking slowly. "I guess you had forgotten that."

When I glanced up from the picture, I saw that the blood had rushed to Peter's face, and his cheeks were red and puffed. His nose was shining under the light and his lips were pulled taut and pale. Suddenly I saw him for the old man he had become.

"He would have been seventeen this year," I said, looking quickly again at my dead son while the tears began to slip down my face.

Peter slowly folded his hands together over mine in a soft embrace. "You hid so much away when he died. You need to go home now, Rosie, and stop being afraid of what really happened."

Finally, I looked up at his old face.

"I don't think I can, Peter. I'm just too scared."

"I don't believe that. We're not babies, Rosie. We are required to do the best we can."

Marta had been standing in the door in a long, rumpled t-shirt the color of a robin's egg, her shoulder-length grey hair pulled into pigtails over her ears. She had grown even plumper over the years.

"Maybe Rosie doesn't need to know what you think, my darling." She walked to me and put her arms across my shoulders, the gentle, easy kindness of her rippling across me.

Peter tapped his bald head with his index finger, making a wooden, hollow sound. "Of course not. I am a gormless stupido." He smiled at her, a shy, beloved smile, and for an instant the slumbering youth in both of them was lit again by their deep affection.

"We love you so much," Marta said. "We know this has never stopped hurting you. But none of us can change what happened."

"What happened," said Peter, "is that Sam died and it broke our hearts forever." He stared at me and opened his mouth slowly to speak again, closing it quickly in silence.

"You know," I said, trying to sound like I was in control but I had begun to cry again in hard aching waves. "There is so much I haven't done. I'm alone out here by the beach or in Oakland in a darkroom. I wanted a family. I thought I would have big Thanksgiving parties. I never raised a child. I never even saw his clothes again."

"Oh my love," said Peter. "I wouldn't hurt you for anything in the world, but you have to go back, you have to get past this."

* * *

By the start of March the storms closed in over the northern coast in California, bruising the sky with deep grey unbroken rain clouds. This was weather that burst across the sea, bloating the horizon with warm, black squalls, and I spent that time at school in the darkroom, leaving the house before the winter daylight and not returning from Oakland until the hard night rain. I hadn't seen David in a couple of weeks, but we talked to each other most nights. He was at Zaca finishing the music for a television movie, and I would imagine him working on the score after dinner, sitting at the piano by the open porch window and composing late into the night, repeating the same sounds over and over, relentlessly searching out that perfect chord.

One night he called me around two in the morning. I had been sleeping heavily for a long time like a drugged person. I had been so exhausted those last weeks, I would climb into bed without eating dinner and fall asleep. At first I thought it was a function of the weather, like hibernation, but slowly it dawned on me that I might actually be pregnant again.

"I'm sorry to wake you, baby. I needed to hear your voice."

"It's okay," I said. I was only barely awake, and my whole body felt heavy and warm.

"I guess I'll always be that same selfish guy from the '60s."

I smiled, lying in my warm bed with the northern rain pitching at the windows, remembering nights at Zaca when he had leaned across me after midnight, spreading the cover like a soft net in a half-spun kind of embrace.

"Are you coming up on Friday, David?"

"Not this weekend, Rosie. I won't be finished for another week or so."

"I need to talk to you."

"What's up?" he asked. "We're okay, aren't we, baby?"

"Yes, of course," I whispered. "At least I think so." I sighed, "I guess I need to tell you now, then. I'm late this month, and this morning when I got to school I went into the bathroom and threw up. I was going to do a test tomorrow. I know it could be anything, but I have a feeling I'm pregnant."

It seemed like he didn't speak for such a long time, and every silent second drained more hope from me.

"Oh, baby, and we thought we were too old. What do you want to do?"

"Well, we shouldn't start worrying yet. I could be wrong."

"I'm not worried, Rosie. Are you?"

"No. I don't know. There's a lot to think about."

"Rosie, if you want this baby then the only thing we have to think about is a name. I'll fly up this weekend and we can figure everything out."

In the middle of the week I arrived home on a rain-drenched evening and stood in my living room with the water caught on my clothes dripping to the floor, my arms full of baggage, my keys, my purse, my coat, my shopping, and I let it all fall to the table as I saw the flashing message button on the phone. I pressed it immediately, wanting to hear David's voice.

"It's Peter. I'm looking for David. Tell him to call me right away. We're at home tonight."

I called Zaca Creek, but there was no answer and so I phoned Peter and Marta in Los Angeles. "He's not here."

"Do you know where I can get him? It's important."

"I thought he was at home. I don't really know. What's up?"

"His father showed up in town last week. Maranova told him about our little film and he came, wanting to be included . . ."

"But you would never do that," I said in a sudden, high voice. "You wouldn't see him, would you?"

"Nikolai was taken to St. John's Hospital, Rosie. It seems he's had prostate cancer for a few months and he had a bad day yesterday. You know, these old Europeans here on the beach have nothing better to talk about. They are all being melodramatic about it, but just in case, I thought David ought to know." There was a long, silver pin sitting on the table beneath my damp fingers, and I picked it up and began to flick it across the skin of my fingertips, flicking just deep enough to scrape without drawing blood, like a taste of the past scattering sick dust.

"Okay. If I hear from David I'll tell him."

"You understand that he has a right to know this."

At first I didn't answer, but I could hear his breathing growing impatient, and so at last I said only, "Sure. Look, I better go, Peter. I just walked in and I'm getting rain all over the floor."

I turned on a lamp that threw deep, amber light into the room, standing still like in a thick, old curved lens before the sulphur-bulb flash. Both hate and longing worked in me. The truth is, I think they became the same thing. I imagined this old man lying in a bed, dying in a hospital, and it ripped open a fire of pleasure in me.

* * *

I did not talk to David that night, because I took a plane myself to Los Angeles, and arrived at the hospital finally near eleven. The security guard at the information desk was reluctant to give me his room number, but I said, "I am his daughter-in-law. We didn't know he was here until this evening." This was a lie I could even prove, that I was his family, and when the nurses on his floor called back immediately to allow me in, I knew that they were expecting this to be Nikolai's last night. The ward was quiet by that time of the evening; the doctors were cloistered and the few nurses on the shift kept their voices low.

His room was dark except for the angled light from the hall, and I sat in shadows without speaking, in a chair shoved back against the wall and out of his line of vision. In that cool light Nikolai's skin became luminescent, irradiated by the warm sickness that was killing him. The sheets over him were spread smooth and close, as though someone had recently come to comfort him. His small body, deflated lungs, and the caved form of his ribcage were outlined by shadows thrown across the linen.

Once through the night a nurse came to change the drip bag for him, propping him up to give him water as well. Then, the room flooded with the scent of ancient alchemy, of amber spice and linden, as the soul of him unraveled around us. I watched him for a couple more hours, and somewhere around three in the morning he died, quietly. His even, shallow breathing slipped away and the malice in him simply disappeared from the world. Then I understood that I had not come for revenge, but to free myself.

I sat in the room until five, when the smoggy Los Angeles dawn began. The morning shift came on and a new nurse, a thin Latin woman, arrived to change Nikolai's drip. She nodded at me, and lifted his wrist to take his pulse. She placed it back on top of the pale blue blanket and turned to me.

"I'm sorry," she said to me quietly. "Your father has passed away."

"Do you want me to go?"

She smiled kindly, and softly said, "No, my dear. You can stay as long as you need." She took my hand in both of hers. Her fingers were cool and soft as she stroked my hand, quietly giving me this calm veil of her grace.

* * *

I drove out through the early morning, up the coast to Zaca Creek, into the lush winter meadows of the Santa Ynez. The valley was filled with fog banks that morning, and the fresh, white-painted fences of the horse breeding farms glowed through the deep mist. As I reached Zaca, one of the fields near our ranch was lit with fire, a farmer's careful burn-off, and the smell of the smoke haze spread over the north edge of the property.

When I came to our turning the old entry-gate by the cottage was tied wide open with rope that had weathered into place through several winter seasons. At the top of our drive

I pulled up next to a new little blue pick-up truck. When I climbed from the car I immediately smelled a faint tinge of lemon in the air that cast me back a decade, breath that knotted my gut with sudden flashes of memory. The scrub up the far hillside still held wild lemon mint, this fragrance spreading out around me.

I went straight for the porch and stopped to sit down on the top step. After a couple of moments David came through the front door beside me.

"My God. Rosie, are you okay? When did you get here?" He squatted next to me.

"I'm all right. I just drove up from LA. David, your father died last night."

"They said it was coming. The hospital got hold of me yesterday." He shook his head. "I finished with all that years ago. What were you doing in LA?"

"For that." No matter how hard I tried I couldn't contain the rising panic that seemed to break Zaca around me into a thousand pieces.

"Why?" he asked.

"I don't know. I just went."

He took off his jacket and put it over my shoulders. "Well, I'm really glad you're here now."

Sam's dog, Joe, lay at the back of the porch, nestled between his food and water bowls. "Hey there," David called out to him. "Look who's here, Joe," but the dog merely lifted his dirty snout and went back to his half-drowse. "Are you sure you're okay? And our baby?" A thin shaft of winter light sliced across the porch and David shifted to see my face clearly.

"Yes." A red dragonfly skated over the lip of Joe's water bowl, hovering beneath his huge, benign teeth. Its transparent wings flickered a hundred times, and then carefully it spun into the air. "The truth is I'm half-expecting Sam to walk through the door, all grown up. I used to imagine that years ago, but I finally made myself stop. Maybe nothing will fix it for me," I said. "I'm sorry."

He knelt beside me. "The answers aren't always just handed out, baby. You know it takes longer than that."

"Don't be angry at me."

"I'm not," he said. "I believe that I can make you want to stay. I don't want to live here for the rest of my life belly-up without trying." He stood up, reaching his hand out to me. "Come on. You look exhausted."

On a table alongside us was a set of delicate teacups, each painted with a different pattern in deep blue and green and yellow, tiny intricate flowers across them. The split pine floor was clean and polished, and along the wall of the old house sat several huge clay pots holding miniature rose bushes. The only thing out of place was the new green hose which hung across the porch railing. David began to coil it around his arm in neat circles. The bench in front of the house was gone, and my old lavender garden, too. Where the big pond had been, he had planted a tousled patch of high-stalked wild anemones, pale pink and still in the breezeless morning.

"Those are pretty," I said quietly. "That was the right choice."

He nodded. "I'm sorry about your garden. I did a lot of crazy things then." My fingers were curled tightly over the edge of the step. "Would you like to sleep for a while?"

"No. Maybe some coffee, though." He took my hand automatically and led me into the house, down to the cool, dark kitchen where I sat at the center table. "Nothing's changed in here," I said.

"I always liked this place the way we had it." He handed me the coffee and sat with me. "I have to go and feed the geese. If they miss a meal they get nervous and go somewhere else. They're kind of fickle like that."

"So you got your geese?"

He smiled sheepishly and said, "Yeah, I got them. About five hundred now every year."

"That's amazing." I slipped my arm around his waist. "You're a magician."

"Not really. It won't take long. I'll be back in about an hour."

I followed him out to the terrace where he had left his boots and watched him as he bent over to pull them on. He stood up and put his hands on my shoulders, leaning forward to kiss my face. After he had gone I walked back through the house past those quiet, empty rooms that for years had been my secret stations. I passed back through the front door and down the steps to sit at last at the edge of Sam's anemones, spreading my hands and legs out on the damp grass. The wild blossom field in front of me was flecked with tiny, crazy skipper butterflies, darting ferociously like sharp quills driven by light. I closed my eyes and knew that the pond was still there, brimming just beneath the earth like an underground spring that could never be dammed. Old pictures began to burst through me, a collection that had waited, glowing and alive, for so long. And when every last picture had escaped, I sat, shaking, by the place where Sam had died.

I did want to sleep then, and I went into the old house to find a place to lie down, to my bed upstairs in the big corner room that looked to the coast cliffs and the wide beach. The room had been freshly painted a rich ivory color, and was empty of furniture except our old pine bed frame and a bare mattress. I stood at one window for a moment, then shoved it open to watch the sweep of headland and sea, allowing the room to fill with the softer smell of the landscape. Beside the far window David's telescope was trained to the north, on the hill beyond the pasture, and I took hold of the barrel, holding it as he had taught me years ago.

I put my eye to the lens, and at first I couldn't see anything but black. I pressed closer, anchoring my face and moving the angle until at last the landscape came to view. David stood on the wide meadow at the far headland. Careful not to flush the grazing geese, he moved slowly, pushing a wooden wheelbarrow of feed through the high grasses. The geese gathered around him. He bent down, digging the grain shovel into the barrow, and flung the feed across the land in a huge arc. He repeated this many times, bending and lifting rhythmically through the red morning light. When he had finished he knelt beside the barrow, absolutely still, watching the birds as dozens more swooped in from the sky to graze.

Then a hawk descended to rest on one of the trees, and suddenly the songbirds waiting in the trees rose, squawking and flapping crazily, flying in a huge ball of noise and chaos to the sky. The waders rose as well across the horizon, and it seemed like the end of the world, the sky seething with this frightened frenzy. The geese bolted from the headland, thrashing their thick wings, and all of them flew in circles in the air, rushing toward our house and the lake beyond.

David stood calmly in the field and picked up the barrow handles. He began pushing it back over the ground toward the muddy path, moving as patiently and methodically as he had come, a lean, dark outline healed by the silent sky. I stood up slowly, and sat on the cool, stripped mattress to wait.